Praise for *The Genius Who Saved Baseball*

"I was really looking forward to reading *The Genius Who Saved Baseball* in part because I have for a long time wished we had a lot more old-school and a lot less analytics in baseball. I had a feeling this book might bring me back to some of those good old days. It absolutely did just that. My plan was to read fifty pages each night before bed. Those plans changed as the story picked up momentum and then quickly gave me a serious burst of excitement. At that point, I was all in. I couldn't put it down until I got to its thrilling conclusion. I got emotional in different ways at different points throughout the story. As a huge lover of baseball, it was right up my alley, and it hit all the right notes for me. This book and I were a match made in heaven."

— Loren Palmroth, Real Estate Agent
and Coach of La Sierra Little League

"I'm not even a baseball fan, but I felt like I'd hit a home run when I read *The Genius Who Saved Baseball*. The story of Charlie Collier and his ideas that lead the Nashville Knights to victory had me cheering on everyone. Great story. Great character development. Great feel-good storyline. What's not to love? Robert Ingram took me out to the ball game, and frankly, I didn't care if I ever came back."

— Tyler R. Tichelaar, PhD and Award-Winning
Author of *When Teddy Came to Town*

"Whether or not you're a baseball fan, the truth is that *The Genius Who Saved Baseball* has something in it for everyone, from its adorable title character to a country music superstar and his team of irascible, loveable team members who create a winning baseball team. There's humor, romance, drama, and best of all, that feel-good ending we all crave."

— Nicole Gabriel, Author of *Finding Your Inner Truth* and *Stepping Into Your Becoming*

"In *The Genius Who Saved Baseball*, Robert Ingram introduces us to Charlie Collier, a teenage genius who proves that we can all create our own destinies when we take a chance on our ideas and have confidence in ourselves. Ingram's fast-moving story makes it hard to stop reading."

— Patrick Snow, Publishing Coach and Best-Selling Author of *Creating Your Own Destiny* and *Boy Entrepreneur*

THE GENIUS WHO
SAVED
BASEBALL

- A FEEL GOOD BASEBALL NOVEL -

ROBERT E. INGRAM

AVIVA
PUBLISHING
New York

The Genius Who Saved Baseball

Published by:
Aviva Publishing
Lake Placid, NY
(518) 523-1320
www.AvivaPubs.com

Robert Ingram
(253) 651-2089
Bobingram7@aol.com

ISBN: 978-1-63618-037-3
Library of Congress Control Number: 2020924254

Editor: Tyler Tichelaar, Superior Book Productions
Cover Designer: Nicole Gabriel, Angel Dog Productions
Interior Book Layout: Nicole Gabriel, Angel Dog Productions
Author Photo: Debbie Gilman

Every attempt has been made to properly source all quotes.
Printed in the United States of America
First Edition

To my wife, Cara, and sons, Jason and Taylor,

Your love of family and love of the game inspire me.

ACKNOWLEDGMENTS

This book would not have been possible without the contributions of many people, both personally and inspirationally. I wish to thank:

America's Founding Fathers, Dick Andrews, Mayo Attick, Chuck Boley, Tom Bresnahan, Jeanné Broxton, Don Byrd, David and Julie Clark, College Park Boys and Girls Club, Frank Cumberland, Jeff Cumberland, Matt Cumberland, Paul Dickson, Abner Doubleday, Bob Dylan, Chris Emery, Tina Ferrera, Susan Friedman, Nicole Gabriel, Debbie Gilman, Valarie Harris, Joe Hindes, Bob Hemphill, Frank Howard, Ed and Emma Ingram, Jason and Michelle Ingram, Lee Ingram, Ulys Garfield Ingram, Gail Jones, Mickey Mantle, Karen McNamara, E. C. Murray, Tiiu Napp, Satchel Paige, Norman Vincent Peale, Brent Polkes, Dave and Bonnie Pride, Frank Reed, Cal Ripken, Pete Rose, Jim Ryan, Robert Schattner, Ralph C. Smedley, Patrick Snow, Derek and Michelle Thielen, Tyler Tichelaar, Gig Harbor Toastmasters, Mary West, Tammy White, and George Wilson.

CONTENTS

★ INTRODUCTION ★

You *know* the world is upside down when computers have taken over baseball. Have you ever yelled at your television as announcers talk incessantly about pitch count, exit velocity, and spin rate? Are you tired of motor-mouthed blowhards in the broadcast booth trying to be witty? You might remember watching games before this madness began, a time when less was more, when baseball was baseball and pitchers' arms didn't fall off after 100 pitches.

Are you drifting away from the game? Do you remember the child-like joy it once brought you? Does it seem to you that a simple game has been hijacked by nerds? If you feel this way, you have company.

In *The Genius Who Saved Baseball*, you'll see what could happen if a major league team went against the group-think and tossed the computer/analytics obsession to the curb. Yes, this is just fiction, but something like it *could* happen.

Main character fourteen-year-old Charlie Collier mixes his love of baseball with his 189 IQ to create a roadmap for the newly formed Nashville Knights to win the World Series. After graduating early from high school, Charlie takes advanced statistics classes at the University of Maryland and presents his professor with a thesis that adherence to analytics has produced a *lower* caliber of play when measured against "instinctual play." Despite his professor giving him a C– on his project,

Charlie keeps working on his theories, eventually gaining the attention of the Nashville Knights, owned by the charismatic, larger-than-life country music mega-star Big T McCraw. Big T takes Charlie under his wing, and with an interesting supporting cast, they set out to save baseball. *The Genius Who Saved Baseball* then takes you through the amazing first two seasons for the new team.

Throughout the book are life lessons to be learned from the characters and situations. The bonus "innings" at the end outline nine bits of wisdom for living a good and prosperous life. Nine seems fitting since there are nine innings to a game and nine players on a team.

My mother planted the seeds in me for my love of baseball when I was three. She would pitch to me in the backyard while my father was at work with his government job. Of course, she was pitching underhand from three feet away and pitching to hit my bat, but I felt like a slugger. Do you have memories of who first pitched to you or whom you played catch with? Growing up on the East Coast, I'd stay up too late on school nights to listen to radio broadcasts of games on the West Coast. I played on teams, beginning at age six and through the over-forty men's baseball bracket. After that, I coached youth teams for a dozen years. You may be like me, just a guy or gal who loves the game. I don't have all the answers to the real or perceived ills of baseball, but I do have strong opinions, and I welcome yours.

If you are inspired to connect, I would love to hear your baseball memories and stories. You can reach me at bobingram7@aol.com. In case the email goes to spam, you may text me at (253) 651-2089.

Your baseball pal,

Robert E. Ingram

★ BASEBALL GLOSSARY ★

Throughout this story, you'll find baseball terms not everyone will know, so I put together a list of some of them. *The Genius Who Saved Baseball* is written to be enjoyed by fervent fans, casual fans, and even non-fans of all ages. These terms will help the non-fan the most. The definitions are my own.

Analytics: In simplest terms, analytics is information. We slice and dice everything today with metrics. Marketers dissect consumers into hundreds of categories. People who run baseball similarly slice and dice players into categories, the theory being that their team will have a competitive advantage, a knowledge advantage. It would probably only be a slight exaggeration if I said they have metrics showing that left-handed hitters performed 53 percent better on days when they ate pancakes and the sky was cloudy. Managers, executives, and even players end up making decisions based on information overload rather than what they see and feel. Baseball is instinctual. Analytics is anti-instinctual.

Batting Average: The number of hits divided into the number of at-bats gives the number of times out of a thousand that the player would get a hit. A player whose batting average is "three hundred," shown as .300, gets a hit 300 times out of 1,000 attempts, or 3 out of 10.

Bunt: A deliberately weak hit by a batter tapping the ball rather than swinging. The batter tries to have the ball roll slowly or stop before the fielder can get it quickly enough to make a play. There are different strategies with bunting. Sometimes the batter doesn't care if he makes an out as long as he advances the other runner already on base. This is called a "sacrifice bunt" because the batter sacrifices himself to advance a runner already on base. Another type of bunt is a "squeeze bunt," which is attempted with a runner on third base who rushes home when the batter bunts the ball.

Blue: A slang term for umpire. Umpires in the early days wore blue, and players call umpires "blue" more often than not. "Hey, Blue! Are you blind? That wasn't a strike!"

ERA: Earned Run Average. This is a statistic measuring a pitcher's performance. The number of earned runs (not involving errors) allowed multiplied by nine (# of innings in a game) divided by the total number of innings pitched by that pitcher. If a pitcher has an ERA of 5.5, it means, on average, he gives up five and a half runs for every nine innings he pitches.

Exit Velocity: The speed (mph) that the baseball attains when hit. For example, an announcer might say, "Wow! That ball had an exit velocity of 111!" rather than "Wow! That was a hard-hit ball!"

Knuckleball: A pitch thrown with the knuckles or fingertips gripping the ball in such a way to create little or no spin. The lack of spin causes the ball to "float" erratically, like a butterfly. A knuckleball can be very frustrating to try to hit as well as to learn to throw. It is rarely seen since few pitchers even attempt to learn it. The knuckleball is generally thrown at a slower speed than other pitches.

Launch Angle: The angle at which the ball is propelled by the bat. You might hear an announcer say, "That ball had a launch angle of about 15 to 20 degrees before it hit the wall and bounced past the outfielder for a triple."

Mound Visit: This usually refers to when the pitching coach or manager asks for time and visits the pitcher on the mound to discuss strategy or take him out of the game. Upon the second mound visit, the pitcher must be removed from the game.

OBP: On-Base Percentage. The number of times the batter gets on base divided by his number of at-bats.

OPS: On-Base Plus Slugging. This is the sum total of On-Base Percentage and Slugging Percentage. This statistic measures a player's power impact. For example, a player who hits more doubles, triples, and home runs has a higher OPS than a player who hits mostly singles.

Pitch Count: The number of pitches a pitcher throws in a game. During games, announcers talk a great deal about how many pitches the pitcher has thrown. This count has been a recent (last twenty years or so) phenomenon. It is generally accepted now, erroneously in my opinion, that it is dangerous for pitchers to throw more than 100 pitches, so pitchers are generally removed from a game at that point. This was never the case in earlier eras when pitchers pitched until they were tired or ineffective. There is no scientific evidence I am aware of to substantiate the 100 pitch concern.

Pitching Rotation: Typically, a team has five starting pitchers who pitch in order. The number one pitcher pitches today, number two pitches the next game, and so on through all five. In the past, teams had four starting pitchers and a four-man rotation.

RBI: Runs Batted In. This measure how many runs are "batted in" by a batter. A batter who produces 100 RBIs in a season is considered to have had an excellent RBI season.

Retire the side: A phrase that means to attain the three outs necessary to end your opponent's inning. In usage: The pitcher retired the side and walked back to the dugout.

The Shift: This refers to moving a fielder on the opposite side of the field from their normal position. For instance, if a batter almost always hits the ball on the first base side of the infield, a team will move a fielder to that side from the side where the batter rarely hits.

* The above definitions are my own and very basic. Readers who want the most complete definitions can consult Paul Dickson's *Baseball Dictionary*, which has over 10,000 entries.

★ **CHAPTER 1** ★

The Café

"It's official. Baseball is ruined forever!" said Frank, walking into the café and throwing down his newspaper in disgust.

"What's wrong?" asked his best friend Dustin, as their favorite barista Maddy brought his coffee.

"All these stupid analytics freaks are messing with the game," said Frank. "Now they want to put clocks in baseball to time the pitcher! What's next? Two-minute warnings and penalty boxes? Have I gone nutso?"

"Well, my friend," Dustin said, "you've always been a little nutso. Are you taking it to new levels?"

Frank Cumberland and Dustin Edwards had been best friends since fifth grade and could read each other like a married couple. The Berwyn Café was where they'd been meeting up and finishing each other's sentences weekly for years.

"I just might be." Frank sighed as he draped his jacket over the back of his chair and sat down. "Maddy, would you bring me an Americano with a shot of vanilla, please?"

"You got it, Frank. Be right back."

"Just before you got here, Frank," Dustin said, "I was thinking about how much baseball has changed from the simple game we played on The Field. Funny, how we just called it The Field. It was our *Field of Dreams*. And now we're sitting in the Berwyn Café, built on that sacred ground, about where third base used to be."

"Yeah," Frank said. "Nobody would understand unless they were with us. Thanks for listening to my little rant. I'll be all right in a minute."

"I know. You just have to grouse every hour or so. Hey, remember when the circus came to town and took over our field for two weeks in the summer?" Dustin asked.

"*No*, I completely forgot about that." Frank laughed. "Imagine that, elephants being unloaded from the train and being marched up Berwyn Road to our field."

"And who could forget the eau de dung?" said Dustin.

"That whole scene almost seemed made-up." Frank said. "What a fun place to grow up. We created most of our own fun, like when the boys from Potomac Avenue challenged the rest of Berwyn to baseball and football games."

"Yes," said Dustin. "Back then, you were skinniest, fastest kid on the field."

Frank laughed. "That was a long time ago. Twenty years in the Air Force thickened me up real nice. I'll bet I can still run the hundred-yard dash in under forty-five seconds, though."

Maddy brought Frank's Americano and wasn't busy, so she sat down with them.

"What's new, Maddy?" Dustin asked. "Now that you've graduated high school early, are you starting college or working for a while?"

"I'm going to enroll at Maryland next semester and knock out some freshman 101 courses. I'll work here still as much as I can. I love my job and my customers."

"How *is* the biz?" Dustin asked.

"It's been okay," she said. "We're shaking up the menu some, and we have a networking group that meets here twice a week. They're starting to bring more people with them. What's new in your world?"

"Not much. I'm just living my retired life, writing some, staying active in our Optimist Club, and trying my best to appreciate my friends, like this galoot," Dustin said, nodding in Frank's direction. "The big news around here is about Frank's nephew, Rex Collier. Rex was chosen to be the director of marketing for the new team in Major League Baseball, The Nashville Knights. He'll be here in a little while to tell us more. Rex worked hard learning the ropes with the Nationals as the assistant director of marketing. Now he's the top dog in Nashville."

Maddy looked surprised. "That's great. I guess he and his family will be moving to Nashville, though; that's not so great. I'll miss them, especially his son, Charlie. He's a real cutie."

"Oh, they'll be back a lot. I'll still be living here," Frank said. "Rex can't go too long without seeing his Uncle Frank."

"So, what's the focus of the conversation today?" Maddy asked.

"Well, I'd say Frank chose the topic when he came in and slammed his newspaper," Dustin replied. "What do you think about analytics in baseball, Maddy? That's what Frank was slamming down his paper over."

"I have a math brain," Maddy said, "so analyzing something seems good to me. Why is it controversial?"

Frank seized the opportunity to educate the young barista. "My dear Maddy, I once had a professor of abnormal psychology who, on the first day of class, said, 'We're all crazy; it's just a matter of degree.' With analytics, it's all a matter of degree too. Baseball is an instinctual game played out in milliseconds. See ball, catch ball, hit ball. When players focus too much on analytics, their instinctual play can take a backseat; they hesitate. That's not good."

"Hmm…I can see that when you explain it that way," Maddy said. "What kinds of things do they overanalyze?"

"Well," said Frank, "by watching a game and listening to the announcers, you'll notice the terms they use. They tell you that the ball made 2,689 revolutions on the way to home plate. They call that the 'spin rate.' When the batter hits the ball, they tell you the ball traveled from his bat at a thirty-seven-degree 'launch angle.' Then they talk about 'exit velocity,' how many miles per hour the ball travels when the batter hits it. Worst of all, though, is 'pitch count.' Announcers remind listeners throughout the game how many pitches the pitcher has thrown. They report on this about as often as they mention the score. Who gives a rat's patootie how many times the ball spins or what the launch angle is?"

"Are the coaches and managers using all this information during a game?" Maddy asked.

"Yes, all the time! You're asking good questions, Maddy," Frank said.

"Somehow," Dustin jumped in, "the analytics people have convinced all of baseball that pitchers can't throw more than 100 pitches a game without risk of injury. I've never seen any evidence of this, but it's accepted as gospel now. Managers take pitchers out of games when they get near or over 100 pitches, even when they look strong and dominant. So many times the relief pitcher comes in and loses the game. Managers decide when to remove a pitcher based on analytic charts rather than believing what they're seeing with their own eyes!"

"There are plenty of other examples of analytics bringing down the level of play rather than improving it," Frank added.

"I see what you mean," Maddy said. "Music is similar. You don't want to think and plan jazz; if you do, it won't be as good. It's instinctual, like baseball. I get it. What does Charlie think? Charlie's a math whiz like me, but he seems instinctual, not a nerd; does he like analytics in baseball?"

Frank laughed. "Charlie hates analytics because they are misused. The boy's got a 189 IQ, but he has common sense too. He's taking advanced statistics at Maryland so he can sort through analytics and separate the wheat from the chafe. Charlie's a brainiac who's a normal kid in most ways. His abnormalities are harmless, like his penchant for puns."

"Who's normal anyway? Charlie's not normal and neither are we," Dustin said.

"True enough," Frank replied. "We did so many abnormal things. I remember the time you got caught sneaking out of your house in the middle of the night to practice your pitching against the brick wall at Holy Redeemer. You wanted extra practice."

"We all wanted extra practice, more baseball," Dustin said. "Heck, for every game we played in the city league, we must have played ten on our field. I think how different our lives would be without baseball. The lessons we learned on the field—how to win, lose, compete, and show good sportsmanship—were game-changers. If not for those lessons, my sales and marketing career would not have worked out as well as it did, and I probably wouldn't have been successful enough to have retired."

Maddy saw another customer coming in and excused herself. "Thanks for the education on analytics."

Frank and Dustin shifted to talk about the Nationals' disappointing season, and Dustin asked, "Are you renewing your same seats or moving up closer next year, Frank? Your eyes aren't getting any better."

"I wouldn't mind being closer, but the ushers in my section have started calling me 'The Mayor of Nats town,' so it'd be hard to start over in a new section. I'm not moving my seats. Rex has been bugging me about moving my seats closer too."

As if on cue, Rex walked in.

Now almost forty, Rex still had his All-American good looks. Imagine a smaller, older version of Angels center fielder Mike Trout, about 5'10" and weighing around 210, with a square jaw, short cropped hair, and a solid build. Rex had played college ball at Towson University and was drafted in the seventh round by the Nationals as a catcher. After five years of riding buses and not advancing past single A-ball, he was able to pursue another path to stay in baseball in the Nationals' marketing department. He was always a "brainy" kind of ballplayer, whose intelligence both on and off the field was a big factor in his being able to play professional ball at all.

Frank offered up his usual greeting. "How's my *favorite* nephew?"

"Uncle Frank, I'm *still* your only nephew," Rex replied.

"True, but even if I had ten nephews, you'd be my favorite," Frank shot back, with his impish grin.

Maddy came over and asked if Rex wanted his usual, an iced Americano with an extra shot.

"Double extra shot, please," Rex told her. "I need a boost today."

"What's up, Rex?" Frank queried. "You just got the big job in Nashville; why the long face?"

"Uncle Frank, I haven't been sleeping enough lately with the back and forth between here and Nashville; that's all. I'm just tired and need a boost."

"Well, have a seat and maybe your fancy coffee and our scintillating conversation will transform your mood and energy," Frank replied with his twinkly eyes, again flashing his impish grin. "First, though, how's that boy of yours doing, my favorite great-nephew?"

"Charlie's having a great summer," Rex replied. "All baseball, all the time, except for a few hours knocking out some Saturday morning col-lege courses at Maryland. Lately, he's been working on some secret baseball white paper for his statistics class. He won't tell me specifi-cally what it's about, but I know he's doing research on the twentieth century history of the game and comparing it to current day. I'll bring him next week and he'll tell us more. He would have come today, but he woke up with a splitting headache. He had one last week too.

"I doubt," Rex continued, "that there's a fourteen-year-old anywhere who knows more about baseball history than Charlie. Except that he's pretty normal, sometimes he reminds me of Dustin Hoffman's char-acter in *Rain Man* when he memorized the phone book. Once the data is in Charlie's head, he calls it up at will, as needed. He would kick butt if he ever got on a baseball-themed *Jeopardy* show. I tease him sometimes about using his gifts for good, not evil. Last week, we watched *Batman*, the one with Batman and Robin versus The Riddler. I was teasing him and asking if he thinks he could outwit Batman, or would Batman defeat him, like the others?

"Here's what the goofball said, 'I wouldn't *defeat* Batman. He would recognize my talents, and we'd be partners, fighting for justice across the globe, and we'd keep Robin as an assistant. And The Riddler's jokes wouldn't stand a chance against my puns.'"

They had a laugh over that, and then Rex said he wanted to change the subject.

Maddy brought Rex's drink just as he switched gears.

"Maybe you two guys can help me with ideas to sell out the ballpark in Nashville, channel your inner Bill Veeck. Then I can keep this cool job!"

(Bill Veeck, who owned the Cleveland Indians and Chicago White Sox, was known for being baseball's greatest promoter. He is best remembered for sending dwarf Eddie Gaedel to the plate, all 3' 7" of him. Gaedel batted once and walked on four pitches, all high.)

"Charlie," said Rex, "was telling me this morning that he's working on an idea to lead the league in attendance. Maybe it has something to do with his white paper!"

Frank and Dustin both laughed, always amused by Charlie's endeavors.

They raised their glasses and toasted, "To Charlie's project and to Nashville winning the World Series and leading the league in attendance."

"I can't wait to hear Charlie's theories," Dustin said. "Be sure to drag him along next time. I miss the rascal."

After they finished their drinks, they said bye to Maddy, who said, "Bring Charlie next time."

"That seems to be the consensus," Rex said. "I'm pretty sure he'll be with me next week."

★ CHAPTER 2 ★

The Café
Next Saturday

Dustin had just settled into his seat and taken his first sip of coffee when Rex sauntered in with his athletic stride, Martha and Charlie in tow. Charlie had Norman Rockwell-ish, all-American good looks… square jaw, moderate number of freckles, dimples, thick sandy brown coarse hair, and even with the braces, a lady-killer smile.

"CHAR-LEEE!" Dustin yelled. "Long time, no see! Where've you been hiding?"

"Hey, Mister D! I'm not hiding; I'm right here. I came here today because I knew you'd drop some nuggets of sage advice on me, right, Mom?"

"He did tell me that on the way over," Martha affirmed.

"Okay, Mr. Brainiac, I've got your sage advice: Get your head out of the books some and have fun! Got any of your jokes for me today?"

"You bet, Mister D! Have I ever let you down? What did the glove say to the baseball?"

"I don't know, Charlie; what *did* the glove say to the ball?"

"Catch ya later!"

"Groaner!"

"Okay then, here's another: Why was it so windy at Candlestick Park? Because of all the Giant *fans!*"

"That's enough for today, Charlie. One more groaner and you're going to the *pun*itentiary!"

"I'm sorry, Mister D. It's true I go overboard with the puns. They just keep coming to me, sometimes out of the blue, at the oddest times. I have thousands stored on my hard drive," he said as he tapped his head.

Martha said her goodbyes and headed off for a meeting of the Berwyn Civic Association at the Holy Redeemer School across the street, leaving Charlie to hang with the menfolk. Frank walked in just in time for a quick hi and bye with Martha. They all settled in to talking baseball and reliving old times. Maddy came by and took orders. As usual, she gave Charlie some extra attention and a little teasing.

"So, Charlie, you picking up the tab for the old coots today?" Maddy asked with her best deadpan expression.

Charlie searched his pockets, turning them inside out, and said, "Nope; looks like it's on Mister D today."

"Well, one of these days, Charlie, you'll be able to buy and sell all of these guys," she replied, nodding toward Frank and Dustin. "So, for now, let them pay for everything." She laughed and sashayed to the kitchen.

"You got it, Charlie," said Dustin. "I'm buying today, *but* my price for buying your drink is you have to tell me something about this top-secret white paper you're working on. I hear you're analyzing stats from bygone baseball days and comparing different eras."

"That's part of it, Mister D," said the whiz kid, with an air of mystery.

"C'mon, Charlie; gimme something here."

"Okay, Mister D, *just for you*, here's my tidbit of the day and a fun story. Yesterday, I was looking at innings pitched and pitch counts from the early days compared to today's game and, ultimately, trying to determine if there is statistical validity to limiting pitch count due to its relationship to injury and longevity. I'm hoping to be able to prove one of my theories: There is no statistically significant difference in results when comparing pitchers from 1979-1999 and 1999-2019, despite the pitch count obsession of the latter period. I'm not finished yet, but I did find a random story from the pre-pitch count days that you might enjoy. It doesn't prove or disprove my hypothesis, but it's a fun story.

"So here it is," Charlie said as he leaned in like an old, wizened storyteller. With a gleam in his eye, and a pregnant pause to signify that he was about to drop something worthy on them, he continued, "This is a true story. The Providence Grays were a major league team in 1884 whose owner gave them an ultimatum…*win the pennant or disband*. The Grays had a pitching staff led by their ace, Charlie Sweeney. One day, Sweeney was enraged when he was pulled from a July game in the seventh inning and quit the team on the spot. Another pitcher, Charles "Old Hoss" Radbourn, told the manager that if the team gave him a raise, he would pitch *every* game for the rest of the season. They obliged him. Old Hoss threw 678 innings over seventy-five appearances. He finished the season with eleven shutouts, an ERA [earned run average] of 1.38, and a record of 59-12! That's when men were tougher and pitchers pitched until they were too tired or ineffective. The Grays won the pennant and didn't have to disband. Old Hoss had a sore arm, but I haven't researched yet how he did in subsequent seasons. And did you notice that the ace pitchers in the story were named Charles and Charlie? I'd have changed Hoss to Charlie *Horse* Radbourn."

"So, what's your angle on your paper, son?" Rex asked.

"Well, Dad, my goal is to prove statistically that the analytics so widely revered are without evidence to support that they enhance team-winning percentages, as measured by results. I'm starting with the hyper-focus on pitch count, but I will look at several other key areas."

"So, you're saying analytics in baseball is hogwash?"

"Well, not totally, but 90 percent of it is, and I think I can prove it."

Chatty Maddy brought our drinks in time to hear Charlie's statement and responded with one of her typical odd quips. "Yeah, Charlie, you tell 'em; show 'em how a *real* genius rolls, and then just grin at 'em. It'll drive 'em nuts."

The men laughed and Charlie shot right back at her, "Maybe you can come along when I present my research to Professor Jacobs, Maddy. You can bring poms-poms to cheer me on; that'd be extra special! What fourteen-year-old has a personal cheerleader? In fact, who of any age does? I'd like that!"

On the way to the kitchen, Maddy got in the last word over her shoulder. "I'm a free agent, Charlie, just like Mike Trout. Pay me enough and I'm yours."

Rex let out a howl and Charlie blushed.

Recovering, Charlie changed the subject, "Mister D, did you talk with my Uncle Frank today? Is he stopping by?"

A second later, almost on cue, Frank burst through the door, waving an envelope Cosmo Kramer-style, "Hey, guys! Look what I just scored—four seats right beside the Nats dugout for the final game of the season! My pal Brent invited us. Let's all go. *Remember*, Jordan Zimmermann pitched a no-hitter in the final game one year, saved by the diving catch by Stephen Souza, Jr. with two outs in the ninth. We don't get seats like this often; maybe something great will happen."

It was settled; they were going!

Frank ordered a poppy seed bagel with butter and no cream cheese, and water with a slice of lemon. He had turned over a new leaf, cutting down on caffeine and drinking more water, per doctor's orders. They talked for forty-five minutes, dissecting the final two months of the season since the tailspin had begun in late July. Frank made the analogy that the previous night's game had been a microcosm of the season. "Our boys led 6-2 after six innings and lost 7-6 with three errors over the final three frames and another blown save. They just didn't finish, and again pulled defeat from the jaws of victory."

Charlie was more engaged than usual today. He got agitated talking about the team's underachieving season and lack of fundamentals, saying it didn't have to be. "*Imagine* if Casey Stengel, Walter Alston, or Connie Mack could rise from the grave and manage a modern team. They would *dominate* today's game. And imagine *this*—starters pitching until they tire rather than counting pitches, hitters hitting behind the runner, everyone being able to bunt, a four-man rotation, and hitters putting the ball in play, taking pride in not striking out. And managers believing what they see with their eyes instead of what's on the stat sheets. *That's* just the beginning!"

Charlie was in full rant now. "We'd win the pennant! Every team in baseball has joined the Church of Analytics. We could win two or three pennants before other teams start copying us. My research has convinced me that today's method of managing based on analytics results in a lower caliber of play, just the opposite of what was intended."

Frank's jaw dropped. "That is fascinating, Charlie. Do you know that one of Henry David Thoreau's most famous quotes could be applied to your take on the use of analytics in baseball?"

"Which one"?

"Thoreau said, 'Our life is frittered away by detail…simplify, simplify, simplify.' It is simple, right? *See ball, hit ball, catch ball.*"

"Uncle Frank, Thoreau was profound. I remember reading that he had a thing for baseball, too." Charlie reached for his iPhone and searched Thoreau Baseball. "Check this out…on April 10, 1856, Thoreau wrote in his journal about checking on a baseball field. I'll read this, *his* words: *April 10, 1856, Thursday. Some fields dried sufficiently for the games of ball which this season has ushered in. I associated this day when I can remember it, with games of baseball over behind the hills in the russet fields toward Sleepy Hollow….*

"It says he was thirty-eight at the time. He had left Walden Pond nine years earlier, published *Walden* two years earlier, and the Civil War was five years away. Wow. How cool would it have been to see those early games?"

Charlie paused for a moment, giving Rex the chance to ask, "So, when do you turn in your white paper, son?"

"Next Thursday, but I'll continue my research. It's been fun."

"Is it as much fun researching baseball as playing it?" asked Frank.

"No way, Uncle Frank; there's *nothing* as fun as playing baseball! I hope to make The Show myself."

Maddy brought their check just as Martha walked in from her civic association meeting. Frank said he had to roll, so they paid Maddy, and high-tailed it out of there.

★ CHAPTER 3 ★

Under the Lights

"Mom, have you seen my cleats!" Charlie yelled from the mud room.

"Yes, Charlie. I cleaned them up for you. They're on the back porch. And your cap is drying. I cleaned that too."

"What?" Charlie shouted. "You *cleaned* my cap? People don't clean their baseball caps. I have dirt and sweat on that cap from the last two years; that's my lucky cap! It's a *seasoned* hat, and we're playing for the league championship tonight. I'm superstitious!"

"Son, you're so good you don't need luck."

"Yeah right, Mom. Everybody needs some luck, like a weak grounder in just the right spot between infielders. It's okay; I'll rub dirt on it before tonight's game, and it's humid so I'll get fresh sweat on it. Will you be there?"

"I should get there an inning or two late. Your dad will be home in about twenty minutes to take you; his plane was late taking off in

Nashville. I have to scoot now; it's my turn to stop by Ledo's to pick up pizza to drop off at my writers group meeting. I'll skip the meeting itself to come to your game. I like to be there when you're pitching. Please feed Gandolfini before you leave." (Gandolfini was their retired racing greyhound.)

Martha kissed her boy and told him the same thing she told him before every game. "Don't you dare come home with a clean uniform!"

Charlie smiled and said, "If a kid shows up here with a clean uniform, send him away; he's an imposter. See you at the game, Momma Bear."

Charlie plopped on the couch and called out, stretching out the syllables, "Fiiiii-Niii! Hey, big boy, come to your favorite human!"

Fini bolted around the corner and jumped on the couch for his loving. "You're a good boy," Charlie told him. "You're a magnificent athlete." (Fini had been a winner on the greyhound track in Tampa.)

Fini appeared to understand and looked at Charlie with his soulful eyes, seeming to smile. "I'll take you out and throw the Frisbee to you later, big boy."

Charlie flipped on the TV to the MLB channel where Bill Ripken and Harold Reynolds were discussing launch angles and exit velocity. Ripken was making the point that focus on the long ball and launch angles had resulted in too many strikeouts, and there was no longer shame in striking out. He lamented that this season was the first time in history when there had been more strikeouts than hits—not good for the game.

Just then, Rex arrived home and gave Charlie his usual greeting,

"Hey, Charlie Hustle (Pete Rose had been his favorite old-time player), how's my boy today?"

"I'm good, Dad. I just can't wait to pitch against Beltsville tonight." Charlie played for College Park in the fourteen and under select league. "Beltsville has some hitters who can mash the ball. I think I can shut them down if I can change speeds, paint the corners, and move the ball around the zone. When can we leave?"

"Give me about fifteen minutes and I'll be ready. Please feed Gandolfini while I'm getting out of my monkey suit," Rex said.

Fini's ears perked up, and he jumped off the couch with Charlie close behind. Charlie dished out Fini's food into the oversized silver dog bowl and said, "Here you go, big boy. Chow down like the big dog you are!"

The starving canine cleaned his bowl like he might never eat again, rearing up excitedly like a horse, his signal he was ready for dessert—two bacon-flavored doggie biscuits.

A few minutes later, father and son piled into their dark green Honda Accord. Driving to and from games was a ritual they enjoyed because they talked about the game on the way and dissected it on the way home. Rex was coaching because the coach from last year had a drinking problem and had mostly quit showing up; the times he had, he had whiskey on his breath. The parents removed him and recruited Rex to finish the season, so this was his first full season as coach. The Nashville job meant that assistant coach Mr. Hoover would fill in when Rex was away. Charlie loved playing against rival Beltsville, especially when they played under the lights at Fletchers Field. This would be the third straight year the two teams would be playing for the league championship with each team having won once. It would be the rubber match. Fletchers was the only field in the area where kids got to play night games, and the championship game was always at Fletchers. It was special because Fletchers had a beautifully manicured infield, a full-fledged press box, and a public address announcer. The boys loved having their names announced. They felt like *big dogs*.

As usual, Rex and Charlie were the first to arrive. Charlie carried the equipment bag to the home dugout. Rex posted the starting lineup on the back of the dugout wall. A few more cars pulled into the parking lot, and players from both teams piled out of cars, carrying their gear.

"Good, Alfred's here. We can warm up early," Charlie said.

Alfred was an excellent catcher; he had grit and wasn't afraid to get down and dirty to block balls. He was a tough kid who came from a challenging family environment with an alcoholic father. He loved baseball every bit as much as Charlie. The boys were battery mates and best friends.

Alfred always knew when to call time to make a mound visit to offer encouragement or tell a random joke. During mound visits, he called Charlie by his nickname, "Suster," often shortened to "Sus." A couple of years ago, Charlie had been trying to say "Buster" but got tongue-tied so it came out as "Suster." The nickname had stuck on him and he'd grown to like it. Although it was still an hour before game time, Alfred and Sus walked down the right field line to the bullpen area to talk about the Beltsville lineup and start to loosen up. The two teams were familiar with one another from the previous season and because some of the boys went to school together.

As it got closer to game time, the teams took extra batting practice because the umpire was late. Finally, he arrived in a beat-up, old yellow Volkswagen with peace stickers all over the front bumper. As the umpire got out and lugged his gear toward the field, the College Park third baseman, Bennie Nutwell, yelled in his direction, "Hey, Blue! Where'd you get the hippie car? Woodstock?"

Bennie flashed a sly smile and turned away, thinking nobody would figure out he'd made the remark. He was the guy—every team has one—who made wisecracks and played grab-ass. But Rex called him over to the bench.

"Bennie," said Rex, "do you think it's wise to insult the umpire?"

"I didn't insult the umpire," Bennie replied. "I insulted his car, which is an inanimate object, Coach. *Technically*, you gotta admit, I'm right."

"Well, tell ya what, Bennie; *technically* your ass is gonna be sitting on *this* inanimate object (slapping the bench) if I hear one more smart-ass word or action from you. You might be riding the pine next game, too, picking splinters! Get back out there, keep your nose clean, and show some respect."

Bennie trudged off, seemingly still amused by his Woodstock crack, judging by his sly smile.

"And wipe the smile, Bennie!"

Playing at Fletchers Field meant having the national anthem played to start the game, just like in the big leagues. Charlie loved that. College Park, being the home team, lined up on the first base line with Beltsville lined up down the third base line, facing the flag just beyond the center field fence. The lights were older lights obtained from long-gone Griffith Stadium in Washington, so they took about twenty minutes to gradually reach maximum brightness. The PA announcer asked all ladies and gentlemen to stand, remove their caps, and honor America by singing along, and they all did, followed by robust shouts of "Play ball!"

It was dusk as Charlie threw the first pitch of the game.

"*Stee-rike one!*" Blue yelled. Charlie and his teammates had seen this umpire before. He was a good one, and was always entertaining. He tended to strut around home plate like a bantam rooster. Last year, he had umpired a game, and when Alfred had checked his swing on a close pitch, he had jumped to the side of home plate, pointing at it, and shouted, "Yes, you did! Yes, you did! Yes, you did!"

Charlie retired the side in the first inning with a pop-up to first, and two long fly balls to center. Three up, three down, but two of the outs were rockets. Thank goodness for having Jimmy Ryan in center; he was so fast he ran down almost every ball hit near him. Jimmy was a natural. His older brother Pat was the team's right fielder. Charlie sailed through the next two innings but struggled with control in the 4th, walking two, both of whom scored on a double by the Beltsville clean-up hitter Jesse Binnall, which tied the game 2 to 2, as College Park had scored 2 in the 3rd. Charlie was done for the day on the mound due to the league maximum innings rule for pitchers. Charlie moved to shortstop, and Lee Ingram—everybody called him "Big Lee"—came in to pitch. Big Lee threw hard and had a tendency to be effectively wild. He kept them loose in the box. Sometimes he'd throw at the hitter's feet. He said he loved to make 'em dance. Big Lee pitched the 5th inning, hitting two batters, but striking out the side, and holding Beltsville scoreless. Alex Dickson and Donnie Sauls combined to shut down Beltsville's bats in the 6th and 7th innings, keeping the score deadlocked.

In the bottom of the 7th, Charlie led off with a walk, in an eight pitch at-bat. Always a threat to steal, Charlie took a good lead at first. The Beltsville southpaw threw over, in a lackadaisical way, and Charlie easily got back, so he stretched his lead another half step. He looked to the third base coach for the steal sign. It was on; he had the green light. The pitcher threw over again, this time with his quick move. Charlie got back, barely. He now had his lead measured. Wary of a pitch-out, Charlie decided not to go on the first pitch. The Beltsville lefty went home this time. Passed ball! Charlie scampered into 2nd. The next hitter was Taylor Tobias, a lefty singles hitter who rarely struck out. Taylor was patient and worked the count to his favor 3-1. Charlie was getting a good lead and secondary lead at 2nd base, playing cat and mouse with the shortstop and 2nd baseman. The 3-1 fastball to Taylor got too much of the plate and the sweet spot of Taylor's bat. Taylor hit a screaming line drive up the middle for a base hit and almost took the pitcher's head off. Charlie was off and running and rounding third. The centerfielder had been playing shallow for this exact situation—to make a play at the plate. He fielded the ball cleanly and came up throwing. It was right on line, a perfect one-hopper to home plate.

The ball and Charlie arrived at the same time. Charlie slid, the catcher applied the tag, a cloud of dust rose, and all eyes were on the umpire. He hesitated, peering through the dust. Then he gave the crowd a flamboyant dance step, pointing at Charlie, who was on his back, looking up expectantly. "You scored! You are *safe!*" the umpire screeched, with another dance step for emphasis. The College Park bench erupted into a swarm of delirious ballplayers converging at home plate. A walk-off win and another league championship!

"Final score, College Park 3, Beltsville 2, winning pitcher Charlie Collier, game-winning RBI, Taylor Tobias," the PA announcer informed the crowd. "Thank you, fans, for supporting youth baseball, and be sure to stop by the snack bar for your post-game treats."

After shaking hands with Beltsville, the team and coaches took the team down the right field line, away from parents and other fans, to have the usual post-game team meeting. Rex told the kids how proud he was of all of them. He brought them into a circle for a last cheer. "Champions! All hands in, all at once…. *Champions!*"

★ CHAPTER 4 ★

Statistics Class

As she'd done every Monday morning for the last few months, Martha had scrambled eggs, hash browns, bacon, and toast with blackberry jam waiting for Charlie when he came down for breakfast. He'd put that in as a special request when he graduated from high school. It was his favorite breakfast, and he said it made a psychological difference in his weekly performance.

"As soon as you're done, son, we have to leave. I just heard on WMAL that traffic is backed up more than usual this morning. I'll feed Fini while you're eating so we can save time. Do you have everything you need for class in your backpack?"

"Not quite everything I need, Mom," Charlie said with a grin. "I could use a teeny-weeny person to massage my feet and back while I'm in class, someone who could hide in my backpack until the proper time. Maybe like in that old TV Show, *I Dream of Jeannie*. She was invisible to everyone but her master, I think. I'd like that!"

"Keep on dreaming, son."

"I'll never stop dreaming, Mom, and I have some real outlandish dreams. Dreaming is good; Albert Einstein said imagination is more important than intelligence, and Walt Disney believed that too."

Charlie could have been lazy with his genius IQ; he could get by without much effort in most endeavors. He fought that tendency, though, and studied other high IQ people to learn how to maximize his gifts. Creativity fascinated him, and he wanted to discover how to unlock unused portions of his brain. He had read about the greatest inventor of all time, Dr. Yoshiro Nakamatsu of Japan, with more than 2,300 patents to his credit, more than double that of Thomas Edison, who comes in second at 1,093. Dr. Nakamatsu had specific methods, including going into all-white rooms, writing on tablets while underwater, and listening to classical music at certain megahertz levels. Charlie studied other inventors and methods, too, and was able to gain insights into how to enhance his creativity. He had, on two occasions, been able to get into an "enhanced state of being" and was hoping to learn to do so on demand, as needed.

Living with a fourteen-year-old certified genius can be challenging. Rex and Martha viewed their role as guiding more than teaching Charlie, and seeing that he had as normal a childhood as possible.

"Let's go, Charlie! I'm getting in the car. We have to leave *now*."

Charlie bolted around the corner and flopped into the car, buckled his seat belt, and said, "Let's go, Mama. Channel your inner Danica Patrick! Professor Jacobs loves to pick on people who are late. He usually says, 'Glad you were able to grace us with your presence, Mr. or Ms. Tardy' to everyone who walks in late. It's embarrassing. And the way he pronounces *tardy* makes it sound like *turdy*. I think he does it on purpose."

Although they lived only about four miles north of campus in the Sunnyside Section of College Park, it often took 25-30 minutes by car because Route One was backed up. Charlie's statistics class was in the Glenn L. Martin Engineering Building on campus, near the Route One entrance to the university, so taking the alternate route of University Boulevard wasn't an option. Martha dropped off Charlie just in time. He got in under the wire and avoided Professor Jacobs' jab about being late. Only one student was late and on the receiving end today. Professor Jacobs seemed to enjoy giving that student a particularly robust "*Mr. Tuuuuurdy*," after which he said, "Class, today you'll be getting back the papers you handed in two weeks ago. Most of you will not like your grade. I am known to be a tough grader. Grade inflation doesn't happen in my class, and there are no certificates for participation. I do not grade on a curve system. I'll give your papers back at the end of class."

Making them all wait seemed cruel to Charlie. When the class finally ended, one by one, they were called before the Great Math God, Professor Jacobs, to be handed their grade.

"Charles Collier," Professor Jacobs bellowed. He was a tall man with spindly legs, a Babe Ruth potbelly body, and mutton chop sideburns. He looked like a computer-generated morphing of The Babe and Disney's animated version of Ichabod Crane. His facial features were even sharper than Ichabod Crane's, with his pointy nose and beady eyes. Charlie dutifully marched to the front of the room with perfect posture and was handed his graded paper. Professor Jacobs had silently handed out papers to those preceding Charlie, but as he gave

Charlie his paper he said, "Nice attempt, Mr. Collier. I'm a baseball fan and I *like* analytics." Charlie knew that remark didn't bode well for his grade. He bolted for the door and exited the building, crossing Campus Drive, and then sat down in the grass on the knoll between the Chapel and Route One. Finally, Charlie turned his paper over and looked: C–!

Charlie was dumbstruck—an odd experience for the child genius. He sat there, motionless for several minutes with a thousand-yard stare. Raindrops started to fall, and then the sky opened up. The rain awakened Charlie from his stupor, and he sprinted toward McKeldin Library where he usually spent the hour between Statistics and Spanish class. He found a desk on the second floor in the study area, where he sat down to read the comments explaining his grade, but the only thing Professor Jacobs had written was "I'm not convinced; your research is inadequate." Charlie could feel the blood rising in his head and told himself to let it go. This was one of those life situations where Charlie's brain power allowed his intellect to override his emotions, something he had trained himself to do after reading *Control Your Mind and Master Your Feelings* by Eric Robertson. The blood rising was a signal to think through the situation rather than react, and a calm came back over him. Charlie took out his Spanish study materials, and for now at least, put Professor Tuuuurdy out of his thoughts. After Spanish class, hunger pangs hit, so Charlie walked to Hungry Herman's for a Cheese Steak Sub and to wait for Martha to pick him up.

After a few minutes, Martha parked her gray Subaru Outback in the open space just in front of the restaurant and came in to grab a quick bite herself. Finding Charlie seated in a booth, she said, "Hi, son!

Want me to give you a kiss and embarrass you?"

"If you want, Mom. Why should today be any different?"

She smiled. "I'll refrain; too many students in here now." She slid into the booth. "So, how was your day? Did you get your statistics paper back?"

Charlie held the paper up silently with the big fat C– clearly visible. "My first C ever. Oh, well, I still believe in my theory and think I made a good case for it."

"I'm sorry, Charlie. Maybe you're in the same category with Fred Smith."

"Who's Fred Smith?"

"Fred Smith wrote a paper in college outlining a new business model he thought would revolutionize the delivery industry by using a hub and spoke system. He got a C on his paper. He continued to believe in his theory and started a company based on it. You might have heard of his company; it's called FedEx!"

Charlie's eyes widened. "Holy smokes, Mom! Maybe I can be the Fred Smith of baseball. If only I can get my theory implemented, but I can't exactly start my own MLB baseball team."

Then he had a thought. Martha noticed his faraway look, as though he'd just discovered something new. He whispered just under his breath, "But Dad *works* for one."

★ CHAPTER 5 ★

The Final Game

The final game of the Nats' regular season was bittersweet. It was a beautiful Sunday afternoon, perfect for baseball, seventy-five degrees, and not a cloud in the sky, but it *was* the final game. No playoffs! Nonetheless, the foursome of Dustin, Frank, Rex, and Charlie were delighted that Frank's friend, Brent Polkes, had offered them tickets for the final game against the Braves. Brent owned a successful agency in Bethesda that specialized in insuring large apartment buildings, condos, and shopping centers. A native New Yorker, his childhood dream had been to play second base for the Bronx Bombers, but at 5' 7" and 150 pounds, the cards were stacked against him. The foursome met up at Brent's home in Bethesda where Brent and his wife Cheryl showed them the memorabilia room. Autographed photos of Hall of Famers adorned the walls, along with signed bats and game-used jerseys. Brent shared his story of how he had been able to acquire a couple of game-used bats.

They walked the short distance to the Bethesda Metro Station and boarded a standing-room-only train filled with fans going to the game. Brent's seats were halfway between the home team dugout and home plate, in the second row. Walking to the seats, Brent chatted with the ushers; he knew them by name and they knew him. Brent treated everyone like royalty and was a generous tipper; hence, he and his guests were always well cared for at the park. They found their seats as the grounds crew finished manicuring the area around the batter's box. Rex was studying his phone with a furrowed brow when he said, "I've got to go upstairs and sit in the Owners Suite. Mr. Rockledge just texted, saying he sees us, and he's inviting me and Charlie to join him in the Owners Suite."

"Maybe he wants to try to talk you into staying here instead of Nashville, Dad," Charlie said.

"Whatever the reason, it's a nice gesture, so c'mon," said Rex. "Let's head up there. We'll meet up with you guys at the gate behind home plate after the game."

The game was a slugfest. Entering the ninth inning, the Nats led 10-9. The Nats closer Sean Doolittle came in and struck out the first two hitters; then he had to deal with the dangerous Freddy Freeman. Doolittle got ahead 0-2, but Freeman took two close pitches for balls, fouled off a couple, and then took ball three for a full count. Two more foul balls and the tension mounted. On the tenth pitch of the at-bat, Doolittle threw a fastball that Freeman hammered. Goodbye, baseball! Tie game. Doolittle retired the next hitter and it was on to the bottom of the 9th. Turner led off and was hit by the pitch. On the 2nd pitch from the Braves pitcher, Turner took off for second and arrived a split-second before the throw for his forty-third stolen base of the year. On the next pitch, Juan Soto hit a line drive over the head of first baseman

Freeman. It looked like it might be foul, but it clearly hit the right field line, as evidenced by the small cloud of chalk that puffed up. Blue signaled fair; Turner scored. Game over, season over. The long dark abyss, aka, off-season, was starting too early for the Nationals.

Making their way to the gate behind home plate Brent, Frank, and Dustin reunited with Rex and Charlie. They exchanged high-fives on the victory and headed to the exit. The Navy Yard Metro Station had extra trains running, and they caught one of the first back to Bethesda. A light rain began to fall as they walked from the station back to Brent's. Along the way, Rex said that Mr. Rockledge had invited him to the Owners Suite to thank him for his contributions to the team and wish him well in Nashville.

★ CHAPTER 6 ★

The 8:07 Zoom Session

Rex was up at 5:30 a.m. the next day. He wanted to prepare for the call. Since all the executives with the Knights had not yet moved to Nashville, the Zoom sessions came as close to being face-to-face as possible. All participants had their faces in the boxes on the screen, reminiscent of the old *Hollywood Squares* TV show. Country music legend Tommy "Big T" McCraw was the majority owner of the new team. Big T was a tall, large-framed man with thick, curly gray hair, model good looks, and a deep, twangy Southern drawl. Originally from Oklahoma, he had moved to Nashville as a teen with a guitar and a dream. Growing up in the Golden Age of Baseball in Spavinaw, Oklahoma, birthplace of Mickey Mantle, McCraw could not help having baseball become his first love. After achieving everything he had ever dreamed of in the music business, he turned his attention to baseball when the chance to own the Nashville franchise was within his grasp.

Thomas McCraw was all about getting up early and being on time. He scheduled early meetings at unusual times like 8:07 a.m. so people would remember them. Rex fed Fini first, then quickly downed two cups of coffee, a bowl of oatmeal, and two slices of rye toast with butter and honey. Fini was skilled at acting like a starving dog and tricking his humans into feeding him twice, so Rex left a note to Martha and Charlie that the canine con artist had been fed. Rex then padded to his office in the spare bedroom for the call.

At 8:03, Rex connected. Big T McCraw was already on; he occupied the box in the upper left corner of the screen. Big T looked big, even in the little box on the screen; in person, at 6' 6," he was usually the tallest in the room. Rex was in the box next to him. Rex had met Big T twice during the hiring process, and he was already a fan of his passion for the game and desire to win.

"Howdy, partner," Big T drawled. "How's the family?"

When Rex had taken Martha and Charlie to Nashville for the second interview, Big T had given them a city tour.

Rex hit the unmute and said, "Everybody's doing well. Charlie's doing his thing at the university. Martha's chauffeuring him around and doing her volunteer work."

"Well, I sure enjoyed meeting them both, and the baseball conversation with Charlie was quite intriguing. Tell them howdy for me."

It relaxed Rex that Big T was so down to earth and easy to talk with, in contrast to the owner in Washington. He even asked his staff to call him Big T rather than Mr. McCraw.

At 8:05, Larry Wenzel popped onto the screen in the box to the right of Rex.

Larry had been a decent fielding outfielder and a .240 slap hitter who had a year and a half in The Show. Previously, Larry had been the infield coach for the Texas Rangers. He was a devout Christian who was known to preach on street corners, completely incognito on his rare off-days in away-cities. Once when there was a rainout in Detroit, someone recognized him preaching on a corner in a tough neighbor-hood that same night. Managing the Knights would be his first shot at being the skipper. Lean and angular, with glasses perched halfway down his nose, Larry greeted everyone with a mellow, "Good morning, gentlemen!" He had the pipes of an FM disc jockey. Sometimes listeners had trouble staying focused on what he was saying because his voice distracted from the words. If he'd had a dollar for every time somebody had asked if he was a DJ or suggested he should be a DJ, he would have been rich!

At 8:06, the other attendees popped onto the screen almost simul-taneously…David Clark, Senior Data Analyst; Butch Dory, Director of Minor League Player Development; Kurt Grimmer, General Manager; and Wally Rupp, Director of Scouting.

All said "Good morning." Their names and titles were beneath the boxes. This was the first time the entire executive team had been on a call together, and a couple of them were meeting for the first time.

Big T did what Big T does. Like a big, friendly dog, he took charge. His box lit up, indicating he was about to speak. He leaned in so that his face filled up most of the screen. Everyone else was on mute.

"Hey, y'all! Welcome to this historic call. I'll get us started by telling you a story I told Kurt Grimmer recently when he asked how I got the name Big T. It started when I was eight and a big ol' twelve-year-old was picking on me every day. One day, out of the blue, I told him "*I'm Big T*. Don't mess with *me*," and I punched him in the nose. He left me alone after that. Nobody had ever called me Big T before, so I have no idea why I called *myself* Big T that day. I guess I wanted to scare the kid with a tough name. I'm the son of a trucker and have been blessed beyond my dreams to make it in this big, beautiful, capitalistic society we call America. We hit the birthplace lottery to have been born here, during this era. Everyone on this screen has traveled more than Marco Polo ever did. Think about that.

"These are wonderful times to be alive in *so* many ways, but to me, owning a baseball team is my slice of heaven on earth. There's nothing I'd rather be doing. Y'all are muted, and I'll be doing most or all of the gum flapping for now. I'll share my vision today, which I already partially did with you during your interviewing process. Also, I'll talk about each of you and the strengths you bring to the party. Y'all have distinct, strong personalities. I believe you'll mesh and complement one another, and we'll win sooner than anyone thinks. We'll shock the world! Muhammed Ali said he would shock the world. Only a few believed him. He did it. So will we. We will shock the world!"

Big T paused, took a swig of his Dr. Pepper, and paused again for a second sip before continuing. "One of the main traits I was seeking when choosing each of you was that you'd be open to doing things differently than the other teams, with one possible exception I'll get to later. In my opinion, those who achieve the most are almost always different; they're the oddballs, ridiculed until they are declared overnight successes and geniuses by the same masses who mocked them. That's why I always loved that song by my pal Toby Keith, 'How Do Ya Like Me Now?'

"I grew up playing baseball and music, my lifelong true loves. I've done everything in music and retired from live performances. Now, it's baseball time. In recent years, baseball hasn't been as much fun to watch—too many strikeouts and a lack of fundamentals. *The Nashville Knights* will be fun to watch. We'll win early and often."

"We'll win because of *you*, the people on this call. Let's start with Mr. David Clark, a man with crazy analytic skills, which we'll be using in a different way than any other team. I first met David when he was the keynote speaker at the annual SABR (Society for Baseball Research) convention two years ago. He delivered a spellbinding speech that evening about how analytics are great but sometimes can damage performance when overused. He maintains that analytics have a major place, but they shouldn't be the tail wagging the dog. David served in the US Navy, hails from the Peach State of Georgia, and a little-known fact is that he's a prepper. If the world goes to hell in a handbasket, David Clark will survive. I expect vigorous debate between David and some of you, which in the end will bring better decisions."

"Let's see; who is next? I see Butch Dory sitting there in the box just below David. How ya doing, Butch? I got y'all muted, but give us a wave for now, Mr. Dory."

Butch obliged with a wave and lifted his coffee mug in a toasting motion.

"Mr. Butch Dory, the man with the most eloquent silver goatee ever to adorn a face! What a blessing to have talked this gentleman out of retirement. Butch managed the Nationals AA Harrisburg Senators for seven years. He accused me yesterday of being a 'silver-tongued, sweet-talking, slick salesman' for talking him into hopping aboard this crazy train of an adventure. Isn't that what you called me, Butch—a slick salesman?"

Butch grinned, nodded, and raised his mug again.

"Hey, Butch, hold up that mug again. Was that your old Hot Rod on there?"

Butch held the mug close to the camera, nodded again, and lip-synced "'71 Duster."

"Butch and I," Big T continued, "grew up in the same town in Oklahoma and went to a rival school. Butch was a catcher and the only local guy from our generation to make it to The Show. He played for the Twins, Royals, Angels, and Nationals. Butch is beloved by everybody he played with and managed. He's in charge of Minor League Player Development. He's an old baseball soul, well-schooled in fundamentals and even better at teaching them. Butch is a maker and molder of young men. In addition to his baseball knowledge, he brings intangibles and wisdom that we'll need as we grow quickly from an expansion to a championship team. I'll also tell you Butch plays a *mean* blues guitar and sings in his church choir when he's not restoring muscle cars…an interesting, multi-talented gentleman, and one of my oldest friends.

"And occupying the lower, left-hand corner, we have our general manager, Mr. Kurt Grimmer. Kurt was the best ball player to come out of Hawaii Community College-Hilo. He was drafted in the fifth round by the Mariners. He played in the minors for seven years before getting his 'cup of coffee' with the big club when he had twenty-nine at-bats, four singles, and three RBIs. He did get to play on the same team with Ken Griffey Jr. and Sr. in Junior's rookie season and drove in

Junior with one of his four singles. After he got released, Kurt earned his MBA and CPA designation, and ventured into banking, where he rose to be CEO of Jefferson National Bank. We met when he was on his way up, managing accounts for the entertainment industry. When I learned of his baseball background, we bonded even more. After a few years of Kurt handling my account, his baseball itch was too great to resist, and when he heard the Tacoma Rainiers (the Mariners' AAA affiliate) were looking for a bench coach, he threw his hat in the ring. Kurt's former teammate, David Mirisch, was the manager, and he hired Kurt over several candidates with more experience. Kurt took over the reins when David left. Kurt was named Pacific Coast League Manager of the Year three times. When I decided to pursue ownership of the new MLB franchise, Kurt was the first person I thought of. The only question was how to best use all he brings to the table. He's the perfect choice for GM because he is a visionary who also sees and understands all of the small details needed to build a perennial contender. He's been lobbying me to do a duet, with him on the ukulele and me on my steel guitar. I told him when we win the World Series, we'll write and record a song about it."

Kurt gave a toothy smile and the shaka sign as a wave. Big T responded with "Aloha, my Hawaiian brother; greatness awaits us!"

"Now," said Big T, "let's say howdy to Larry Wenzel, whom all of you know from either meeting him in Nashville or from his days as infield coach with The Rangers. Larry's a solid baseball man and, as importantly, a man of character, the kind of leader I want in the dugout. As I put out feelers to find the best candidate, Larry's name came up several times. I invited him to Nashville, and we spent two days talking baseball. I didn't even want to interview anyone else after that. Larry's our guy.

"Our guy heading up our Scouting Department is Walter E. Rupp. Wally was an excellent collegiate player with a good shot at making The Show, but a heart issue derailed his career as a player. It's a long, impressive story on how he got here. If you talk to Wally for more than a couple of minutes, you'll learn that his focus in life is faith, family, and baseball, in that order. You heard me use the phrase 'man of character' earlier, and it applies to Wally as well. It applies to *all y'all*, as we say in Oklahoma. Character counts. We've hired high character baseball men, and some women, throughout the organization."

Big T then gave a drum roll.... "And noooooow, batting clean-up, we have Mr. Rex Collier! Rex had a five-year minor league career with the Nats and parlayed that into an entry level marketing position. He's the man who dreams up fun promotions and puts butts in seats. As the special promotions manager with the Nats, Rex originated the most effective campaigns leading to their attendance, growing more than any team in MLB over the last three years. Of course, nothing puts butts in seats more than winning baseball, and we'll have that too. Between winning baseball and having Rex at the marketing helm, we'll be successful at the box office. *Wildly* successful!"

Big T swigged from his Dr. Pepper again and went on. "I've scheduled a two-day conference at one of my favorite resorts, Wintergreen, in the Blue Ridge Mountains of Virginia, not far from the stomping grounds of Patsy Cline and The Statler Brothers. The dates are October 25 and 26. You'll be getting an email with more details shortly after this call. I picked Wintergreen because it's about halfway between Nashville and DC, where a couple of us still reside. I'll be in New York City for some MLB meetings, but I'll fly into one of the small local airports. I've hired a professional facilitator named Timothy Ramage. He's a pal of mine and very skilled at maximizing efficiency at conferences. We'll leave Wintergreen with the basics of our plan in place to be immediate contenders. You have two weeks to prepare. I want a *bold* plan—a path that is different from every other team. Don't give me a bunch of *happy horse-pucky!* I want us to *zig* while everyone else is zagging.

"Gentlemen, that's it for now. Look for that email and prepare for an adventure."

Big T tipped his cowboy hat, said, "Happy Trails," and vanished from the screen.

★ CHAPTER 7 ★

Breaking News

Rex romped down the stairs for his coffee refill.

"How was the call, dear?" Martha asked. "Was there anything newsworthy?"

"Give me a minute to change clothes and I'll tell you; yes, there's news," he said, giving her a kiss.

With that, Fini galloped around the corner to greet him. "Hiya, big boy! How ya doing?" said Rex.

The canine athlete reared up on his hind legs like greyhounds do and seemed to smile. "Where's your buddy, Charlie?" Rex asked Fini, as though expecting an answer. This was normal family communication, and Martha knew it was her cue to answer.

"Charlie went over to Holy Redeemer to throw the ball against the wall. I told him it seems like a good way to scuff up a perfectly good baseball, but he says throwing at single bricks in the wall improves his control."

"That's true, baby," Rex told her. "Berwyn boys have been aiming at bricks on that wall ever since Dusty started doing it when he was a kid, and he probably picked it up from some older kid. Fortunately, that section of the building doesn't have windows! Lemme go change and I'll be right back down to tell you the news; it's exciting."

A few minutes later, Rex came downstairs in casual attire, meaning workout sweats and a hoodie since he would be working from home that day. Martha was sitting on the couch watching *Jeopardy* reruns with the world's best greyhound stretched out beside her.

She lowered the volume, patted the couch on the other side, and said, "Take a load off and give me your news, Mr. Marketing Director."

"Sure you have room for me?" Rex asked. "I wouldn't want to take space away from your number one over there." He nodded toward Fini. "Look at *him*. I swear he smiled when I said that!"

"You know you're his equal, Sexy Rexy; now give me the news, will ya? 'You're killin' me, Smalls.'"

"Well, it's like this—to quote renowned Renaissance man Yogi Berra, 'The future ain't what it used to be!' This morning's *8:07* meeting with Big T McCraw changed it. In two weeks, my presence is required at Wintergreen Resort on October 25 and 26. Big T wants to win, and he doesn't want to wait; he wants to contend immediately, which no expansion team has ever done. We need to do something dramatic, and he gave us marching orders to come up with a plan, something different from what all the other teams are doing. He says we need to zig while they zag. In one sense, baseball is a simple game—see ball, hit ball—but he's right; we need to make a dramatic shift…somehow. He told us to all think individually for the next two weeks and to think way outside the box. That's my news. How was your day?"

"Wow, Sexy Rexy! Well, maybe it *will* lead to something good. My day was productive. Mary West agreed to take over as civic association president for the next term, and Jeanné Broxton said she'll help me with the literacy program. Also, I visited a Toastmasters meeting that Karen McNamara has been inviting me to for a year. I'm thinking about joining. She says it will improve my presentation skills, and they seem like a fun group of positive-minded people. My most important accomplishment of the day, though, was getting Charlie scheduled for a doctor's appointment. His headaches are getting worse. I agree with what you said last night, and I'm trying to get him into the HMO to see the cancer doctor instead of the regular doctor. He'll refer us to the cancer doctor anyway, to get the MRI and rule out a tumor."

Fini's ears perked up, and a nanosecond later, he jumped off the couch and bolted for the door, just as Charlie opened it to come in. "Hey, big boy, you almost got knocked on the noggin; we might have to put a helmet on you. You'd look pretty fancy in your red coat with matching helmet! What do think about that, big ol' boy?" Charlie said as he vigorously scratched Fini's ears. Fini smiled in agreement, or so it seemed. "When's din-din, y'all? I'm starving!" Charlie announced.

"Your dad and I haven't gotten that far yet, but what if we make it a pizza night? What do you think, Rex?"

"That works for me. How about if Charlie and I ride over to Continental in Kensington and bring it home?"

"I'll call it in so it's ready when you get there," Martha said.

"Let's roll, Dad!"

Forty-five minutes later, they were sitting at the kitchen table. Charlie was emptying half of the hot peppers bottle onto his slices and had a huge glass of lemonade ready to cool the fire about to ensue. Martha didn't know how he could tolerate that much heat, but she accepted it as another of Charlie's exceptional abilities. The peppers did get stuck in his orthodontics sometimes. Rex was on his third slice, and Fini stretched out under the table because he liked to be near his humans, and as importantly, near their falling crumbs. When Charlie had finished his first two slices, he said, "Hey, Mom, Dad told me about his business retreat at the fancy resort in two weeks. I looked the place up. I wish we could all go; they have an indoor swimming pool and all kinds of cool stuff to do—horseback riding, hiking, and tubing on the Shenandoah River."

"We'll have to tough it out here, son. I don't think Dad will be doing any of those activities. It sounds like he'll be locked up in a room all weekend thinking of ways to bring a championship to Nashville."

Rex nodded in assent between bites. "Yeah, it's going to be an intense two days. I looked up the man who will be the facilitator, a guy named Timothy Ramage. Big T mentioned him briefly and has known him a long time. They call him The Rammer. Apparently, he knows the game and had a brief stint in single-A ball and then a couple of years in independent leagues. After that, he became a lawyer specializing as a corporate turnaround artist, someone who goes into troubled companies and resets their courses. He's renowned as a guy who's fixed companies in a wide range of industries. Maybe he's a good choice. If we need to think outside of the box, it makes sense to bring in someone like him. I've read he's a real curmudgeon, though—a get-off-my-lawn kind of guy. But, hey, if he can help us win, I'm all in."

★ CHAPTER 8 ★

Wintergreen

As soon as the DC traffic heading west on I-66 let up, Rex felt the tension leave his shoulders and he let his mind wander to thoughts about the team and the upcoming meeting. His phone interrupted his reverie with his special ring tone for Martha, "What a Wonderful World" by Louis Armstrong. "Hey, baby, how's my beautiful wifey?"

"Missing my man, but other than that, I'm happier than a bird with a French fry!"

"Any news?"

"No, things are routine. Charlie's showering and Fini is doing his couch potato thing. I just wanted to see how far down the road you are. Text me when you get to the resort. I'll be awake until at least ten-thirty."

"I just saw a sign that said seventeen miles to Charlottesville. Another hour or so. I love you, baby," he said. She gave her usual reply, "Love you more!"

After the call, Rex turned on the radio and landed on country music WMZQ, playing Big and Rich's hit "Six Foot Town," a song with catchy lyrics about feeling ten feet tall in a six-foot town. Rex was tapping the wheel and singing along. He liked Big and Rich because they wrote and sang fun songs. After Dustin and Leanne had talked Rex and Martha into going to Big and Rich's concert a couple of years ago, they had become fans.

Traffic was thinning as Rex got farther from the city. He bounced around the radio dial, back and forth, from country music to talk radio, motoring through the countryside on Route 29 south before exiting onto I-64 West toward Charlottesville. Once past Charlottesville, it was only another forty miles or so to the resort. Rex exited onto state road 151 for the final ten miles. It was nine-thirty when he arrived at Wintergreen, starved, and hoping they were still serving food. The two granola bars he'd eaten in the car weren't cutting it. Rex parked and went into the lobby to register. A bellman greeted him promptly and asked if he needed assistance. Rex asked if the restaurant just off of the lobby was still open and was relieved to hear yes. He thanked the bellman, went over to the desk to register, and went quickly to his room to drop off his bag. The intention was to go right back to the restaurant, but as he stepped into the hallway, the phone in his room rang. He ducked back in to pick it up. It was the front desk clerk saying he had forgotten to give Rex an envelope at check-in. "Thanks. I'll be right there," Rex replied.

After stopping at the desk, Rex walked across the lobby into The Copper Mine Bistro. He decided to wait until he was seated and had ordered before opening the envelope.

The hostess showed Rex to a table, gave him a menu, and told him his server would be there shortly. The server arrived quickly and asked to take his drink order. Rex told her he was ready to order his entrée too, asking for her recommendation for a hungry man, something filling. Without hesitation, in her sweet, Southern Virginia accent, she replied, "Well, sir, I *strongly* recommend our lamb chops served with our house specialty sautéed eggplant, a side salad, and our home-made multi-grain bread that came out of the oven five minutes ago."

"Sold. Honey mustard dressing on the salad, please, and no olives," Rex said, handing her the menu. "Oh, and hot water with lemon, please."

Rex picked up the envelope with its ornate, thick paper and the embossed name *Timothy J. Ramage* in black letters with gold accents in the upper left-hand corner. He ripped it open with no regard for its regalness, pulling out the three neatly folded pages. The stationery matched the envelope, of course. The top page was in handwritten gold cursive:

Nashville Knights, World Champions

The next two pages were the agenda and a welcoming note from Big T. Famished, Rex looked it over quickly, put it back in the envelope, and wolfed down his salad. The lamb chops, sautéed eggplant, and homemade bread were as good as advertised and knocked out the hunger monster. The triple scoop of butter pecan ice cream was just for fun. Rex went back to his room, called home, and hit the hay. He would need all of the energy and mental focus he could muster over the next couple of days.

***

Six-thirty a.m. came early. The light creeping through the curtains got Rex's attention moments before the alarm went off, making it official. Rex slapped the clock and stretched in bed, much like dogs and cats do before rising, then said his morning prayers. Properly stretched and prayed up for the day, he put feet on the floor and turned on the coffee. While it dripped, he opened the curtains to a gorgeous sunrise over the Blue Ridge Mountains. It seemed prophetic. Rex had the sense he was about to participate in the dawning of a new day, something significant and historic. He flipped on the TV as background noise. He left it on *Shark Tank* while he shaved and showered. The irony that he might be in the shark tank in a few hours wasn't lost on him. He went about his morning rituals, always needing an hour and a half before being ready to properly greet the world. Room service helped because he didn't have to deal with pre-meeting happy talk should he run into others in the restaurant.

The farmer's breakfast platter with three scrambled eggs, hash browns, a poppy seed bagel, and fresh blueberries arrived and really hit the spot. Rex sat at the desk enjoying breakfast as he channel-surfed, catching the news and weather. Fully caffeinated, rituals completed, and breakfast consumed, he headed downstairs. He was excited and anxious at the same time. Something extraordinary was about to happen.

CHAPTER 9

Rammer's Hammer

Rex was five minutes early when he entered the Shamokin Board Room. *Shamokin* is a Lenape Native American term meaning "welcome," as Rex had noted from the *Wintergreen Magazine* in his room. Seated around the table were his colleagues GM Kurt Grimmer, Manager Larry Wenzel, Head of Minor League Player Development Butch Dory, Director of Amateur Scouting Wally Rupp, and Senior Data Analyst David Clark. At the head of the table was a new face Rex recognized from his online search, Timothy J. Ramage. Rex nodded and said good morning to the group, and his colleagues did the same.

Timothy Ramage was silent. He did nod slightly. He had *presence*, even without speaking...a chiseled face, rugged good looks, and a salt-and-pepper, Ronald Reagan style haircut. He'd just turned fifty. His glasses had frames making them almost invisible. The character lines on his face suggested he'd weathered many storms and was unafraid to face another. Rex had the impression that this was a man used to accomplishing difficult things.

BANG! Ramage pounded the table with a gavel!

"Good morning, gentlemen! I'm Timothy Ramage, and for the next two days, I'll be the ringleader of this conclave of professional baseball visionaries. During our time together, things might get a little crazy. Let's just not become the guy on the porch in his underwear yelling at squirrels."

He chuckled at his own awkward joke and continued….

"You can call me Timothy or Rammer, my nickname. We begin with a quote from Albert Einstein: *'You have to learn the rules of the game and then you have to play better than anyone else.'*"

The Rammer read the quote twice and then added with a laugh, "Who's smarter than Einstein? You knuckleheads might be smart, but you're not Einstein smart. Imprint that quote in your brains. Everything we talk about over the next two days should circle back to that quote."

The Rammer pounded the table with the gavel again. *Was this gavel-pounding going to be a regular thing for the next two days?* Rex wondered.

"You like this gavel?" The Rammer asked no one in particular. "I was given this by some executives at a company I restructured a few years ago. They had it engraved with 'Rammer Hammer,' a nickname one of my favorite clients bestowed on me. I used to pound my fist, so they decided I needed something more dignified. They were probably right. If I pound my fist, I'm a maniac, but if I pound the gavel, I'm dignified and smart. Get used to The Rammer Hammer; you'll hear it a lot.

"I was born and raised in Southern California. I was equally good at baseball and soccer in high school, and I had scholarship offers in both, but I chose soccer. Yes, I know," he said, holding his right hand up, palm facing the group, "sacrilegious in these circles. Despite my soccer distraction, I was able to play single-A ball one year. Being a soccer goalie wasn't too different than diving at balls at third base. I also like '80s punk music…Social Distortion, Johnny Rotten & The Sex Pistols, The Ramones. My favorite movie is *Fight Club*, and I *don't* like long walks on the beach, puppies, or rainbows. I've worked in IT, I've worked as a roughneck in the oil fields, and I've turned around Fortune 500 companies that were quickly dropping off the list.

"Along the way, I met Big T McCraw. As you can see and hear, *I'm not normal*. And I don't deliver normal results. We…" He pointed his index finger around the room, "are going to produce a plan that will make The Nashville Knights into the team that shocks the baseball world. Are you willing to join me?" He stared around the room at everyone. "Are you willing to be pioneers to transform us into a team that plays better than anyone else? Are you willing to leave your egos and your turf defenses at the door to help us play better than anyone else? Are you willing? You need to be able to answer yes to those questions. We need total commitment and then total buy-in to The Plan. Winning isn't just about the players on the field; it's also about us, right here in this room. We are the difference makers!" He pounded the gavel again for emphasis. "We are *the ones, the ones* to come up with *The Plan* that starts the story, the story of the Nashville Knights, World Champions! Let that sink in, Nashville Knights, World Champions!" He pounded the gavel again, this time harder and with a crazed look in his eye.

The Rammer paused and centered himself before continuing. "I will assume we are all in the same state of mind. Are you willing to enter the mosh pit of creating The Plan?" He looked around the table again. "Gentlemen…Mr. McCraw believes in you. I asked him when he first called me if he felt he could bring a championship to Nashville with his current executive team. He unequivocally said yes. He believes this team is capable, but he said you need a stroke of brilliance, a path not traveled by anyone else. Those were his words. He says we need to zig while they zag. Let's get started. The ground rules for our time together are…*there are no ground rules.*"

There was a soft knock on the door. The Rammer motioned for someone to enter that only he could see from his seat.

"Ah, perfect timing, Ms. Scully," he said. "Gentlemen, meet my brilliant assistant Rebecca Scully, and yes, she's related to Vin; she's his distant cousin. She's the only woman I know who carries a baseball around in her purse for good luck and fidgets with it when she's thinking. She calls it her 'thinking ball.' It's an old ball with grass stains and a stitch missing. Don't offer her a new one; she won't take it." Ms. Scully proudly held up the ball, smiled, and bowed slightly as a way of introduction.

"Ms. Scully will be in the room with us most of the time. Having someone with her skill set will help us keep track of ideas as they start flying around the room. Ms. Scully will be writing on the giant Post-its on the wall and helping me keep you knuckleheads in line. That's said with love and affection, so don't get all offended on me. Let's get going. First, I know you've each prepared for this meeting and have some ideas. I want to go around the room and get One Big Idea from each of you as a way to get started. You can give more than one idea, of course, but I want to know which is the one you deem most important."

★ CHAPTER 10 ★
OBI
One Big Idea

The Rammer, feeling he had properly set the stage, turned to Rex and said, "Rex Collier, what's your OBI—your One Big Idea? What *OBI* of *yours* will contribute to us playing the game better than anyone else?"

Rex paused for a moment before answering, a skill he had learned in Toastmasters meetings when answering impromptu questions. He began with a Captain Obvious disclaimer, stating that his area, marketing, didn't have a role in on-field talent and thus had lesser opportunity to contribute directly to Ws. It sounded like an excuse.

The Rammer's body language said he was annoyed, but he checked himself and motioned for Rex to go on.

"My OBI is to become a blend of Bill Veeck and Charlie Finley and create fun, unique events and experiences for fans *and* players. I'd like to see a different look from other teams too, with old-school uniforms, congruent with our style of play. Veeck and Finley were the two most innovative owners in the storied history of baseball. There's nobody like them among today's owners! Players are more likely to perform at optimal levels in a fun, uplifting environment."

Timothy J. Ramage hit the table with his gavel again, this time softly. "Let's move on as soon as Ms. Scully completes her calligraphy. We'll come back to each of these," he said, pointing to the Post-its, "after we go around the room."

Rebecca Scully wrote in lovely cursive on one giant Post-it on the wall:

> Marketing OBI
>
> Emulate Veeck and Finley
>
> Special Events
>
> Fun, unusual experiences
>
> Old-school uniforms

The Rammer turned to Larry Wenzel, who would be managing for the first time after coaching for several years in the Rangers Organization. "Mr. Wenzel, what OBI of yours will contribute to us playing the game better than anyone else?"

Larry, lean and angular, leaned forward on his elbows and pushed his glasses up the bridge of his nose. Rex would soon learn that when Larry spoke, everybody listened. In his DJ voice, he said, "I've seen the game change and everyone move like sheep when it does. I detest the inability or unwillingness to beat the shift. If the defense plays all of their fielders on one side of the field, then the hitters can learn to, as Wee Willie Keeler said in the 1890s, *'Hit 'em where they ain't.'*

Wee Willie hit over .300 for thirteen straight seasons. My OBI is to beat the shift so that nobody even dares to try it on us. This *one* thing would probably add twenty-five points to our team batting average and would put ten-plus more games in the W column. Another idea is to add another left-handed power hitter on each team throughout the minors. It would give us versatility in late innings with a pinch hitter coming off the bench. We'd have to give up a relief pitcher slot, but I think the benefits outweigh the costs."

Timothy J. Ramage tapped his gavel again, this time not hard, not soft. He liked to switch it up, like a pitcher changing speeds. "Thank you, Mr. Wenzel."

Ms. Scully finished putting Larry's OBI on the second Post-it:

Manager OBI

Beat the Shift

Will add 25 points to Team BA

Will mean 10+ more wins

Add left-handed power hitter

Next, The Rammer turned to David Clark, Senior Data Analyst. David, a self-described introvert and geek, originally from Georgia, resided in the condos across from the ball park and team offices. He could crunch numbers like nobody's business and provide reports from all kinds of angles that management would use to assess players. Though an introvert, he had worked hard to become an accomplished public speaker and could be very persuasive when arguing for a position, and he *always* had numbers to back up his theories.

"What say you, Mr. Clark? What OBI will you throw into this smoldering fire of ideas? Heave away; start a bonfire. Let's get this party going."

David Clark fidgeted a bit, not sure what to make of The Rammer's style. He thought while he fidgeted, pushing his Coke bottle-bottom glasses up the bridge of his nose, stalling for time before speaking.

"Well, we've been encouraged to throw out any idea, no matter how outrageous it may be. So here you go; this may get a bonfire going or it may douse the flames; we'll see. A friend of mine, Dr. Suzie Proctor, is a professor of Artificial Intelligence at Harvard. Dr. Proctor's program is in development, and we might be able to participate as a beta user. If successful, her work will result in a quantum leap in AI and put all of our pictures on the cover of magazines."

Timothy J. Ramage sat up in his chair and leaned in, looking either intrigued or bewildered; it was hard to read his expression. "Before going any further," he said, "would you please explain how AI will help us play the game better than anyone else? Will robots be play-ing? Paint me a picture of how a game would be different. And just so you know, I don't give three turds about being on the covers of magazines."

David ignored the turds comment and looked pleased to have the op-portunity to go on. He chuckled at what he was about to say. "Well, ro-bots might not be playing, but they could be managing and coaching."

A weird silence followed. He continued, "The amount of data that can be analyzed is going to be hundreds of times what we have now. We will even be able to tell which players are more likely to perform the best on a given day based upon non-invasive medical scans. AI could figure out best matchups, exactly where to position fielders based on satellite GPS integrated with all of the data on every nuance of every player and matchup. It won't predict the future yet, but it can give us ways to predict that an outcome is extremely likely, if X, Y, and Z moves are made. AI could make better, more informed, more-likely-to-turn-out right decisions than a human manager could. And, yes, we could have robot coaches coaching first and third with automatic stop and go lights for runners as well as signals to steal, bunt, or tag up on a sacrifice fly. I see all this being reality in ten years, but what if we could go there sooner? I have one other idea. We should prepare our players for working within the coming time parameters as clocks and timing come into the game."

David paused.

Around the table, the others weren't sure if he was finished, but Larry Wenzel was incredulous, and *really* pissed. He glared at David. "You're saying I'm out of a job then, and probably some of the rest of us in this room too? That's your idea of building a championship team? No manager or coaches? And we prepare players for working with clocks? Did you get hit on the head this morning? Yeah, let's just let all the computer geeks take over baseball! We don't need no stinkin' manager, no baseball men with decades of experience. We just need more data and bigger computers, and clocks; yeah, that'll make us winners!"

David looked at Larry with a blank "I'm just stating the facts" look. The rest of the room went silent again, expecting The Rammer to take control, which he did.

The Rammer rapidly clapped his meaty hands in robust applause. "Now we're getting warmed up! I love the passion; let's get raw in here. Let's throw some gasoline on this fire!" He turned and pointed to the Post-it that Ms. Scully had just written:

<u>Sr. Data Analyst OBI</u>

Partner with Harvard Professor

Implement Artificial Intelligence System

Replace Managers/Coaches with AI "robots"

Prepare players for timing, clocks

Butch Dory, Director of Minor League Player Development, politely cleared his throat and said, "I don't see the robot thing. We'll never replace humans with robots. We've already gone too far with analytics. Baseball statistics are a lot like a girl in a bikini; they show a lot, but not everything. The pendulum needs to swing back. That's my opinion. Maybe some middle ground would be the better approach."

"What about you, Kurt?" The Rammer asked.

Kurt pushed back in his seat, looking like the relaxed surfer dude he'd been, growing up in paradise. The Hawaiian shirt and longish thick mane of dark curly hair completed the look. He laughed, covering his face as if to apologize for laughing inappropriately. "I'm sorry for laughing. I know David is serious about the robots, but it just hits me funny. I had a picture in my head of the robot in that old show *Lost in Space* standing in the third base coaching box, lighting up and blinking, with a robotic voice saying '*Proceed home, please.*" Kurt giggled for a good fifteen seconds, and Butch caught the giggles too. "Okay, let me clear that out of my head," Kurt said as he waved his hand in the air above his head. "There, it's gone."

Kurt continued, "I probably come down on this somewhere close to what Butch said; there must be some middle ground between old school and analytics that doesn't go off the deep end. 'Just Say No' to robots in baseball!"

Everyone laughed at that one; even David Clark smiled. The Rammer had a wry smile, too, as he turned his attention to Wally Rupp. "So, Wally, what's your Wally's World reaction to Mr. Clark's robotics? What say you?"

"I call bullshit on it; in fact, double bullshit."

The Rammer laughed. "Speak up, Rupp! Big T *told* me you're a no-bullshit kind of guy, and here you are *calling* bullshit! He said you like to talk and interrupt a lot...get it? Inter*rupt?*"

Wally didn't look amused as he leaned forward, saying through narrowed eyes, "I *should* have interrupted him and saved us from having to hear the excrement flow from his pie-hole. I exercised *extraordinary* restraint."

The Rammer laughed louder this time. "By the way, Wally, did you see the movie with Clint Eastwood playing the old crusty scout? I think it was called, *Trouble with the Curve.*"

Wally gave him the stink eye. "Yes. Why?"

"You just remind me of him, that's all—a younger version."

Annoyed, Wally said, "That was so random, *Timothy.*" Just the way he said *Timothy* let everyone know he didn't appreciate the old, crusty comparison.

"I know, Wally. I'm sorry. It'll be okay. You're right; I do get random sometimes. It's my curmudgeonly side. You'll grow to love me…maybe. I do recall Eastwood saying something that applies to what we're talking about. He said, '*Anyone who uses computers doesn't know a damn thing about baseball. What's next? Computers telling you when to scratch your ass?*'"

That hit everyone as funny—except for David Clark. Timothy tapped his gavel lightly. "Let's move on. We got sidetracked with robot base coaches. We haven't gotten OBIs yet from Wally, Butch, or Kurt. Mr. Rupp, since you just e*rup*ted, keep going. What OBI can you add to this mosh pit of brilliance?" The Rammer pointed at the Post-its.

Wally had played baseball and football at the University of Richmond, as a center fielder and wide receiver. He had been equally good in each sport, but baseball was his first and true love. Unfortunately, doctors had discovered a heart murmur during a routine exam his senior year, which had ended his dream of playing pro ball. He would have been too small and a half-step too slow for the NFL, but a baseball career was a real possibility. He had been on the radar of the Cincinnati Reds and the Baltimore Orioles, but the heart murmur nixed that. It didn't stop him from teaching in Baltimore for a year and going on to be a mail carrier. The baseball itch never went away, though. The opportunity had come when his old college hitting coach, Fred "Smokey" Fields, heard that Wally wanted to get back into baseball. Smokey helped Wally change his swing between his sophomore and junior year, which resulted in raising his batting average seventy-three points and being named Offensive Player of the Year for the Colonial Athletic Association. Even more importantly, Smokey led Wally back to the Lord during his senior year, changing his life forever. The two had regularly stayed in touch. Wally threw caution to the wind, putting his Post Office pension aside when Smokey called Big T to recommend Wally for a scouting position.

Wally swiveled in his chair to better face everyone down the table from him. His eyes went wide and his face lit up. "*Speeeed!* Speed *disrupts* on the base paths and speed in the field means we reach balls other teams don't. Imagine a team with speed throughout the batting lineup *and* in the field. That's my OBI…*speed*. Be the *fastest* team on the field, always. Another idea is for us to ready ourselves for the inevitable Designated Hitter rule to be adopted. We need to recruit more RBI-producing power hitters to fill the DH spot. That's it. Two ideas from the crusty old scout."

Scully wrote down Wally's comments.

> Director of Amateur Scouting OBI:
>
> Speed
>
> Recruit RBI-producing power hitters for DH spot

Another light gavel tap and Timothy looked across at Kurt. "Your turn, surfer dude." Kurt looked ready to go, like a school kid with his hand up, saying, "Me, me, call on me please!" His face switched expressions, going from happy and excited to serious and intense as he spoke. "*Exploit the bunt!* How would you like to have an .800 batting average? Bunting against all these shifts should produce about an .800 bunting average. Every hitter in the lineup should be able to lay down a good sacrifice bunt as well as bunts for hits. We could win another ten games a year if we master the art of bunting! Heck, ten wins is the difference between making the playoffs or sitting at home eating Moon Pies and drinking Yoo-Hoos. And here's my second idea: Let's add a couple of relief pitchers so starters won't have to go past five innings. They get tired and that third time through the batting order is tough."

"*Exploit the bunt!*" shouted The Rammer as he clapped his catcher's mitt-sized hands again. I *like* it! Moon Pies, I like that, too; that's funny. Are those still around?" He turned toward his assistant. "Ms. Scully, put 'exploit the bunt' in bold letters up there." He pointed to the Post-it. "Right under Mr. Grimmer's OBI."

Scully wrote on the Post-it note:

General Manager's OBI

EXPLOIT THE BUNT

"Got anything else for us, Kurt?" asked The Rammer as Scully wrote.

Kurt furrowed his brow and said, "Just to add that this strategy would reduce or eliminate the shift, which means other hits go through, like the line drive up the middle. It galls me to see a screaming line up the middle caught because of the shift. We can minimize or eliminate the shift if we become 'black belt' bunters. These are professional ball players, the best in the world; they should *all* be able to lay down a bunt, sac bunts, squeezes, bunts down the line, and push bunts past the pitcher. Pitchers have historically been able to bunt pretty well, so real hitters should master it with a little effort. Maybe we incentivize them with a thousand bucks every time they effectively lay one down."

The Rammer barely tapped the gavel and turned to Butch. "It's your turn, Mr. Dory. What's your One Big Idea?" Butch, sitting upright, looked dignified, as usual. It was just his way; he could look dignified eating spaghetti.

Butch looked around the room and spoke in his deep, baritone voice. "Three words: *Eliminate the strikeout.*" He continued, "In all my years, I've never seen a time like this, where there's no shame in striking out. Sure, everyone strikes out sometimes, but it's accepted now by too many players. Where is the *shame?* So-called sluggers in today's game have *more strikeouts than hits.* The extreme other side is a guy like Tony Gwynn who faced Greg Maddux 106 times and *never* struck out. We need guys to put the ball in play. I'd like to see us look at strikeout averages as equally important to batting average or OPS. If you put the ball in play, you got a shot. It might find a hole. If we could cut our strikeout rate in half, it could result in an extra 6-10 wins a year. My second idea is training more geared toward adding muscle, and that would give us more home runs and extra-base hits. I know we have a big ballpark, but we play half of our games in smaller parks, and beefing up a little would help us compete when we're away from home."

The Rammer turned to Rebecca. "Ms. Scully, make that big bold letters under Mr. Dory's OBI: Strikeout Shame and Beef Up!"

Scully wrote on the Post-it note:

<u>Director of Minor League Dev't</u>

STRIKEOUT SHAME

BEEF UP

The Rammer rapped the gavel again and said, "Gentlemen, let's take a break; we're making a little progress. At this point, it's like pieces of a giant jigsaw puzzle laid out all over the table, and a few pieces are starting to connect, but we can't see the big picture yet. It's my job to guide us through so that we have the puzzle completed and the picture is clear. To accomplish that, we need nourishment. It is now 12:37. Our hosts here at Wintergreen will be bringing in lunch at 12:45. You can stay here the whole time or you may want to check your emails, call home, or hit the porcelain convenience, but be back here at 1:59! Class dismissed!"

***

By 1:55 p.m., everyone was back in the room and the staff had finished clearing the dishes. The Rammer and Ms. Scully finished a hushed discussion, and then she went back to her seat as his eyes darted around the room. He clapped his hands, causing thunderous, one-man applause to fill the room. The guy could clap louder than any three normal people. Whether he was using the gavel or the meaty hand clap, The Rammer seemed to relish being abruptly loud to redirect mood and attention.

"Pardon me if I woke any of you up," The Rammer said. "After filling your bellies like you did, I'm just making sure you don't nod off with a post-lunch nap. Ms. Scully, would you please get the cooler with the healthy energy drinks and pass them around? I used to be a Gatorade guy, but these give me mental focus. If you prefer coffee, we have that, too.

"Now, let's see if we can shape this mish-mash, mosh pit of ideas," he nodded toward the Post-its on the wall, "into something that will help us learn the rules of the game and play them better than anyone else. Like I said this morning, it all has to come back to that quote by Mr. Einstein. We all have to leave our turf defenses at the door. I heard and felt some turf defense this morning, so I'm reminding you to keep it in check. Got it?" When no one answered, he added, "I'll take that as a yes."

Boom! The gavel sound rattled the room. The Rammer jumped on his chair, shouting, "Nashville Knights World Champions!" He beat his chest, ape-like. "We *will* win! *Why?* Because we have the *will*, and soon, *we'll* have *The Plan!*" He sat back down, sipped his energy drink, and calmly said, "Sometimes you have to show some passion.

"Here ya go, grasshoppers; I'll drop another quote on you. This is from one of the great philosophers of our time, Tyler Durden, the main character in *Fight Club*: '*It's only after we've lost everything that we're free to do anything.*'" The Rammer paused again to let the quote sink in; then in a near-whisper, the master of vocal variety said, "Gentlemen, my lovable knuckleheads, do we really have to wait until we've lost everything to be free to do *anything*? Let's not wait until we're desperate from losing to be free to be bold. Let's put ourselves there from the get-go. Let's say we've lost everything *already* since we've won nothing. Combining the wisdom of Albert Einstein and Tyler Durden, here's a quote, put together by yours truly." He paused, looked around the table, and said in a hushed, this-is-important tone, "We have to be ready to *do anything to play the game better than anyone else.*" His eyes squinted in steely-eyed determination as he stressed each word.

One thing Rex knew for sure, as he sat in that room and reflected on the day so far, was that other teams wouldn't be doing this, and they wouldn't have anyone like Timothy J. Ramage to challenge them. It did feel like the beginning of zigging instead of zagging. Though he couldn't see exactly how this plan would shake out, Rex sensed something special was in the works.

"Ms. Scully," The Rammer said, "please prepare to demo your calligraphy skills again for us, if you would be so kind. We're going to winnow down some of the OBIs from this morning and maybe expand on some of them. Let's review each Post-it and decide which ideas we keep and which we shit-can. Oh, I'm sorry. I shouldn't talk like that. I need to be more *sensitive*. Better said, let's start new Post-its with our keeper ideas that we'll use to build The Plan.

"Which ones can we all agree will make this first cut? I'll go through first and make my cuts, and then you can hash it out with me and defend your positions. Let's take them in order." He pointed to Rex's Post-it. "I don't think Rex's list brings much to the party. Yeah, we could do special events like they do in minor leagues if we're looking to be lovable whether we win or lose. Just *win*. We don't need gimmicks.

"Looking at the other OBIs, I see some old school tactics we'll probably be incorporating in the final Plan, so old school uniforms would be congruent. I do like the old-school uniform look."

Rex added, "Yeah, maybe a *Field of Dreams* look."

"Good one! Ms. Scully, would you please set aside Rex's original Post-it and start a new one for all of us? Title it 'KEEPERS' with your beautiful script, please. Write 'OLD UNIFORMS' down. Frankly, that's going to be the least important keeper; no offense meant, Rex. Your role doesn't impact what happens on the field and whether we win or lose. Win and 'They will come.' Winning makes marketing easier. I don't mean to diminish your role; it's just a fact. In discussing who would be at this meeting, Mr. McCraw insisted you be included. He told me you have insights and observations that others miss. So please don't get your nasal passages out of joint because I'm not embracing all you said. We will need your insights. See, I'm not always a curmudgeon; I can encourage people today because it's Saturday. I'm nice one day every week, and this week, it's Saturday. Aren't you glad it's Saturday?"

The Rammer looked around the room. "Did the turkey sandwiches have too much tryptophan? Do you need some caffeine? There appears to be an energy dip, or maybe you just don't like the way we're doing this. What say any of you?"

Larry spoke first, pointing to the Post-its. "I don't see anything up there that by itself would take us to the Promised Land: bunt more, beat the shift, more team speed. All of that," he said, waving his hand dismissively, "seems like obvious things most teams would try."

Kurt, ever the optimist, said, pointing to the Post-its, "Maybe these can get us started, and maybe we'll come up with something special if we keep working and believing the answers will come. Also, if we can execute some of these ideas, it's possible to win it all. Isn't it all about execution? Most teams are trying to do the same or very similar things."

Butch was quiet. Maybe it was the tryptophan.

David sat quietly, too, looking smug before saying, "I believe AI can be a difference maker."

David's comment was just plain annoying and brought on another weird silence, which The Rammer ended by refocusing attention with his mighty gavel. *BOOM!* Satisfied he had everyone's ear, he said, "Okay, team. We need to shake something up. Let's break for forty-five minutes. During that time, I want each of you to go outside and find a place where you can be alone. It's a perfect day to be in such a gorgeous setting. Go out, breathe some fresh Shenandoah Valley air to reflect and clear your mind. Meditate, pray, chant, hum, pick lint from your naval, do whatever it is you do to bring forth your best. We'll reconvene outside on the veranda to see if that helped stimulate our thinking apparatuses. Recess is over in forty-seven minutes; that's three-thirty. Don't talk to each other until we reconvene, and don't ask why. There's a method to my Rammer madness. Trust the process.

"Ms. Scully, if you would stay here with me, please. The rest of you lovable knuckleheads I'll see on the flip side."

★ CHAPTER 11 ★

The Veranda

During the break, Ms. Scully had the resort staff set up seven Adirondack chairs in a circle, two red, two white, two blue, and one multi-colored (red, white, and blue). The circle was about twelve feet in diameter, and along the rail was a table with pitchers of lemonade, sweet tea, water, and cheese and crackers.

Timothy J. Ramage and Rebecca Scully spent their free time on the veranda enjoying the view of the Blue Ridge Mountains and the magnificent hundred-year-old oaks, in all their glory. They were ruminating on the multitude of colors before them when David Clark sauntered along, dressed in black, looking like Johnny Cash. The others pretty much followed en masse. All were present by the appointed time. Ms. Scully gave up her seat to be the "Vanna White" of the whiteboard. She looked different this time. She'd put on makeup, changed into a medium-brown leather skirt, a midnight-blue flowy top, and a pair of leather half-boots.

Everyone poured their chosen drink, but no one touched the cheese and crackers. They all looked expectantly to Timothy, who leaned back in the red, white, and blue chair. "I suppose you're expecting me to start barking orders…woof, woof, woof! Let's get at it, you lovable dogs.

"Here's a question for you. Have you ever been to a Quaker church service? I see the answer is no. I bring that up because I want us to try something I witnessed at the only Quaker service I ever attended. The congregation sat in chairs around the room's perimeter. No one individual led the service. People just sat and spoke whenever they were moved to do so; there was no order to it. There were long periods of silence when no one spoke. Most of the time, one person spoke while the others listened thoughtfully before responding. Let's give this a shot. The only leadership I'll give is to keep the focus and discussion on the merits of the OBIs, if we get sidetracked. I'll start the silence. Let's be quiet for a minute or two. I won't give any signal; just pretend we're all Quakers, and whoever feels moved to speak first can do so and we'll see where it goes."

It was quiet for about forty-five seconds, which felt like five or six minutes.

Kurt: "I'll break the ice. We need more arms. Two or three more relievers would allow us to save our starters' arms so they aren't pitching on fumes at the end of the season. Wally and Larry are asking for more power hitters. That's just like everybody else; all teams compete for power hitters, and they don't grow on trees. I don't want to give a pitcher's roster spot to a power hitter. Pitchers have more impact on winning."

The group was quiet, unsure whether Kurt had more to say. He didn't, and this time the silence held for ten or fifteen seconds.

Butch: "I have an idea about how we might get more RBI power *without* adding players. If we brought in a kick-ass strength coach, we could beef up our existing players, add ten or twenty pounds of muscle to each one, and we'd increase power without giving up a pitcher's roster spot."

More silence.

Wally: "Sorry, Kurt. I'm not buying that we need more relievers. I'd rather see us put the emphasis on starting pitching and free up the spots for some RBI-producing guys."

Kurt: "Butch, I don't think our goal should be to turn our players into muscle guys. Baseball players come in all shapes and sizes. We've already hired a trainer/conditioning coach, Chris Emery, who doesn't believe in adding muscle like so many teams are doing. Chris specializes in stretching and movement exercises to minimize injuries. I don't want our strength coach beefing guys up. It changes their swing and has messed up many a player."

Butch: "I disagree. If guys are stronger, they'll hit the ball farther, and our power numbers will go up."

Kurt: "Maybe, maybe not. If their swing changes because of the muscle mass, they're less likely to hit the ball well *and* be more prone to striking out. Even if they did hit the ball a little farther, what's the point if they put the ball in play less often?"

Butch: "The point is that more exit velocity means a better chance of a hit. Even on ground balls, if guys are stronger, they hit it harder, and the ball is more likely to get through the infield."

Kurt: "So our goal is to muscle up and hit hard ground balls? And Butch, your own OBI says to *eliminate the strikeout* and put the ball in play. Your idea to muscle up is at odds with your idea to eliminate the strikeout. Muscling up will *increase* strikeouts."

Butch rolled his eyes but didn't respond further.

David: "Scoff if you will, but other teams will be getting used to clocks and other technology advances, and we run the risk of falling behind. I think we should keep a close watch on AI advances. I think embracing AI would serve us far better than getting extra power hitters as Wally and Larry suggest."

Larry: "I don't know anything about being a Quaker and when to be silent and when to talk, but I'm sick of hearing about AI, robots, and clocks in baseball…those are *not* keepers. Yes, I'd like to see us have the option to have a couple of left-handed power hitters available off the bench in late innings. You can debate whether we should spend the roster spot on a reliever or a power hitter; that's a legitimate debate, but robots and clocks? Gimme a break! What was the word you used earlier, Timothy? Shit-can? Yes, shit-can the robots and clocks! And how about some *real* intelligence instead of artificial intelligence? We're playing real baseball, *not* artificial baseball. I don't want to get into it with David again, but all that stuff has to go."

David folded his arms and set his jaw, saying nothing.

Rex: "David, I wish you'd focus your analytic skills on giving us basic data we can use. Maybe that means just giving us an opponent's general tendencies. For instance, a certain hitter pulls the ball to left and struggles with hitting the off-speed stuff. Basically, the same type of information we could get in the days before the analytics era. I don't want to know about launch angles, exit velocity, or any of that mumbo-jumbo. Keep it basic."

For another hour and a half, they went back and forth, arguing the same points in different ways, disagreeing more than they agreed. The Rammer got his exercise pounding the gavel as things got heated. Ms. Scully appeared to be getting a kick out of the arguing, especially when The Rammer was being his robust, Rammer-Hammer self. Larry wanted to slug David over the AI argument, and Wally would have liked a piece of him too. The Rammer was having fun egging them on, saying, "It's never cool to die without any scars, so you boys have at it." Ironically, his comment calmed them just in the nick of time. Maybe they envisioned really having scars, who knows, but they got out of each other's faces. No fists were thrown.

Timothy rapped the gavel twice on the arm of his chair—two snappy ones, different than any of the raps. The gavel was an instrument to him, another form of communication. In this moment, his face took on a different countenance, a troubled look.

Staring at the mountains, he slowly turned, redirecting his gaze to his "lovable knuckleheads."

"Gentlemen and lady (nodding toward Rebecca), I have been a part of and led dozens of people through experiences similar in many ways to the one we currently find ourselves in the midst of. I've kept hoping for a breakout, but I'm not seeing or feeling it. And, I can tell you, what we've come up with so far is not good; it's crapola. *Crap-o-la.* Have you forgotten the quote from this morning?

"'It's only after we've lost everything that we're free to do anything.'

"Gentlemen, we've lost everything *if this*," he said, pointing to the Post-its "or any amalgamation *of this* sees the light of day. It's pablum, plain vanilla, and I'd be embarrassed to show this to Mr. McCraw. Remember, too, he will be here tomorrow to hear our final recommendation. This is *not* a plan. Mr. McCraw wants to be unlike any other team in baseball. We need a plan that is bold, that will excite our fan base and our players, that will take us to the top, and stun the baseball world! So what are you holding back on? We've already almost had a fist-fight. We've lost everything with these results." He pointed at the Post-its again. "Mr. Collier, Big T said he values your insights and you look like you've got something going on between your ears. If you have a genius thought, now is the time to set it free. Set it free, man. Set it free."

Rex looked eager and uncertain at once. He stood, smoothed out his shirt, and gathered himself before speaking. "I can relay my thinking better if I stand. I do have a thought that is so far out there it borders on bizarre. I think all of you know that Charlie, my fourteen-year-old son, is extremely gifted—literally, a child genius. We downplay it so that he can have a normal childhood, but he is a certified genius with a measured IQ of 189. He's taking advanced statistics classes at the University of Maryland. Bear with me here; you'll see where I'm going in a minute. Charlie is also a baseball historian with a savant-like memory for almost anything about the game that he saw or read even once. For his statistics class, he compared baseball statistics from 1979-2019, and his hypothesis is that the analytics craze has actually produced a *lower* caliber of play. He believes he has statistically demonstrated that. I don't profess to understand all the mathematics, formulas, and assumptions that go into it. Charlie believes if a MLB team went back to playing 'old-school' baseball, they would become the dominant team in baseball within two or three years. He's been working on an actual plan to implement old-school baseball, starters pitching every fourth day, no more pitch count worshiping, and other changes. Last week, Charlie and I had a long discussion about it, and I can tell you he has a real vision based on numbers. Sometimes he goes into what I'd describe as almost a trance-like state where everything shuts down except his brain and he writes his ideas down like a madman. He did that a couple of weeks ago about a plan to dominate baseball. He taped art paper to his walls and scribbled all over them for a couple of hours, and then he told me he thinks he's discovered the Holy Grail of baseball. What if we looked at his work? That would be zigging instead of zagging. It's the eleventh hour; Mr. McCraw will be here tomorrow afternoon. This may be our Hail Mary."

The Rammer motioned collectively to everyone except Rex. "So what do you think about what he just said? Is it *crap-o-la* or genius?"

Wally said the idea was intriguing, and Butch agreed it was worth a look.

Then David Clark puffed up. "My friend, Mr. Collier, must believe the earth is flat too!"

The Rammer called for a vote. "Show of hands; who says we pursue this?" He paused to count. "Three hands up. Three hands down. We have ourselves a tie. My vote is the tiebreaker, and my hand is up. Sit tight for a couple of minutes while I put in a call to Big T. I believe he'll be coming down on his private plane. Be right back," he said, walking away, phone to ear, calling Big T McCraw.

Five minutes later, The Rammer returned with a wry smile. "Big T is delighted with this direction. He wants Charlie and his mom to join him on his plane to come there. All they have to do is be at the airport at ten tomorrow morning. Big T will be flying from New York to Nashville and can pick them up in College Park. Can you make that happen, Rex?"

Rex nodded excitedly.

"Okay," The Rammer said. "We're done for now. Tell you what, since we need to wait until Big T and Charlie get here tomorrow, let's meet for breakfast at nine-thirty, and maybe we'll partake in some lawn bowling afterwards. They have a professional lawn bowling green that's as perfect as any golf green. It's a sport for the highbrow crowd, so you knuckleheads will fit right in." He chuckled.

"Gentlemen, I bid you good evening. Ms. Scully, please stay behind so we can chat. Tomorrow is a big day. As they say in *Fight Club*, 'We'll evolve, let the chips fall where they may.'"

★ CHAPTER 12 ★

CHARLIE
Gets the Call-Up

Martha opened the mudroom doggie door to let the regal greyhound outside to do his business. Then she called for Charlie a third time. "CHAR-LEEEEEE!" He romped around the corner. "Sorry, Mama; I had my headphones on listening to some old tunes from the '80s. How may I be of service?"

"Well, you can pay the pizza guy when he shows up in a few minutes; here's a twenty. While we're waiting, would you look at the calendar to be sure all of your activities for this week are on there?"

"Sure, Mom!" Martha's phone rang. She'd left it by the calendar so Charlie picked it up without answering. He saw it was his dad and handed it to Martha. "Mom, it's the man who makes your heart go pitter-patter."

"*Howdy, Big Boy,*" Martha said.

"Howdy back," Rex replied. "You call me *and* Fini your big boys, so I'm never sure if you're talking to me or him." He laughed. "Listen, babe; I have some amazing news. Is Charlie there?"

"He's right here with me. We're waiting on a pizza."

"Excellent! I have big news. If you put me on speaker, you can both hear at the same time."

"Hi, Dad! It's your favorite son here. It's me, you, Mom, Fini, and the cricket in the mudroom."

"I hardly know where to start," Rex began. "First of all, both of you, this is top secret stuff, so not a word of it to anyone. Okay, so we're down here, ya know, to figure out how to bring a championship to Nashville so quickly it'll stun the world. We were unable to figure out a path to a title; nothing unique, we got stuck. And Big T McCraw is coming down tomorrow afternoon. At the end of today's session, our facilitator, who calls himself 'The Rammer,' told us we'd failed. He said our plan *wasn't* a plan; it's *crapola*. That's the word he used. He said we had to explore any idea, no matter how bizarre it may seem. So, I told them about your white paper, son. Based on the conversation you and I had last week, I shared your vision of old school baseball producing higher-caliber play versus analytics-driven baseball producing lower-caliber play. I told them I don't understand the numbers behind any of it, but you've put together a credible plan. We voted to have you come down to Wintergreen to present your ideas in person! You're an MLB consultant! And, of course, you too, Martha."

Rex paused for a moment. There was silence from the other end.

"Hello?" said Rex.

"Er, sorry, darling," said Martha. "I've never seen Charlie like this; he is completely slack-jawed. Wow! Wow, wow, wow. When is this going to happen?"

"Before I tell you *when*, let me tell you *how*. You and Charlie are going to be traveling *with* Mr. McCraw in his private jet to Wintergreen!" In his best game show host voice, Rex added, "*You and your son will be traveling in style* in Mr. McCraw's private jet! The *when* is tomorrow. You need to be at the College Park Airport and ready to go at 10 a.m. Mr. McCraw's plane will be coming from New York where he's attending MLB meetings. It's okay to say you're going to Wintergreen to hang out with me; just don't breathe a word about Big T McCraw, how you got here, or that Charlie is actually here, as unbelievable as this sounds…as a consultant to a Major League Baseball team! Not a word."

Charlie was in full stupor, even more than that day on the grassy knoll when he saw his C– grade and it took a downpour to break it. This stupor was different; it was a *happy* stupor. In the end, though, a stupor is a stupor, and he was temporarily stuck there.

Rex continued, "Be sure to get there early; nine-thirty at the latest. Dress is casual, nice casual, business casual. Take Uber to the airport. You'll be picked up on this end at Charlottesville Albemarle Airport, thirty-nine miles from Wintergreen."

"That sounds great, babe!" said Martha. "I'm kind of speechless like Charlie. Just *amazing!* I'm going to have to scramble to get us ready. Fortunately, tomorrow the only thing on my schedule is my weekly bingo at Branchville firehouse. Just before you called, I asked Charlie to look over the calendar to be sure we're on top of everything for this next week. Then the phone rings and everything changes! That's life, and probably divine intervention in ways we'll see later. I'm so happy for you and for Charlie. Doors are opening!"

"Indeed, they are, my darling. Thanks for being such a loving wife and mom! Without you, none of this would be happening. You are the glue. Who knows how this will play out? Tomorrow might be a day that changes the baseball world! You and our boy are in for a big adventure! We all are. I love you!"

Martha blew an audible kiss, and Charlie, still shaking his head, managed, "Love you too."

The pizza arrived from Continental Pizza and helped snap Charlie out of it. The rest of the evening at the Collier residence was a whirlwind. Martha did her mom thing, making sure everything that needed to be done *got* done. She also arranged for the neighbor, Germaine, her friend and fellow dog lover, to check in on Fini, feed him, and let him go potty. Germaine had helped out before and liked to hang out with the canine couch potato.

Oh, what tomorrow would bring! A shift was coming.

★ CHAPTER 13 ★

CHARLIE
and the Jet

Martha had set her alarm for six-thirty, an hour earlier than usual to get herself and Charlie to the airport on time. When she opened the bedroom door, she was shocked to hear Charlie downstairs talking to Fini. She went down, turned the corner, and saw Charlie rolling a tennis ball for Fini to fetch.

"Hiya, Mom! Bottom of the morning to ya! I've been up for forty-five minutes. I could hardly sleep. I'm not nervous at all, though, which is *strange*. Mom, even though it's Sunday, would you make my special Monday breakfast? Today is monumental, and I need to be properly fueled. Plus, I consider it my lucky breakfast. Isn't it funny that I have this high IQ, and yet I consider my good fortune will come by luck, based on what I eat for breakfast? We humans are weird creatures. I blame baseball; baseball players might be the most superstitious people of all."

"Sure, Charlie!" Martha replied. "I'll start breakfast. You make sure you've got your bag packed with whatever you need for overnight at Wintergreen. Bring your swim trunks and best hiking shoes in case we have time to use them."

After Charlie wolfed down his scrambled eggs, hash browns, and wheat toast with blackberry jam, he savored the three strips of Hemplers hickory-smoked bacon that remained. He always saved the bacon for last and viewed it as proof of his ability to delay gratification. Martha had a scrambled egg and English muffin. She went upstairs to shower and do her makeup just as Rex called.

"Hey, Sexy Rexy! This is a nice surprise. We're getting ready to go."

"I'm glad I caught you. Are you by yourself now?"

"Yes, why?"

"I've been worrying about Charlie's headaches. I think we need to call the HMO and get an appointment with a neurologist. I'm thinking we should have a brain scan done; it's just not normal to have as many headaches as he's been having."

"Yes, I've been worried too. That's a good idea. I'll call to get it scheduled."

At eight-thirty, Martha went back downstairs. Charlie was ready with his gym bag at the door. Martha sent Germaine a text to let her know they were leaving and that Fini had gone potty and been fed so she wouldn't have to stop by right away. Martha called for the Uber, which arrived three minutes later.

Charlie and Martha climbed into the backseat and told the driver their destination was College Park Airport. The driver was a woman in her sixties at least, with a long gray ponytail and a Detroit Tigers baseball cap on backward. She introduced herself as Detroit Doris.

Martha said, "Nice to meet you. I'm Martha, and this is my son, Charlie."

Doris was missing a couple of bottom teeth and had the look of a gal who'd lived a lot of life and survived. A sign on her dashboard said, "Granola bars, chewing gum, breath mints, and advice." She pointed to the sign. "They're free, courtesy of *Dee*troit Doris."

Martha couldn't resist asking, "What brought you to DC, Doris?"

"Ah, it was a man, a real charmer. An age-old story. He left me in the dust when he found a younger model, but I'm livin' my life and having fun, so to heck with the scraggly goat. I hear that sweet young thing's getting tired of him, so he might just get kicked to the curb soon. It'll be karma kickin' him in the head! So how 'bout you two? Where you flying to? Not many people fly out of College Park."

"We're off to Wintergreen, Virginia, to meet up with my husband, Charlie's dad, who is already there. He's there on business, and we're going down for fun."

Seizing a momentary lapse in conversation, Charlie piped in… "Ms. Doris, are you a Detroit Tigers fan?"

Detroit Doris lit up. "Am *I* a Tigers fan? Does a big ole' bear go poo-poo in the woods? I'm a Tigers fan through thick and thin, young man!"

"Did you see Rocky Colavito play?" Charlie asked.

"*Did I see Rocky Colavito play?* He was my daddy's favorite player. Had a cannon of an arm; one of the greatest right fielders of his era, right up there with Clemente!"

Charlie leaned forward so that Detroit Doris could hear him better. "Yes, ma'am. From what I've read, he's never been given his due. Playing in Cleveland and Detroit, he didn't get the attention he would have in larger markets, but he's adored in those two cities. When he retired, he went on to live a quiet life in Reading, Pennsylvania, as a mushroom farmer."

Detroit Doris cocked her head and looked at Charlie slack-jawed. "Young man, how in heaven's name would someone your age know about Rocky Colavito, let alone what he did *after* baseball? A *mushroom farmer, huh?* Are you some kind of baseball whiz kid or something?"

Martha and Charlie both smiled at that last remark, and Charlie sheepishly mumbled, "Yes, ma'am, sometimes."

"Well, here's the airport, you two. It's been a pleasure transporting you. Young man, I have a strange feeling I'm gonna be reading about you or seeing you on TV soon. Have a great flight!"

Charlie and Martha got out of the car, collected their luggage, and then walked through the airport's double door with a sign above that read, "Welcome to College Park, The World's Oldest Continually Operating Airport!"

Rex would have been proud of them because they were early. It was only 9:25 a.m. Charlie was immediately drawn to an area with exhibits on the airport's history. On the wall was a list of "firsts" associated with the airport that briefly captured his attention until an urgent vision popped into his brain, and he whirled around to find his mom, who was right beside him. He hugged her and said, "I can see it *all*, Mom. I feel that everything is happening like it's supposed to. I'm not even nervous. That's the surprising part. I can't explain it, Mom, but you and Dad are in this too. I'm meant to change baseball."

Martha smiled at her boy…. *I know, son. I know*, she thought.

The reality of the moment hit them at the same time, and they shifted gears to watch the planes landing, especially Big T McCraw's. One small red plane landed as they waited, and then a small yellow plane took off. Martha commented on how the two planes blended in with the red and yellow foliage surrounding the airfield.

While Charlie was enthralled with watching planes, Martha went inside to make the call to the HMO. She was able to get through to the HMO neurology department quickly and set up the appointment while Charlie was occupied. Martha walked back outside. They kept their eyes to the skies, and a few minutes later, they saw a larger plane approaching. It had a white body with a dark blue nose and the same blue on the wing tips. As it got closer, they could see the letters "TG" in blue on the white body. Obviously, this was no mere plane; it was generations removed from the bi-planes the Wright Brothers had flown here and even the red and yellow planes Charlie and Martha had seen a few minutes ago. This was a *jet*, Charlie's jet, the jet coming to pick up the *fourteen-year-old* MLB consultant. This was happening. This was *really* happening! They heard the sweet sound of the engine as it touched down ever so gently. Charlie and Martha could see a face in one of the six windows on the right side. It looked to be music legend and MLB baseball owner Big T McCraw himself. Charlie's eyes were as wide as silver dollars!

Martha put her arm around Charlie and whispered, "You might not be nervous, but I am. I've always been a fan of Big T McCraw."

"It'll be fun, Mom; you'll have a blast. *Look* at this cool jet we're going on!"

Charlie and Martha were standing behind the red line that said "Authorized Personnel Only." The jet came to a stop, and a minute later, the door opened and out came Big T. He was wearing gray slacks and a blue Western-style shirt that matched the accent blue on his jet. He looked every bit the part of a highly successful businessman/civic leader as he descended from the plane. Squinting into the sun, he saw them, turned, and started walking their way. When he got close enough, he extended his big right hand to Martha and then to Charlie. "That's a fine handshake, young man. Your daddy must have taught you that! What a beautiful day for a plane ride! Martha, I am so excited for you and Charlie to join me on *The Glider*; that's what I call her. She just glides effortlessly through the sky. We'll take off in about ten minutes. I'm going into the airport for a couple of minutes. My pilot, Captain Larry, is still in the cockpit working his checklist. I'll be right back out. Is that okay? Can y'all hang out here for a while so I can take care of a little business in there?"

When Big T came back, Charlie and Martha were chatting it up with Captain Larry, who had finished his checklist and introduced himself. Captain Larry Fickel was easy to like. He knew passengers feel less anxiety when they know their pilots know what they are doing, so he had the smarts to work into the conversation that he was a retired commercial pilot, had been a fighter pilot in the Air Force, and for kicks, even had flown bush planes in Alaska for two years. Larry's nickname was "SAS" (Smooth as Silk) because nothing ever rattled him.

When Big T returned, he said in his deep twang, "I see you met Captain Larry, the only pilot I let fly *The Glider*! Captain Larry, I love this airport. I only flew out of here once before. It's called the Cradle of Aviation."

"It's my first time here," Larry replied. "What a feeling to be at the same airfield the Wright Brothers used. Flying out of College Park is bucket list stuff for pilots! I have goosebumps. Let's get going!"

Charlie wasn't even trying to play it cool. "Yeah, let's go!" he said as he started toward *The Glider*. Captain Larry, Big T, and Martha got in line behind him and followed.

"Go ahead and get in the cockpit, Charlie," Captain Larry said. Charlie bounded up the stairs with a gleeful grin that just about made the rubber bands fly off his braces. When all were aboard, Captain Larry asked if Charlie would like to sit in the cockpit during the flight. Pausing for a millisecond, Charlie pointed to the sky and said, "If it's okay with Wilbur and Orville."

Thirty-five minutes later, Captain Larry gently touched down on the runway at Charlottesville-Albemarle Airport. Charlie had probing questions for Captain Larry throughout the flight, so he was disappointed that it ended up being so short. They mostly talked about the specifics of the aircraft, which was an Eclipse 500, manufactured in 2019, and was in the VLJ (Very Light Jet) category. It was sleek and sexy, with leather interiors like a Corvette, and Charlie was smitten.

After exiting the plane, Big T and Martha waited on the tarmac for

Captain Larry and Charlie, who were both still in the cockpit. Captain Larry descended the stairs a minute later with his arm around Charlie's shoulder. "Thank you, Captain Larry," said Martha, "for such a fun, smooth flight. And thank you for letting Charlie sit in the cockpit with you."

"It was my pleasure, ma'am. You might have a future pilot on your hands with Charlie."

As they finished saying goodbye to Captain Larry, a tall, easy-on-the-eyes young blonde woman approached them with a big smile and sweet Shenandoah Valley Southern accent. "Hi, Mr. McCraw, Mrs. Collier, and Charlie. I hope you had a delightful flight! My name is Charlene McDermott, and I'll be your driver for the entire trip, *all the way to Wintergreen*, which should take us just about the same amount of time as your flight here from what I understand, about thirty-five minutes. If y'all will please follow me, we can walk right out to the car. Or perhaps you'd like to use the restrooms here first." Big T said yes, he'd make a pit stop, so they all did.

Soon they were all comfortably seated in a brand-new Lincoln Town Car and ready to go. As soon as Charlie got in, he blurted, "This car smells new."

"Your nose knows, Charlie," Charlene replied. "This car *is* new. It only has 287 miles on it, and most of that is from picking it up in Richmond. The resort buys all of our vehicles from a dealership there."

Charlene explained that she worked part-time at the resort. "I heard that the baseball executives for the new team in Nashville were here for a couple of days and that you, Mr. McCraw, were coming in, so I asked if I could pick you up. I'm from a baseball family and the only girl of five. My dad played, my brothers played, and I played for as long as they would let girls. My brother Matt was a teammate of Ryan Zimmerman of the Nationals when he was at UVA. Anyway, I talk too much sometimes, but I'm really trying to say it's an honor to meet y'all and be your driver. I can offer you bottles of water if you're thirsty, and I can provide any music genre you'd like, or we can go without the music and y'all can talk among yourselves while I drive."

Big T chuckled and said, "I like Beethoven. What do you like, Mrs. Collier?"

"I like country—Big T McCraw, Garth Brooks, Little Big Town, and Josh Turner," Martha replied.

"How about you, Charlie?" Big T asked.

"Hmm…definitely hard to choose one genre or group, but I'm going with the first one that pops into my head—The Clash. Maybe some other '80s punk too."

After a few keystrokes, Charlene said over her shoulder, "Done. We'll hear about twelve minutes of each genre, starting with classical, followed by country, and ending with The Clash. That is the logical order, in my opinion, for the flow of those three genres. I'll set the volume at a comfortable level for having a conversation too, and y'all let me know if you want it up or down." As Charlene pulled the car away from the curb, she surprised them with a perfect-pitch soothing rendition of Willie Nelson's "On the Road Again." She just did a couple of lines and then trailed off. Big T started the applause, and Martha and Charlie joined in.

Everything about this journey would go down in the annals of Collier family history and storytelling…Charlie getting the call-up, Detroit Doris, Charlie's jet ride, lovely Charlene just being lovely Charlene, and what was about to come.

Charlene chauffeured them through the gates of Wintergreen with The Clash's "Should I Stay or Should I Go?" blaring from the speakers. She had been right; the flow worked beautifully.

★ CHAPTER 14 ★

MLB CONSULTANT
Charlie Collier

Rex was sitting on the veranda when he saw Martha and Charlie driving into the resort. He jumped up and rushed to hug them. The Rammer and Ms. Scully were in the lobby coffee shop. Seeing the Collier group hug, they waited the appropriate time before approaching. "Howdy, Mrs. Collier. I'm Timothy Ramage, and this is my administrative assistant, Rebecca Scully."

"Hi, Mr. Ramage, Ms. Scully! I'm Martha. This is our son, Charlie."

"Hi, Mr. Ramage! Hi, Ms. Scully! I'm Charlie."

Timothy Ramage extended his hand, and Charlie shook it like a man. The Rammer smiled broadly. "Young man, I'm looking forward to working with you and hearing your ideas. I'm the facilitator for the group. Let's you and I spend a few minutes together before the group meets. I'd like to get to know you and have a little pre-game pep talk. Is that okay?"

"Yes, sir, Mr. Ramage! That's what every great coach does. I love pep talks!"

"Mrs. Collier, is it okay if I take Charlie for an ice cream after you check in? The ice cream shop here has thirty-seven flavors. It's through the door behind the coffee shop."

"That'd be great, Mr. Ramage. It would surely hit the spot for Charlie, but trust me, he'll get plain vanilla, even if they have 137 flavors."

"Charlie, meet me there at eleven-fifteen, okay?"

"Yes, sir, I'll be there!"

* * *

Thirty minutes later, following some chit-chat with Mr. Ramage, Charlie had finished his vanilla ice cream.

"Charlie," said Mr. Ramage. "I've enjoyed having this time to get to know you. We'll go with the plan where everyone holds their questions to the end. You're only fourteen, and my team is made up of grown men, so I want to make sure you are at ease and not intimidated in any way. I don't want you peppered with questions. That way, you get to fully present your thoughts without possibly being derailed by interjections. The whiteboard will be there for you to use, and Ms. Scully and I will be there to help you if you need anything else. Think of it like you're the teacher and they're your students, no matter the age difference. Tell us what your research shows and what you think we should do. Let's see your stuff, kid!" As they parted, Timothy Ramage reminded him, "We're meeting at noon in the Shamokin Board Room; see you then. All the cool kids will be there!"

Charlie laughed and replied, "That's a funny name, Shamokin; makes me think of Jim Carrey in *The Mask*…Smokin'!"

The executive team and Big T reconvened in the Shamokin Room, which was stocked with juices, water, coffee, protein bars, and a beautiful watermelon. The watermelon had been carved to look like a basket with a handle, and the melon inside it was cubed into bite-sized pieces. The chairs were around the table in a U shape with the open end by the American flag and the whiteboard. Around the table sat six top executives of an MLB franchise who were about to be given a presentation by a fourteen-year-old kid with nothing but a theory. That they were open to listening showed their belief that the only way to win quickly is to go against the grain, against prevailing baseball thought.

Ms. Scully escorted Charlie into the room. By happenstance, they were color-coordinated. Charlie wore a pair of crisp blue jeans and a gray long-sleeve baseball jersey with red sleeves that read "Baseball Is Life." Ms. Scully was clad in hip-hugger jeans, a red top with gray geo-metric designs, and her soft leather half-boots. Charlie had his gym bag with him, which he placed on the table beside the whiteboard.

An air of expectation and a slightly awkward silence filled the room as Charlie sat down. Nobody knew what was coming next. Normally, The Rammer would pound his gavel, but Mr. McCraw had asked to open the meeting and introduce Charlie.

Big T stood, took off his jacket, and laid it on top of the table, next to Charlie's gym bag. He took a sip of sweet tea, looked at Charlie, and began. "Charlie, thank you for being here today. I believe you all know that Charlie, at age fourteen, is already an underclassman at the University of Maryland majoring in statistics. Obviously, he's not a typical kid. He is also a baseball historian who probably knows the game as well as the rest of us in the room, and he's a pretty darn good pitcher from what I hear. Let's give him the respect of a peer while still remembering he's only fourteen. Let's consider him an extremely talented rookie. Our team is new, so we can go in any direction without any of the encumbrances established teams have. This can work to our advantage. I want no part of taking ten, twenty, or even just five years to win a championship. I want nothing less than to shock the baseball world by being contenders immediately. Charlie, we know you're quote, unquote, just a kid, but we are going to consider what you have to say today. Mr. Ramage and I have spoken about and decided upon the format for this afternoon. We want to be sure you are put in the best position to put forth your theory. I want all of you to hold questions and comments until Charlie says he is completely finished. At that time, you can ask questions and discuss what we heard. Ms. Scully will videotape the session. Are there any questions now, before we begin?"

Surprisingly, Charlie was the one who had a question. He raised his hand just like in school.

"Yes, Charlie," Big T said.

"Mr. McCraw, would it be okay if I just pretend I'm with my dad and his friends? Sometimes I go with him to his favorite coffee shop where we meet up with my great-uncle Frank and a couple of other friends of theirs. We always talk baseball. Since this is my first business presentation, I think if I pretend I'm talking to them, I'll be better able to explain it to you without nervousness." (His voice cracked on the last word.) "Oops. That's the teenage voice thing there. Sorry."

"Of course. *You be you* and just give the info and vision to us in whatever way works," Big T replied.

The Rammer added a robust "Hear! Hear!" All the while, Ms. Scully was grinning at the cuteness of Charlie's voice crack, and of Charlie in general. The rest of the group didn't know what to think, especially Rex. Here was his fourteen-year-old son being introduced as the whiz kid to tell a major league team how to win! On what planet does that happen?

★ CHAPTER 15 ★
CHARLIE
Makes His Pitch

Big T turned to Charlie and said, "The floor is yours, Mr. Collier."

Charlie stood and smoothed out his pants and shirt. He held up his right index finger and said, "One moment please," as he reached into his gym bag and pulled out his glove. It was his best glove ever, and at three years old, it was perfectly oiled and broken in. He rooted around a little more in the bag, "Hmm….thought I had a ball in here too. Oh, well."

"Okay, so this will just be me, Charlie, talking to my dad, my great-uncle Frank, and their friend Mister D in the coffee shop."

Ms. Scully's voice broke in. "Excuse me, Charlie. Would this help?" She held up a baseball—not any baseball, but her special baseball, the old ball with a stitch missing, which was always in her handbag. It was her "thinking" ball, the one she would flip from hand to hand when contemplating life's major and minor decisions.

Charlie held up his glove with the universal *throw-it-to-me* movement. Ms. Scully obliged and threw a strike. Charlie caught it and snapped the ball into the webbing a couple of times. "Thanks, Ms. Scully."

"You betcha, Charlie! That's a *very* lucky baseball."

"Cool," Charlie said, looking it over. "I can see it has history."

"Okay, I'll just start. There's so much involved in baseball, so many nuances, and the nuances are key. From a historical perspective, the game has changed with the information age, just like everything else in the world. But not all things can be measured. Sometimes, the non-measurables are the things most crucial to success or failure on the field. I believe my research proves that overuse of analytics has resulted in a lower caliber of play. When I examined the data from 1979 to 1999, and compared it to the period of 1999 to 2019, I found that the *overall* performance of players was statistically equal, within the standard deviation. The key emphasis there is on the word *overall*… overall player performance. Yes, one area might be enhanced, such as home runs, but another equally important area of performance might see caliber of play decline. And *then* there are the non-measurables. (Charlie was ramping up, excitement in his eyes.) We all know that some players are great "clubhouse/team" guys. They make players around them better. How do you measure that? Answer, you don't; you can't. Another example of a non-measurable would be cultural differences between players and how they affect caliber of play. The overzealous analytic people would have us believe that with more and more data, they can do an increasingly better job of assembling and managing a team. I disagree. The numbers don't bear that out. When players overthink rather than play the game on a more instinctual level, they aren't as good. Instinctual play is better. A player who overthinks will hesitate, and that means he's out by half a step or late on the fastball, and he's walking back to the dugout."

Charlie was pacing now, gripping the ball with his curve ball grip, slinging it into the webbing as he paced. Meanwhile, Big T was madly scribbling on a yellow legal pad.

"I'm not sure how to say this," Charlie continued, "except to just say it. I mean this with the utmost respect for you gentlemen, but I'm afraid you wouldn't understand the bulk of the mathematics behind my research; it's very complex. I'll just give you the results. Last week, I did a lot of thinking about my research and what it means. I wanted to encapsulate it all in one simple way—one idea that could be easily understood. I was actually in my backyard target shooting with my slingshot when it came to me. The answer was right in front of me. *Total bases!* Our game is called *base*ball. In theory, my plan is simple: Get as many bases as you can and prevent your opponent from getting bases." Charlie wrote Project Baseball on the whiteboard. "Project Baseball, if fully implemented, could bring a championship quickly, in my opinion. The plan is all about capturing *bases* and stopping opponents from capturing *bases*. I've broken it down into *offense* and *defense*." He wrote OFFENSE and DEFENSE on the whiteboard across the top. "Then within each category, I have ways to accomplish the goal. Before I get into that, I will give you some of the *easy* math to show you a couple of the categories under offense and how we can capture more bases.

"Let's take strikeout rate, for instance. In 2019, the average strikeout rate for hitters throughout the league was 26 percent. The Cleveland Indians struck out at the lowest rate of 21 percent while most teams were in the 24-26 percent range. *Now*, let's compare those numbers to 1979. In 1979, the Oakland Athletics had the lowest strikeout rate for hitters at 10 percent, and the San Francisco Giants had the highest rate at 15 percent. The average strikeout rate in 1979 was 14 percent, puny by today's standards. In Project Baseball, one piece of the puzzle is to put more balls in play by cutting down on strikeouts. The plan calls for a team strikeout rate of 15 percent. Based on last year's at-bats of a typical team, this would put the ball in play an additional 462 times, and we know good things happen when we put the ball in play."

At this point, Charlie started to pace and fire the ball into his glove again. He seemed to do this when thinking; Ms. Scully's "thinking ball" was aptly named.

Then Charlie put the glove and ball on the table and started writing on the whiteboard again. Under OFFENSE, he listed:

> Strike-Out rate
>
> Hits
> Walks
> Sacrifice bunts
> Bunt hits
> Sacrifice flies
> Hit behind runners
> Squeeze plays
> Stolen bases

Charlie then turned to the group and continued. "I just showed you numbers for strike-out rates and where I think we should be, at about 15 percent. I could go through these other categories and show you similarly that the caliber of play has declined in most of these areas when comparing 1979 to 2019. For example, take stolen bases. In 1979, the average success rate was 63 percent. Today, the average success rate is 73 percent. That's like having a .730 batting average. You're capturing a base successfully 730 times out of 1,000. I'll take those odds any day. Yet, stolen base *attempts* are down compared to 1979, even considering that there are four more teams in Major League Baseball than existed in 1979—the Rockies, Marlins, Rays, and Diamondbacks. This makes no sense. If something works seven out of ten times, why would you try it less often? Yet, that is *exactly* what has happened. In 1979, across all MLB teams, there were a total of 4,681 attempts, and by 2019, stolen base attempts had fallen to 3,112, despite the additional four teams. When we look at walks by hitters and compare 1979 to 2019, we find the number of walks virtually the same when taking into account the four additional teams. Hits are down significantly, as reflected in lower batting averages today compared to 1979."

Everyone in the room was spellbound. It was quiet except for Charlie's voice, the thinking ball hitting the glove, and Big T flipping over pages on his yellow legal pad.

Charlie pointed toward the whiteboard and continued. "The rest of the items under offense don't lend themselves to comparison because stats don't exist for them. There are no stats from the 1980s that I can find for hitting behind the runner, squeeze plays, bunts, or bunt hits, but I think you agree that these fall into the 'lost art' category and we know they've declined significantly."

Charlie picked up his glove again and pantomimed catching a ball, with the words, "Let's talk about defense."

Keeping his glove on his left hand, Charlie wrote under DEFENSE on the whiteboard the following items:

Pitching Rotation

Hits

Walks

Errors

Balls not reached

Strikeouts

Runners caught stealing

Fielder Positioning

Charlie picked up the ball and snapped it into the webbing again, which seemed to help him stay focused. Then, seemingly out of left field because he sensed the room was too quiet, he blurted, "Hey, I got a couple of jokes for you. That's what we do at the coffee shop sometimes. *What do you get when you cross a pitcher with the Invisible Man?*" Charlie paused for a second, then quickly answered, "*Pitching like nobody's ever seen before!*"

The men and Ms. Scully laughed, and Wally Rupp shouted, "Preach it, brother! Bring on the Invisible Man!" Everybody laughed again.

Like any good comedian, Charlie paused to let his audience enjoy the joke before launching the next one.

"*Why are some umpires overweight?*" This time he waited for an answer.

David Clark, the self-described nerd of the group and also a jokester and punster, guessed, "Do they eat lots of chicken and conduct a *fowl* poll about it?"

"Ooh, that's a good guess," Charlie said over the groans from every-one else, "but that would be incorrect." He drum-rolled his fingers on the table and then gave the answer. "*It's because they clean their plates!*"

The crowd response was half-laughs, half-groans. Reading his audi-ence like a pro, Charlie knew it was time to get back to Project Base-ball. Standing confidently, he asked if it would be okay to erase the whiteboard. The Rammer asked Ms. Scully if she had recorded it, and she replied she had, so he nodded his consent to Charlie.

Charlie put his glove back on the table and erased everything on the whiteboard except the words Project Baseball. He turned and faced the group with his disarming, shiny orthodontics smile and pas-sion-filled eyes.

Next, Charlie picked up his glove again and started slinging Ms. Scul-ly's "thinking ball" into the webbing even harder. He turned toward her and said, "I can see why you like this ball."

Then Charlie faced the group and said, "I could talk about the sta-tistics behind my research until the cows come home, as my uncle Frank says, but there would be no end to the analysis. Instead of look-ing at all those boring, impossible to understand numbers, why don't you come with me on a baseball journey? This is the journey where The Nashville Knights win the World Series!

"Project Baseball, or PB for short, requires a completely different phil-osophical approach from Low-A ball to The Show. It'll be *fun* for the players because it will be something experimental, bringing change to the game in a meaningful way. People like to be part of a movement, something that matters. PB should draw free agents who will want to be part of something no other team will be doing. PB is Old School baseball, the way the game was played before the analytics craze took root. We will be like judo tenth-degree black-belts and use the weight of our opponents' analytics against them. It will be analytic baseball versus instinctual baseball. Does anyone think the 1964 New York Yankees wouldn't be able to compete today?

"Let me rattle off some of the main tenets in the PB plan. Starters will pitch every fourth day, instead of fifth, just like in the old days, and there will be no pitch counts. A pitcher is removed when he is struggling, tired, or ineffective. When a pitcher is cruising, he remains in the game unless there is a really good reason. I believe pitchers would jump at the chance to go Old School and have more starts, opportunities for complete games, and shutouts. Pitchers love to build their career statistics, so we'd attract ace pitchers and young gunslingers. Pitchers might actually win twenty games a year again! And our pitchers from Low A to The Show have to be excellent fielders. We want them squaring off to field their positions. How often do we see ground balls go up the middle for a hit, directly over the pitching rubber when the pitcher has fallen off to one side in an effort to gain an extra 1-2 mph on their fastball? What would be a routine out becomes a runner on first, all because the pitcher wasn't fielding his position. Even worse, a pitcher falling off the mound is more vulnerable to a line drive to the head. After he throws the ball, a pitcher is a fielder. Pitchers and all players will master bunting. There isn't one team in Major League Baseball today that even comes close to mastering the bunt. Oddly, they seem to disdain it. I've watched film of and read about past greats like Mickey Mantle. An iconic slugger like The Mick could lay down a drag bunt for a hit and take pride in it. He didn't think it beneath him like today's sluggers. Part of being a big leaguer should be that, at minimum, players in the organization be excellent bunters. On pitching philosophy, PB calls for a de-emphasis on 95-100 mph fastballs and development of pitchers who know how to change speeds, have an arsenal of pitch assortments, and good control. As Hall of Famer Jim Palmer once said, 'Pitching is the art of throwing the batter's timing off.' My research indicates there are more pitching injuries and more time on the Injured List for high-velocity pitchers due to the extra torque on their arms and shoulders.

"I could talk more about the overall vision and the subsets I erased from the whiteboard and break this down in more detail. I'm working from memory, but I did put this and a lot more detail into a Word document that could be a starting point if the team decides to adopt PB as the path to the World Series!"

At this point, Charlie paused. It felt like a natural stopping point. Maybe it was time to open up the floor to Q and A or whatever came next.

Big T sensed the same thing and said, "Does anyone have questions for Charlie?"

"Yes, sir, I do," said GM Kurt Grimmer. "Charlie, you've seen a copy of the OBIs that each of us came up with at Wintergreen. Which of our OBIs do you think are compatible with Project Baseball?"

Charlie paused to process the question. Here he could veer off to come across as critical of these men he admired, but he surely didn't want to do that. On the other hand, he was being asked his opinion in his capacity as a MLB consultant, so duty required honesty. "Yes, I did review those. Let me look at the list again and give you my opinion about which ones fit. Overall, many of them are what I'd call analytics lite or 'first cousins' of analytics. Let me address the specific OBIs.

"I'll pick on my dad first. Dad, the uniforms don't matter; if we execute Project Baseball, we'll win. We could be wearing bib overalls.

"Mr. Wenzel, your OBI is *Beat the Shift*. If Project Baseball is executed, that will occur automatically. As for *left-handed power hitters*, I say just get players who play the PB way, players who will capture bases and deny our opponents bases.

"Mr. Clark, Artificial Intelligence and robots in baseball? Human intelligence beats artificial intelligence. It's funny, er, punny...yesterday I was reading about a study where AI competed against humans in pun writing contests. The judges, human, concluded that the AI puns were better only 10 percent of the time. AI has its societal place, but not in baseball. I can show statistically that fundamentally sound, instinctual baseball beats analytics-driven baseball.

"Mr. Rupp, yes! Speed is a central pillar of Project Baseball. As for your other idea to bring in power hitters because you think the DH rule is inevitable in the National League, I say that doesn't fit. I believe we just need to find players who *do* fit our Project Baseball system, capture bases, deny bases.

"And Mr. Grimmer, *Exploit the bunt*, yes! Being a great bunting team is another pillar of PB. The other idea, *Add Two Relievers*, does not fit. PB strongly emphasizes starting pitching.

"Mr. Dory, *Eliminate the Strikeout* and *Muscle Up*. Yes, eliminating the strikeout is an excellent OBI. Muscling up is a no. I believe I could show, with more research, that the overly muscled player loses efficiency due to changes in body mechanics. Muscling up will increase strikeouts. Yes, let's *eliminate the strikeout* and not *muscle up*."

Charlie looked to Big T for direction or the next question. Big T asked, "Does anyone have other questions for Charlie?"

David Clark stood up. "Yes, where do you get the authority and experience to declaratively say you can prove your theory statistically? There are people like myself with loads of experience who say otherwise. These men are just taking your word, and you haven't shown me any numbers. And you respond to my comments by just saying human intelligence is better and cavalierly dismissing my opinion with a story about computers writing puns."

"Gosh, Mr. Clark," Charlie replied, "I don't mean to upset you. I thought I gave some statistical analysis and examples in my presentation that are compelling, like the stolen base numbers showing that there was a higher success rate in the latter era compared to 1979-1999. I believe the entirety of my work will be made available to you so you can study it in greater detail."

He looked at David apologetically and said, "I didn't mean to come across as cavalier and dismissive; I'm sorry if I did, but I do believe in my research, and any authority I have comes from my research, which I believe is sound."

David's face reddened, and he stuck out his chin as he turned toward Big T and said, "I don't think this is workable. I am not being taken seriously."

Big T showed no sign of being upset with David. Instead, he said, "It's okay, David. We can have some disagreements. You are taken seriously, but realize that we have a wide range of thoughts. You'll be able to see details of Charlie's research, and even if we adopt Project Baseball, you still may have valuable insights. Let's just sit tight and we'll work through everything." That seemed to relax David slightly.

Butch spoke up. "Not a question. I just want to say thanks for your presentation, Charlie. You got us thinking."

"It's my pleasure," Charlie replied. "It's been fun being here; feels like I'm in a movie."

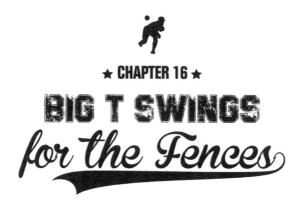

★ CHAPTER 16 ★
BIG T SWINGS
for the Fences

The Rammer started the applause for Charlie's presentation, and everyone joined in, including an enthusiastic Big T. He asked Charlie to come stand with him while someone took their photo. Ms. Scully volunteered and positioned them better underneath a light, taking several pictures that she showed to Big T. He asked Ms. Scully to please send them to his cell phone. Big T then pumped Charlie's hand again, saying, "Thanks, Charlie. Great job! I have one last request, which you can probably do with your phone. Would you please send me an email with the documents for Project Baseball? I want to look them over carefully. The more detail, the better. If you can send it right away, I can study it during the break we're about to take. Your dad can text you my email address."

"I'll send it right away, Mr. McCraw. Thank you."

Ms. Scully escorted Charlie down to the lobby. They sat near the mammoth fireplace while waiting for Martha to arrive. It did give them a chance to talk some more about the "thinking ball." Ms. Scully told Charlie a couple of stories about its power. She said that slinging the ball increases its power and that it helped with his spellbinding presentation. By the end of the conversation, the "thinking ball" had been promoted from a *lucky ball* to a *magical ball*. Charlie thanked her for letting him borrow it. Ms. Scully put the ball back in her purse and said, "My pleasure!" Once Martha arrived, Ms. Scully returned to the board room in case she was needed. Charlie and Martha sat in the lobby to people-watch while waiting for Rex and the drive home.

Alone with his mom, Charlie said, "Today went great, and I'm so happy. Why am I getting a headache now?"

"I don't know, son. We'll find out. I have some Tylenol in my purse that might help some." She took the bottle from her purse and got two capsules. Charlie took them, swallowed without water, and said, "Headache, go away."

***

Once Charlie left, the room felt empty. He had been the most powerful presence in the room without trying or wanting to be. He had brought pure love of the game and of life, and he'd a disarming effect on those in the room. He had sensed this effect a couple of other times in school when giving presentations. It was a weird magnetism he could feel but not explain. Today, though, was unlike any other time. It was *otherworldly*.

With one exception, the seven grown men in the room looked dazed, like people who had just finished watching a gripping suspense movie in the theater; they were so blown away they had to sit there for a while afterwards and regroup.

Big T, all 6' 6" of him, was the only one standing and the only one *not* looking dazed. He glowed like he'd just found a long-lost treasure. "Let's break for three hours. I want that time to thoroughly think through it all and review the documents. Mr. Ramage, please stay with me."

***

Three hours later.

"Team, everything just changed," said Big T. "I made a decision. We're going to swing the *big* bat! If we go down swinging, so be it. I'm swinging for the fences! While listening to Charlie, I was getting ideas of my own. Someone once said a camel is a cow designed by a committee. We're not going to design this by committee. I have decided we *will* adopt Project Baseball, as written by Charlie, as our path to winning. Mr. Ramage and I were able to dig deep into the plan. I love the boldness and all the detail Charlie put into the documents we reviewed. Frankly, I think it's brilliant. All of you can be a part of it, *if* you are all-in. We're not dipping our toe in the water; we're doing a cannonball, and we'll make a splash that will wash all over baseball! As my friend Timothy is fond of saying, 'We're going whole hog!' And, by the way, thank you, Timothy, for your work with us. This will be one of those times we'll look back on and say, 'Remember that meeting at Wintergreen in the beginning?'"

Timothy J. Ramage smiled and sat up in his chair. "My pleasure, boss. It's what I do."

"As soon as we get back to our offices," Big T continued, "we'll plot how we'll go about installing PB from top to bottom. First, we'll need to get copies for each of you from Charlie as an email attachment. Study it as soon as you get it; then we'll spend this week planning the implementation. I can see by the looks on your faces that you're surprised, maybe shocked, by my quick decision. It's going to be a great ride! Mr. Ramage, do you have any final words for the group?"

"Yes, sir, I do. I can't wait to see what you all do with this. I can see it capturing the imagination and heart of the nation, with fans everywhere rooting for the Old School Guys. Yesterday, we began our meeting with the Einstein quote: "You have to learn the rules of the game and then you have to play better than anyone else." Team, now I say to you: Learn the rules of Project Baseball and then play the game better than anyone else. I'm rooting for you! In my not-always-so-humble opinion, Project Baseball is, literally, a stroke of genius by the Kid Genius. It might just work, and if anyone can lead you lovable knuckleheads besides yours truly, it's my friend, the boss man here (motioning toward Big T). Have fun and go conquer Major League Baseball!"

The Rammer silently handed the gavel to Big T, who took it and rapped the table. "Meeting adjourned. Go, Knights!"

The group now said their goodbyes and dispersed to begin their travels home.

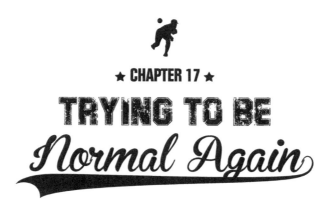

★ CHAPTER 17 ★

TRYING TO BE
Normal Again

Charlie jokingly groused about riding home in such a plebian manner; a Honda Accord just didn't cut it after having traveled in a private Eclipse 500. Nonetheless, all three Colliers piled into their car to begin the drive home. A few hundred yards down the road, Rex turned off the radio. "Who *was* that back there?" he asked. "*Who* gave that presentation? *Where* did that come from? You had no notes, nothing. No experience speaking to groups like that and they, *we*, were spellbound. What just happened? Martha, it was *amazing!* Your boy held court and got MLB executives to adopt his plan! Our Senior Data Analyst, David Clark, challenged his theory and Charlie kindly and firmly held his ground. David ended up almost walking out. How'd ya do it, Charlie?"

"I have no idea," Charlie replied. "It was as though I became another person and was observing myself. Maybe it was Ms. Scully's thinking ball after all. Dad, can you turn back on the radio and find some music for the ride home? My head hurts. I just want to relax for a while and close my eyes."

Rex turned on the radio through the back speakers. A high school football game was on, so he hit the FM button for music. "Should I Stay or Should I Go?" was playing.

"We heard this song yesterday," said Charlie. "It must be following us."

"Stay or go where?" Martha wondered aloud. "I wonder what they're talking about?"

At Martha's suggestion, they took the scenic route home via the Blue Ridge Parkway. It was quite a bit slower, but glorious in color this time of year. Charlie dozed in the backseat; his brain was tired. Maybe it was the trait of a genius, or maybe it was just being a teenager, but when he hit the wall, he could have slept at an Aerosmith concert.

When they neared the DC beltway, Charlie woke up. "Hey, looks like we're almost home," he said. "I zonked out. I had a dream Alfred and I were in some kind of big parade. Oh, by the way, Alfred sent me a text while we were at Wintergreen. He'd like to practice some if we get home before dark. I'd like to work on my change-up with him. Is it okay if I tell him to meet us at the house so we can practice right away?"

"Okay by me," said Rex, "unless your Mom has other plans, but I want to stop by Continental for pizza first."

"Fine by me," Martha said, adding, "Charlie, you have a doctor's appointment at the HMO tomorrow at ten. We set it up to see if they can figure out why you're having headaches."

"Good," Charlie said. "I'm tired of these nuclear headaches; they're splitting."

Rex groaned.

**

Half an hour later, Alfred pulled into the Colliers' driveway, parked his old-school bike with its banana seat and butterfly handlebars, and sat down on Charlie's front porch. A few minutes later, the Colliers arrived.

Charlie jumped out of the car and shouted, "Alfred!"

Alfred threw up his arms and cried, "Suster! Let's throw some before it gets too dark."

Alfred had his catcher's mitt and a ball. Charlie grabbed his glove and the boys headed to the backyard pitcher's mound that Rex and Charlie had built at the beginning of the season. They threw for about twenty-five minutes until it got too dark. Alfred, ever the encourager, raved about Charlie's progress with the change-up. "Sus, your change-up is getting better; your arm looks like you're throwing a fastball, but the ball just creeps up to the plate. We're gonna have some fun making batters look like fools!"

Just then, Martha opened the back door to tell them it was too dark to play anymore and to come inside. "Be right in, Mom," said Charlie.

As soon as the boys got inside, Alfred's phone beeped with a text from his mom, saying he had to come home. After walking Alfred out, Charlie came back inside and flipped the TV to the MLB Network where, amazingly, the talking heads were doing a feature on Big T McCraw and the Nashville Knights. "Mom, Dad, come look! Big T is being interviewed on MLB!" They watched the segment together and then talked about their Wintergreen experience.

"Okay, Charlie," said Martha. "I know you're excited, but back to reality, young man. You have to get ready for bed."

"Aw, Mom, do I have to?"

"Yes, sir! You have to. It's in the rule book."

"What rule book? Whose rule book?"

"The rule book that counts—*mine*! Now skedaddle upstairs! You have your doctor's appointment in the morning, and you'll look healthier with a good night's sleep."

"Sleep's overrated, Mom. I'm an MLB consultant now and need time to refine Project Baseball. I can sleep when I'm dead."

"*Go!*" Rex said in his Alpha Dad voice, pointing upstairs.

Charlie feigned outrage, moaning as he complied. "That's not *fair!*"

"Good *night*, son," Rex and Martha echoed.

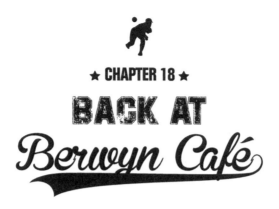

★ CHAPTER 18 ★

BACK AT
Berwyn Café

Three days after Charlie's presentation, Frank, Dustin, *and* Maddy were enjoying their second cup of coffee. When things were slow, Maddy would sometimes sit with the regulars. Today, Frank and Dustin were asking her about her band. Rex rolled in just as Maddy told them she'd just recorded a new song.

"I'm calling it 'Slow 'n Easy on a Beautiful Day.' I wrote it during a particularly stressful time. It came from a deep place, a song of healing. 'Slow and easy on a beautiful day' is the refrain. 'Sloooooow and eaaaaasy on a beautiful Dayaaaaa,'" she half-cooed, half-sang.

Abruptly, Maddy's singer/songwriter face switched to her barista face as she jumped to her feet. "Sixteen-ounce Iced Americano with a shot of vanilla, Mr. Collier?"

"You're good, Maddy!"

"That's what they tell me!"

"How 'bout bringing me a sausage egg sandwich on a toasted poppy seed bagel along with that Americano?"

"You got it, Mr. Collier! How's Charlie doing? And how come you left him home?" She winked. "He's more fun than you old guys, but I do like you *hip oldsters* too. Or is it *old hipsters*? Whatever...there's definitely something to be said for elder statesmen."

"Charlie's either at home catching up on schoolwork or hanging out with his buddy, Alfred. I'll tell him you asked. He'll blush." Maddy smiled knowingly and went back to the kitchen.

"Actually," Rex said, "Charlie's headaches have gotten more frequent. I didn't want to tell her that when she asked how he's doing."

"Bummer," Frank replied.

"Are you having tests done?" Dustin asked.

"Yes," Rex said. "He had a brain scan the day after we got back from Wintergreen. We're waiting for the neurologist to read the results. We expected to hear already."

"Leanne and I will pray for a clean bill of health," said Dustin.

"Amen to that," said Frank.

Frank steered the conversation to baseball, asking Rex what had happened at Wintergreen. Rex had been looking forward to telling Dustin and Uncle Frank; he needed to tell *someone* besides Martha, someone who knew baseball and would understand—a confidante. Who better to tell? First, though, he would swear them to secrecy.

"Okay, I have big news. What happened at Wintergreen was surreal, right out of *The Twilight Zone*, in a good way."

Frank and Dustin leaned in, eyes widening.

"What I'm about to tell you I *shouldn't* be telling you, but I trust you. This is super-secret. The only people who know, after I tell you, are Charlie, Martha, and the executives with the Knights. If word got out, it would be my ass, so please be careful. Even when Maddy comes back with coffee, be careful. We can't risk anything being overheard and repeated, no matter how innocently."

"Wow, Rex. This sounds big. My lips are sealed," Frank said.

"Mine too," Dustin added.

"Here's the deal. We all went down to Wintergreen to draw up the plan to immediately be contenders and shock the world. But we got stuck, hopelessly stuck. We argued, almost came to blows at times, and couldn't agree. We did come up with something, but the facilitator, a gruff straight talker, termed it crapola—his word—and threw it out. Because we were hopelessly stuck, Big T asked us for any idea, no matter how outrageous. So, I brought up Charlie and the research he's been doing. Big T said he wanted something big; that we needed a Hail Mary. Long story short, Big T invited Charlie to come to Wintergreen and present his concept in person. Big T even picked up him and Martha in his private jet and flew them both down."

Frank and Dustin's jaws were on the floor.

Rex paused the conversation as Maddy brought the sausage egg sandwich and Americano. She warmed up Frank and Dustin's coffee just as three more customers came in together, which was perfect because Maddy didn't linger, allowing Rex to continue the story.

"Charlie gave us a presentation on his research and the plan he developed. Then we took a three-hour break while Big T looked over the details of Charlie's plan. After the break, Big T declared we would implement Charlie's plan in its entirety throughout the organization. No vote, no further discussion. Boom! Big T just said we're doing it! Can you believe it? My kid, your great-nephew, Frank, just convinced a major league team to adopt his strategies!

"I got a text from Big T this morning," Rex added, "that David Clark, our IT guy resigned. He had lots of issues with the new approach, so it's not a surprise."

Frank and Dustin sat there, waiting for the rest of the story on David Clark, but there was none.

Finally, Dustin asked, "What's next?"

"Everything's a whirlwind," said Rex, "so I'm not sure what's next. Obviously, we'll be working on the plan implementation, and we have to do that quickly. On top of that, we'll need to move to Nashville sooner, so life will be insane over the next few months. I never would have dreamed anything like this would happen. When we were kids playing ball, we played for the sheer joy of it. I'm feeling sheer joy about this too. It's a dream come true, almost like when we were kids and we imagined hitting the game-winning home run in the seventh game of the World Series."

Frank and Dustin were now all smiles. They understood. Frank teared up a little and cleared his throat before saying, "I am so proud of you, nephew. You've worked hard your whole life, and you've put yourself and Charlie in this position. Just remember to get your old Uncle Frank great seats for the playoffs and World Series!"

"You bet, Uncle Frank! You and Dustin and your fellow Berwyn Boys will be well cared for. Remember, though, not a word. Not one word about this to *anyone*. That means not your wives, siblings, nosy next-door neighbors, or even your dogs!"

Rex's phone beeped, signifying a text coming through. While glancing down at his phone, a slight worried look came over his face. "Hmm…. Martha is asking if I can come home right away. She usually calls with routine news, but if it's bad or *really* good news, she likes to tell me in person. This could be about Charlie's scan. I gotta go. I'll catch you guys later; here's twelve bucks for my tab and tip."

★ CHAPTER 19 ★

The News

Traffic was light, so Rex pulled into his driveway fifteen minutes later. He went in through the mud room, where Fini greeted him. Usually, Martha was a step behind Fini. This time, she wasn't.

Rex called out, "Hi, honey!"

Usually, Martha would immediately answer back, but this time she didn't.

"*Honey*, where are you?"

He heard a faint "In here" coming from the back bedroom.

When he got there, Martha was sitting on the edge of the bed. Her eyes were red. She'd been crying.

"What's wrong, honey?" Rex stroked her arm.

She looked up, tears welling and lip trembling, and said in a barely audible voice, "It's Charlie. The doctor called; it's…ah…b-b-brain can—." The last word never made it to the final syllable. Martha fell into Rex's arms. They clung together, sobbing, hearts pounding. Rex let out an anguished sound, somewhere between howling and crying.

Martha pleaded, "Oh, God! *Please, God*, help our boy, and help us to help *him*." Rex hugged her tighter.

They dropped to their knees and prayed, asking for strength and calm in the storm. They would need all they could muster for themselves and Charlie.

Martha gathered herself and continued. "He wants to do more tests to determine the best treatment approach. The doctor said based on the shape of the tumor he's almost certain it's cancerous. He said we should expect a positive outcome because tumors in that area of the brain, the cerebellum, have high rates of successful treatment."

Martha pulled back and turned to face Rex. Looking into his eyes and clasping his hands, she asked softly, "How do we tell him?"

"Directly, I think. If it's okay, I'll take the lead. We'll tell him together, but I might be less emotional to get started."

"Yes, I agree."

"Where is he now?"

"He just called and said he was leaving Alfred's house. He was going to stop by Mr. Bill's Trading Card Store on the way home. He should be here any minute."

"I'm not so sure. Mr. Bill likes Charlie, so they can talk for an hour or more if the store isn't busy. Mr. Bill gives Charlie cards. Last week, he gave him an Art Monk football card because Charlie told him he liked Art Monk. Sometimes, Mr. Bill's son Loren is there, and he's a talker too."

Martha remembered that nothing had been planned for dinner. "We'd better order dinner to be delivered. I don't want to think about preparing a meal tonight. How about that Peruvian Chicken Rotisserie joint? Charlie loves it, and they just started delivering."

"Perfect—er, that was dumb; nothing feels perfect right now," Rex replied.

Martha called in the order.

The house was chilly, so they turned up the heat a notch and pulled a wool blanket around themselves as they sat on the blue leather couch, two peas in a pod waiting for their boy. They could see through the dining room window and would see Charlie coming.

Martha wanted a serene atmosphere, so she spoke to her new electronic device, a Google Mini that her friend Germaine had given her for her birthday. "Hey, Google! Play soothing music." The device responded, "No problem," and began playing soft, jazzy music.

"Hey, Google! I prefer 'My pleasure' instead of 'No problem.'"

"My, you are polite. I will say 'My pleasure' in the future," the device informed her.

Rex and Martha sat cuddled as they waited. They prayed again, thanked the Lord, and talked about the victory they would have in this battle.

Thirty-five minutes later, the food arrived. As the delivery gal was leaving the porch, Charlie came bouncing up the driveway.

"Yes!" Charlie shouted, and then in his best MMA ring announcer voice, he added, "Rooooooootisserie chic*ken*! I'm starrrrrrrrrrving! Let's eaaaaaaaat!"

Charlie was so hungry that Rex and Martha instinctively knew to eat before delivering their news.

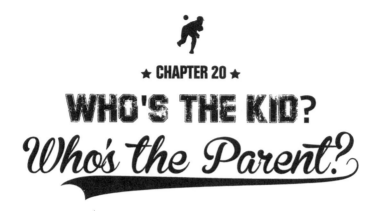

★ CHAPTER 20 ★

WHO'S THE KID?
Who's the Parent?

Rex's phone beeped again. He wiped the chicken grease off his fingers and checked his message. "Here's a text from Kurt Grimmer. He says Big T is being interviewed right now on the MLB network." Rex turned on the TV, and sure enough, there was Al Leiter asking Big T how long he thought it would take for the Knights to contend.

Whenever Rex showed excitement, he would rub his hands together, but there wasn't any hand-rubbing this time, as Charlie noticed. "Dad, you're not rubbing your hands together." Pointing at the TV, he added, "How exciting is *this*? There's Ken 'Bow-Tie' Rosenthal interviewing Big T! Is that not worthy of hand-rubbing?"

Rex stalled for time. "Shh…I'm listening. Let's hear what Big T says."

Martha raised her finger to her lips, signaling to be quiet because she wanted to hear Big T too. They listened as Big T explained to a stunned Rosenthal that he expected to contend in the first year, at worst the second. He dodged questions and spoke, without giving details, about the unique team of executives he'd assembled and how they had devised an approach to winning, but he did not say what the plan would entail. Rosenthal pressed him for details, but Big T was having none of it. He ended the interview by saying, "Hey, Kenny, I appreciate your time today. I gotta run now; gotta get back to Nash-ville." Then, with a twinkle in his eye and a deep Southern drawl, he said, "Stay tuned, Kenny. Stay tuned. It's gonna be *big*!" And he out-stretched his arms as far as they would go.

Big T abruptly strutted away, all 6' 6" of him, 6' 8" with his cowboy boots, and Rosenthal, all 5' 5" of him, turned, looking directly into the camera. With the bow tie, he looked like Pee-wee Herman. "Well, folks, there you have it. Big T McCraw says The Nashville Knights are going to be *big* soon. Stay tuned. If his music success is any indicator, we should take him seriously. Baseball could use a story like this. Back to you in the studio, Harold."

Charlie was finishing off the beans that came with the chicken. He always ate things one at a time, never mixing his food; he didn't even like them touching. Fini was quite comfortable on the couch, his head resting on Charlie's knee, and always alert for food droppage. Martha went into the kitchen to get some more napkins. As she was walking back, napkins in hand, Rex decided now was the time to tell Charlie. Martha knew too. She and Rex communicated with a look and a nod that went unnoticed by Charlie.

Rex turned off the TV. Charlie, Fini, and Martha were all three on the couch, with Charlie in the middle. Rex was in the wing chair that he'd pulled closer. Charlie, sensing something important was about to be discussed, took a guess. "So, Daddio, Mommio, are we gonna talk about moving to Nashville? I'm okay with that now. I'll be able to keep in touch with my friends."

"No, son," said Rex. "The results of your brain scan are back."

The mood changed with those words. Charlie knew they wouldn't be bringing it up if it was all good.

"Uh, oh," Charlie said under his breath. Reverting to humor as a defense mechanism, he asked, "Did they find one? A brain?"

"They found what they believe to be cancer, a small tumor," said Rex. "It's in an area of the brain, the cerebellum where they have good success in treating. The doctor called and talked with your Mom this afternoon." Rex paused. "And she told me when I got home an hour ago." His voice cracked. "We know of no other way to tell you except directly." Rex had his hand on Charlie's knee and Martha's arms were around her son. Even Fini, lying at Charlie's feet, seemed to know. They were quiet in the seconds that followed, except for Martha whispering, "We'll get through this." Charlie was stoic; his mind went elsewhere. Martha had always called Charlie an "old soul"; he sometimes seemed to have the wisdom of the ages. Suddenly, he changed from stoic to animated. "Guess what, Mom? Any tumor in me is gonna be like your Bingo games...B-9!" His parents didn't laugh, but they managed weak smiles. Encouraged, Charlie added, "C'mon, Mom; c'mon Dad; do you completely lack a sense of *tumor*?"

Two more weak smiles.

"I choose not to worry about it now. Alfred's big brother offered to take us bowling at seven-thirty. Can I go? We can talk about this other stuff later. I can walk to his house and his brother will drive me home afterwards. I just want to run upstairs and change into sweatpants—easier to bowl in."

"Sure, son," said Rex. "Just text when you get to the bowling alley, and when you leave, okay?"

"Sure, Dad!"

A minute later, a *blur* named Charlie bolted by and out the front door. A loving, heartsick mother cried out as he bounded off the porch, "You forgot to kiss your mother!" The *blur* reversed course, kissed his mother *and* father, and was gone.

Rex and Martha sank into the couch and looked at each other in astonishment.

"Who's the kid and who's the parent here?" Rex wondered aloud. "He comforted *us*. Your old soul theory is gaining credence with me. Can you believe the jokes he comes up with to assuage *our* fears? And then he chooses not to worry, at least for the moment, about what he can't control. He just goes *bowling*."

Holding Rex's hand, Martha softly answered, "Sometimes he's the parent, and sometimes we are. Tonight, it wasn't us."

★ CHAPTER 21 ★
A TASTE OF
Nashville

Martha unpacked the box of kitchen utensils. She was making progress getting the Nashville kitchen set up. Rex was taking on the heavier boxes not yet unpacked while Google Mini played country music.

"Music always seems to make the work easier, don't ya think, Sexy Rexy?"

"Not all music," Rex replied. "Some of that country music will bring you down quick; somebody's dog dies, wife leaves, they're out of work, and out of beer. Sad stuff. Mostly, though, you're right; music makes the work flow."

"How upside-down is our world since we got the news about Charlie? Thank God for Big T getting us an appointment with Dr. Sievers."

"I *know*. It was crazy how fast he got things going when I told him about Charlie. It hit him hard. He took a liking to our boy and wants to do all he can to help with his network of people we can plug into. Hey, why don't we take a break? I'm tired and hungry. Let's walk to the pizza place a couple of blocks over. It has a funny name—Smokey's Prolific Pies—something like that; they looked busy, usually a good sign. We need to find a few favorite places to eat."

"Let's go, but let's *not* walk please," Martha pleaded. "I've already had too much exercise. I might keel over and pigs might fly. I've been to the gym six days this month."

Aroma beckoned from a block away. The door to Smokey Sam's Prodigious Pies swung open freely much like saloon doors. Today, the weather being unseasonably warm, the outer door had been left open, allowing more smoke than usual to waft into the street with each entry and exit of patrons. This, of course, brought in more patrons, some of whom surely had no intention of eating pizza until the smells of hickory wood-fired pizza saturated their air space. Rex took a deep sniff, let it out, and remarked, "Cha-ching! Brilliant marketing. That's some real *smells-manship*!"

Martha groaned but laughed and said, "Charlie would like that one."

They were seated in a booth by a window looking out to the parking lot, where the Accord sat. Rex liked to be able to watch for "bad guys" who might be messing with his car, that particular year and model Accord being a high theft target. Seeing his baby looked safe, he relaxed.

The pizza was perfect. A smothering of sweet red sauce, real Italian provolone cheese, fresh basil, all baked over hickory wood, *extra* crispy. They ordered another to take home for Charlie. Martha ordered a glass of wine while waiting for the carry-out, and Rex followed her lead.

Their server, a college age girl named Samantha, according to her badge, brought the wine and asked if she could bring anything else. "No thanks," Rex said. "Nothing for me."

Martha placed her index finger on her cheek and with a furrowed brow said, "Hmm. I don't suppose cheesecake would negate six days in the gym this month, do you? You'd split it with me, wouldn't you, Rexy?"

Rex went along with the program and nodded. Samantha smiled and said, "I'll bring two forks."

A minute later, Samantha returned with the cheesecake and two forks. "And we can slow walk your take-homes and even keep them warm for ya. Y'all can hang out with us till closing. We appreciate you coming in tonight. Don't think I've seen you here before. First time at Smokey's?"

"Yes," Martha replied, "and we already know we like it. We moved here this week, from Maryland."

"Well, welcome to Nashville. It's a friendly place; been here all my life."

"We like it so far. How long have you been working here?" Martha asked.

Samantha laughed. "Well, everybody else in here knows," she said as her eyes scanned the two dozen patrons, "so I can tell you too. I've been working here all my life. My grandpa is Smokey—Smokey Fields. He's the owner, the boss man. He opened this place when I was still crawling around on the floor. This used to be a hardware store, but it went out of business and the property was vacant for a long time. My grandpa is a smart man, and he saw opportunity. When he has passion for something, he succeeds at it, and he's passionate about pizza. He's passionate about making money too."

"Well, he must be excited that Major League Baseball is coming to Nashville."

"Oh, my goodness! Are you kidding me? He's like a twelve-year-old boy! And his pal Big T McCraw being the owner makes it extra special."

"Hmm, Smokey Fields; his name sounds familiar." Rex knew he'd heard it before. A Google search gave him the answer. Smokey had coached baseball at the University of Richmond and been Wally Rupp's college hitting coach. Smokey Fields was the one who had recommended Wally to Big T. Rex remembered Wally telling a story about a coach whose nickname was Smokey because he was renowned for his smoked meats. Last year, according to Google, Smokey had won the Dork Smoke Award, a category that combines duck and pork, hence the name Dork.

"Wow, I just googled your Grandpa, and this is bizarro, the connections here. I'm Rex Collier, and this is my wife Martha. I'm the marketing director for the Nashville Knights. I *work* for Big T and so does Wally Rupp, our head scout who played for your grandpa when he coached at the University of Richmond. This is small world stuff. How does your grandpa know Big T McCraw?"

"Well, it's another small world thing. First, I'll tell ya that Grandpa was on the radar of some big league teams as a pitcher. He's a lefty, and they say he had a nasty curveball and an even nastier screwball. Unfortunately, he broke his arm on a screwball; the pitch just put too much torque on the ulna. He was unable to come back from that. As you probably know, the same thing happened to two big leaguers, Dave Dravecky and Tony Saunders. It's rare and hard to fathom breaking your arm throwing a pitch, but it happens. After that, Grandpa got into coaching, and for a few summers, he coached in the Cape Cod College Wood Bat League. He coached the Hyattstown Harbor Hawks, and Big T's nephew was on that team one summer. Big T spent some weekends there watching his nephew play. After one Saturday evening game, my grandpa cooked up his blue rib-bon-winning beef brisket in the parking lot. He actually got to the field at the crack of dawn and got it started. By game time, the enticing smell of Grandpa's brisket hit people before they even got out of their cars. Big T went nuts about the brisket and chatted him up. They be-came fast friends and have kept in touch ever since. It turns out that Big T fancies himself as a pretty fair meat smoker too. He challenged Grandpa to a cook-off competition at one of the games. It wasn't a real competition with judges, so there wasn't a winner, except for the fans and players. They cooked enough for everyone and had a cash donation bucket, which all went to support the team."

"So, why didn't your grandpa open a barbeque joint where he could smoke his brisket? And doesn't he know smoking brisket is bad for his lungs?"

Samantha laughed. "Pizza is easier and we make more money; there's big profit in pizza. I told ya, Grandpa's a smart man and a full-fledged capitalist. He had a broad menu for a while, but he figured out we do better being one-trick ponies with the best pizza pies in Tennessee. Grandpa brings his big smoker to the parking lot for special events, though; he can't give up his brisket completely, and he *loves* to fire up his award-winning Dork occasionally. He dubbed himself the Dork

King. How's that for self-deprecating humor?"

"How'd he come up with the name Smokey's Prodigious Pies?"

Samantha laughed again. The official name is Smokey *Sam's* Prodigious Pies—I'm Sam and Grandpa is Smokey. When Grandpa was getting the business set up and coming up with a name, I was in a spelling bee at school, and I won by spelling the word prodigious. I had to use the word in a sentence, so the sentence I used was, 'My grandpa makes *prodigious* pies.' It hit Grandpa as funny, so that's where the name came from. Most people just say Smokey's, though."

Rex and Martha thanked Samantha for the wine *and* the story. Then Rex told Samantha, "I hope to meet your grandpa someday."

"Definitely, me too," Martha added.

"Oh, you will. He's here quite a bit," Samantha said, and she headed to the kitchen.

The family sitting at the table next to them now left, giving Rex and Martha the sense of privacy they needed. They reached across the old wooden table, clasped hands, and looked into each other's eyes like a couple of newlyweds.

"I *love* you."

"And I love you beyond the moon, RC. Aren't ya glad we have each other?"

"RC!" Rex laughed. "You haven't called me that in a long time. That's so funny. All the time I was hooked on drinking two or three RC Colas a day and didn't realize it was my initials until you pointed it out. I think it was on our third date; you nicknamed me RC because of my cola addiction, and everybody else thought it was for my initials. Then the whole baseball team picked it up and started calling me RC. Even today, when I'm out and about, somebody will yell RC, and I know before I turn around that it'll be one of the crowd we hung with back in my playing days."

"It was on our second date I *crowned* you RC," Martha replied. "I had the thought on our first date, but I didn't say it because after waiting for fifteen months for you to ask me out, I didn't want to scare you off," she said in a teasing way. "We've been through a lot together. It's worked out, though, hasn't it, RC?"

"Yes, it has," Rex said as he flipped his eyes upward, saying, "Thank you, God. We know *he's* with us now. We have so much going on with Charlie, the move, and the job. We haven't even had time to talk it all through; maybe that's not even possible; everything isn't predictable anyway. With Dr. Sievers, I'm confident we're in as good a position as we could possibly hope for. We have three more weeks until surgery. Charlie seems to be handling everything well, almost too well. The whole thing about the brain tumor feels like a beast is upon us, at least to me. It has to be that way for Charlie too. I'm trying to compartmentalize to the extent it's possible. I'll work as much as I can until the surgery, and you're working *so* hard coordinating the move and getting us set up. We're doing all we can. We'll keep moving and leave the rest to God."

She kissed him. "It'll all work out. I know it will."

When Samantha looked over from behind the counter, Rex made a motion like signing a check, indicating he was ready to settle up. She brought the carry-out pizzas from the warmer. "It was fun talking with y'all," Samantha said. "I'm gonna tell Grandpa about meeting you. He'll be excited when he hears you work for Big T. See ya back here soon!"

"Yes, indeed. We'll be back. We're happy we discovered *Smokey Sam's Prodigious Pies*," Rex said, looking pleased that he had mastered the tongue twister.

★ CHAPTER 22 ★

FIVE DAYS UNTIL

Pitchers and Catchers Report

Sixty-seven days had passed since Project Baseball was adopted as the plan to shock the baseball world. The executive team had made rapid progress, and with pitchers and catchers reporting in five days, Big T was in touch with coaches and managers from all levels of the organization. GM Kurt Grimmer did an excellent job of communicating to prepare everyone, including hosting daily Zoom sessions with coaches and managers. Larry Wenzel, as manager of the big club, also played a prominent role.

Gathered in the expanded meeting room were forty-seven coaches, managers, and scouts waiting on Big T to officially open training camp. Normally, the room seated about twenty-four, but for larger groups, a center wall could be opened to double the space. Some people were seated already, but most were still milling around, talking.

Big T came into the room at 8:20 a.m. He gave a "Howdy, y'all" to the group in general, shook a couple of hands, and said, "Let's get started" as he strode to the lectern in his Levi's, snakeskin cowboy boots, and light blue Western-style shirt. A silver turquoise bracelet completed the ensemble, along with his ever-present silver cross necklace.

"Friends, before we start the baseball part of our meeting, I have some news that a few of you know, but most don't. A member of our Knight family needs our prayers and support. The architect of Project Baseball, fourteen-year-old Charlie Collier, Rex and Martha's son, is having surgery in ten days to have a brain tumor removed. Those of you on the executive team met Charlie. All of us in the room know the story: Project Baseball was born from this young man's statistical analysis of analytics versus what I'll call 'old school ball.' It's an amazing story to think that an MLB team would adopt a fourteen-year-old's path to a championship. *When* his plan works, he'll be on the cover of *Sports Illustrated*, and everyone will know his name, but none of that matters now. Charlie faces a challenge no one should have to face so young. The Collier family has an excellent team of doctors and one of the best surgeons in the world performing the operation. So, everyone is optimistic, Charlie too, according to his mom and dad."

Big T paused; emotion was catching up. He had loved Charlie right from the get-go. After a couple of big swallows and a quick eye dab, he went on.

"Charlie's an integral member of our Knight family. Keep him and his family in your prayers." Looking directly at Rex and pausing again, fighting not to choke up, Big T continued, "Rex, please tell Charlie we love him, and we have a seat for him in the Owners Suite at the ballpark on Opening Day."

Rex nodded that he would convey Big T's message to Charlie.

"Now," said Big T, "let's get down to baseball business. We've made amazing progress in a short time. You know that because y'all have lived it since day one. Everybody's all in. I can feel it. And that's good because, as Robert Frost said, we have miles to go before we sleep. Thank you for being *so* totally engaged. Thank you for being on every one of the Zoom calls for all these weeks. There are a lot of thanks to go around, but we *do* have miles to go before we sleep. So we celebrate. We celebrate our amazing progress and we're grateful, but we must move again, take more territory. We have miles to go.

"In a minute, we'll be break out into groups for each specialty…pitching coaches in one room, managers in another, hitting coaches, and scouting in another. You'll see the breakdown on your agendas. Each group will have a group leader, also identified on your agenda. What I want y'all to do in your groups is to talk about your successes and your challenges with implementing Project Baseball. Whiteboards are in every room if you want to use them. Mr. Grimmer and I will be bouncing in and out of rooms to help out and to get a flavor of your insights. You may be thinking, 'Should the owner be doing this? I thought owners should leave the operations to the baseball people.' Just so you know, I *will* be involved, which doesn't mean our GM and managers are going to be told what to do by me. *They* will make the final call, but I will offer input. The first session begins at quarter to nine and will go until eleven o'clock, followed by a thirty-seven-minute break, so we'll reconvene in this room at eleven-thirty-seven. Be on time. I have a surprise for you."

* * *

They were all back in the room a few minutes before 11:37 a.m., except for the boss man. At 11:45 a.m., Kurt Grimmer announced that Big T had sent him a text saying he'd be back in ten minutes. The coaches and scouts had no problem waiting. They were excited; the room was buzzing with energized conversations all around. Kurt had to shout to get everyone's attention over the din of baseball buzz.

When Big T came back into the room, he wasn't alone. He had two familiar faces with him: Timothy J. Ramage and Rebecca Scully. Most in the room were so engaged in their own conversations that they didn't immediately see the three of them walk in. Quickly, though, they started noticing, and then there was a shout of "Rammmmer" and some applause, which came from Wally Rupp, erupting again! Larry Wenzel and Butch Dory snaked through people to go over and say hello. Big T went to the front of the room and said, "Hey, Hey! Let's get back to our seats, please." In a moment, they were all seated. The Rammer and Rebecca sat in the back row.

Big T took the microphone. "Welcome back, everybody! I promised you a surprise, and I now see that my surprises are inconveniently seated in the back row, underneath the exit sign," laughed Big T as he pointed in The Rammer and Rebecca's direction. "You're not skedaddling out early, my friends! Come on up here!"

The surprise guests came up the center aisle. When they got to the front, The Rammer, the self-described curmudgeon, said, "Group hug" and a brief one ensued. Big T then redirected his attention to his seated audience as The Rammer and Rebecca moved to stand beside him.

"For those of you who don't know them," said Big T, "I'd like to introduce you to my friends, Timothy Ramage aka The Rammer and Rebecca Scully. Our executive team already knows them. Timothy was our facilitator in the sessions at Wintergreen and in Nashville, resulting in our adoption of Project Baseball. He's had a long, successful career working with various industries to maximize potential. And Rebecca Scully is his extremely capable assistant who was also with us throughout our planning sessions, and yes, she is related to Vin. They are here for a reason. I have asked them, and they have agreed, to be a permanent part of our team. The Rammer, as most people call him, will help us in a blend of ways. He will report directly to me, as Executive VP, and will work throughout the organization in quality control to be sure all of our teams—the big club and the minors—are adhering to Project Baseball. He will also take on special projects, as needed. Rammer, would you like to say a few words?"

Never one to miss an opportunity, The Rammer reached for the mic, paused, and said slowly in a deep voice, "A few words," and handed the mic back to Big T. They both laughed and Big T said, "That's the first time you've said a few words in your whole miserable life!" They laughed again and so did the audience. Big T, looking at the crowd, said, "We go way back." He handed the mic back to The Rammer. "Here ya go; you can say a lot of words."

Ms. Scully took a seat that was added to the front row. She half-expected Timothy to say, "A lot of words," and hand the mic back again.

"First, thank you, Big T!" The Rammer began. "You're just the man to bring Major League Baseball to the Music City! This opportunity will be a crowning achievement for many of us in this room. We're in a position most could only dream of. It's going to be one whale of a ride. Years from now, when we look back, these will be the "good ol' days." Let's recognize this as something historic and noteworthy that we're doing here. Look, I can be a grumpy pessimist at times; some of you know that. But I'll tell you what; I'm high as a kite on the Nashville Knights and on what I think we can do with this brilliant strategy put forth by young Charlie Collier. I know Big T gave everyone the news this morning about Charlie's upcoming surgery. He is a very special young man; everybody loves the boy. His Project Baseball is a stroke of genius, *literally* in his case." The Rammer paused and looked at Big T. "Does that qualify as 'lots of words'?"

Big T laughed. "For you, that's just a hello."

The Rammer looked back to the audience. "I'm done and I'm excited for all the fun we're gonna have making this dream come true! Here ya go, Big T," he said as he tossed the mic and Big T easily caught it, like a shortstop taking a flip from a second baseman. The Rammer took a seat next to Ms. Scully, who gave him an approving look, a small fist bump, and a gentle pat on the leg.

"Thanks, Mr. Ramage! I am thrilled you and Ms. Scully have joined the team. I know you will contribute mightily. I have to fly to New York in three hours for an MLB meeting, so I'll be unable to be here the rest of the afternoon. You all have your agendas outlining the speakers and breakout sessions. I hate to miss Ricky Henderson when he's here working on base-running with us, but I need to catch this flight. Thank you all for all you do. Yes, we have miles to go, but let's enjoy the journey, too. Play ball!"

★ CHAPTER 23 ★

THE

Big Day

The cacophonous clang awakened Rex and Martha like a slap upside the head, which Rex rewarded with a slap in return, turning off the rude noisemaker. Four-thirty was no time to be awake, but today was no normal day. Charlie's surgery was scheduled for ten-thirty, and he needed to be at the hospital by six-thirty.

Rex kissed Martha on the forehead. "I'll go wake Charlie; you can rest a little longer."

"No, I can't sleep now anyway. I'll shower and then come down. Remind Charlie he can't eat or drink anything except water or clear liquid."

Rex padded down the hall to Charlie's room. He opened the door to the darkened room. The light from the hall illuminated the room enough for Rex to see without turning on the overhead.

"I'm up, Dad. I heard your prehistoric alarm clock go off."

Rex sat on the edge of the bed. Charlie was still under the covers, on his left side, facing away. Rex put his hand on Charlie's right shoulder. "I love you, son. Your mom and I are proud of you for your courage in facing this battle that has been thrust upon you. You'll come through this like the champion you are. Dr. Sievers is highly skilled and at the top of his game."

Charlie turned onto his back with the covers pulled up to his armpits and his hands clasped together on his chest, fingers intertwined.

"Sometimes I don't feel like I have courage," he replied. "Some days I'm scared. Everything was going so well; my life seemed too good to be true, and I guess it was because now this has happened. Everybody thinks I'm handling this well, but inside, I have an ongoing battle between the brave and the cowardly. It's like there's a little guy inside my head with a megaphone trying to tell me things are gonna turn out bad, but I shout him down 99 percent of the time, and he goes away. And I pray and give thanks for all that I have. I'm trying, Dad. I'm trying to be brave."

Tears started to stream down Charlie's face. He wiped at his nose and eyes and shook uncontrollably. Rex hugged him with a deep, long hug.

"It's gonna be okay, son."

"I know, Dad. I'm sorry. That's the first time I've lost it."

"You wouldn't be normal if you *didn't* lose it, son."

"I'll be okay now, though. Just hand me some Kleenex please; maybe a paper towel."

Fini bounded into the room and reared up like a horse, his way of saying good morning. He seemed more exuberant than usual, perhaps sensing stress relief was needed. It worked. Charlie's face lit up with his first smile of the day. "How ya doing, Big Boy! Are you coming to see your best bud?" With an ear scratch, Fini was in doggy heaven until Charlie got up to dress and temporarily ended the doting. Charlie was already in the bathroom when Rex yelled after him, "Remember, nothing but clear liquid; no food this morning. I'm going to go get ready myself. Wear your comfortable clothes; sweatpants would be good. See you in a few. We'll need to leave by six."

"Ten-four, Daddio," came the muffled reply through the door.

CHAPTER 24

The Hospital

The nurse in charge of surgery prep was a muscular man about forty named Adam. He had a tattoo sleeve on his left arm, a man bun, and a patient, kind smile. Adam went over with Rex, Martha, and Charlie what to expect in the operating room. When the buzzer went off indicating it was time to take Charlie there, Adam asked the parents to go to the waiting room. He pushed Charlie on the gurney to Operating Room 2.

"Ah, number two—that's a good sign; it's my number in baseball," Charlie said as he rolled through the doors.

Beyond those doors was a strange, foreign world; eight people were wearing masks, in surgical uniforms, and illuminated in intense light. Nothing was comforting until Charlie saw familiar eyes above one mask. It was Dr. Sievers.

"Good morning, Charlie. I know you've been asked already, but not by me; how are you feeling now?"

"I feel like I'm in a sci-fi movie, in a spaceship surrounded by aliens."

Dr. Sievers and the nurses laughed.

"We do have that sort of look, don't we, team?"

"I'll be Spock," one of the nurses replied.

"More importantly, Doctor," said Charlie, "how are *you* feeling this morning?"

"That's a question I get asked a lot, Charlie. I feel great. I'm a morning guy. My best mornings are *Wednesdays*, so you're in luck. I get to solve people's problems every day, and I feel great doing that. I'm going to solve your problem. You have a problem with a growth that isn't supposed to be there. I'll have it fixed for you when you wake up. You'll take some time to heal and get back to your normal self, but your problem will be solved. How 'bout them apples?"

"I like them apples, Doc."

"Do you have any questions?"

"Yes. Do you know why the brain surgeon stopped following baseball?"

"I have no idea, Charlie. Why?"

"Because it was too complicated!"

Doctor Sievers had a joke of his own. "What do you call an eight-sided operating room?"

"I don't know, Doc. What *do* they call it?"

"A doctagon."

"Oh, I should have gotten that."

Charlie had another. "Did you hear about the conversation between the brain surgeon and the anesthesiologist?"

"No, tell me."

"It was mind-numbing."

Dr. Sievers laughed. "Perfect segue, Charlie. Your anesthesiologist, Raquel, is a few feet behind you, and she's dripping your sleepy drops into the IV. You met her in the pre-op meeting. Raquel's been working with me for years; her nickname's Knockout. By the time I finish this sentence, you'll be...zzzzzz."

★ CHAPTER 25 ★

The Wait

The surgery waiting room at Nashville General had a cushy, yet minimalist feel to it. Blues and grays interplayed, creating a soothing feeling. A large TV was built into the wall, tuned to the local Nashville news station. The couch, love seat, and chairs were fine leather, comfortable seating for nervous souls switching between pacing the thickly carpeted floor and collapsing into a soft refuge. Rex paced more than he sat, back and forth through the lunch hour and into the afternoon, occasionally flipping through television channels. Martha sat curled up on a small sofa with a quilt pulled around her, courtesy of a local quilter, Betty Young, to comfort worried souls.

Ten after two and *no word yet.* It wasn't supposed to take nearly this long. Rex touched Martha's knee, communicating, "Move over please." He sat, his hand still on her knee. He started The Lord's Prayer and they prayed it together, followed by specific prayers for Charlie and Dr. Sievers. Beyond prayer, they felt helpless. Time moved like a herd of turtles.

Finally, one of the nurses on the surgical team, who looked to be from central casting, came into the room. If her oval face were a word, that word would be *compassion*. Nurse Emma Grace still had her scrubs on, except for the mask.

Her kind eyes met theirs. "Mr. and Mrs. Collier, Charlie is in recovery now, and he's doing well. It took longer than anticipated. Dr. Sievers will be out to see you before he does anything else. Charlie should be in recovery for a while."

"Why did it take so long? Did something go wrong?" Martha asked.

"We never really know how long a procedure might take, and there's no such thing as perfection in surgery, but Charlie is doing well. The doctor will be here soon. God bless."

"God bless you, too, and thank you," Martha replied.

"Yes, thank you," said Rex.

After the longest twenty minutes in eternity, Dr. Sievers entered. "Mr. and Mrs. Collier," he began, speaking kindly but in a straight-up way. "Charlie is still in recovery. We'll keep him in recovery for another forty-five minutes. He's fine, but we ran into some challenges. We had two issues. When we got in there, we found that the tumor had broken through the outer membrane of the cerebellum. Remember in our pre-op meeting I said we thought the tumor was attached to the cerebellum, but had not broken the membrane? We found that it *did* break the membrane slightly in an area difficult to see on the computer images.

"What does this mean?" he asked rhetorically like a professor. "It *means* we had to take out a very small amount of matter from the cerebellum to get all of the cancer. When I say very small, it's an amount that would fill about one-third of a thimble. Another few months and it would have been a different outcome because this type of cancer grows fast. I'm confident we got it all. As far as cognitive abilities, he'll be the same gifted Charlie. We may see an issue with balance. The cerebellum is central control for balance and physical coordination. Because we took such a small amount, I'm optimistic any coordination issues will be minimal. We'll have to see. It's above my pay-grade now; somebody else has it," he concluded, pointing his index finger skyward to indicate who was in charge.

"You said there were two issues," Rex replied. "What was the second?"

"We had problems with the anesthesia. We needed to give Charlie more about three hours into the surgery due to the unexpected length of the operation. In rare cases, a second dosage triggers mild reactions that we monitor. In even rarer instances, the reaction can be severe. Charlie's vitals dropped suddenly. I've only seen such a rapid drop once before in my career. Fortunately, my anesthesiologist Raquel is the best of the best. She's seen this before, so she knew exactly how much of an antidote to administer, and she acted quickly. It was a close call. Charlie's heart stopped for seventeen seconds. He should have no ill effects from that at all since it was under a minute. People who have experienced that do sometimes report it to be life-changing in a spiritual way."

Martha was staring oddly, fixated on nothing, in a way Rex had rarely seen. Her face looked heavy, tired, and in shock. They were both between emotions. On one hand, Charlie had survived brain surgery and would still be Charlie with all of his brilliance. They were lucky they had caught the cancer early. On the *other* hand, he might have physical limitations and they had almost lost him on the operating table. Rex and Martha were beyond drained. The last twenty-four hours had felt like two weeks.

"Thanks, Doctor," Rex said, fighting the lump in his throat.

Martha started to cry, half sobs at first, then full ones, before she managed to get out, "Yes, Doctor. Thank you."

"No thanks needed, Mrs. Collier. It's what I do."

"Well, I want to hug you, Dr. Sievers. May I?" she tearfully asked.

"You may hug the doctor," he replied with a sheepish grin. And she did. Rex followed with his own hug and pat on the back. "Thank you, Doc. Thank you!"

"I'll be doing my rounds tomorrow morning and will see Charlie first thing," Dr. Sievers promised. "He'll be carefully monitored throughout the night by our excellent team. I encourage you to get a good night's sleep tonight after you see him. He'll be safe and well cared for."

Rex and Martha made their way to the elevator to go back to Charlie's room to wait for him. Two women, looking to be mother and daughter, one fiftyish, the other thirtyish, were standing close together in the elevator's left rear corner. They both tried unsuccessfully to stop crying when Rex and Martha got on. Hospitals can be sad places. Rex and Martha got off on Charlie's floor and went directly to the nurse's station to ask about Charlie and where they should wait. A young nurse, who looked all of eighteen, but might be twenty-eight, said they could wait in Charlie's room since there were two chairs, and he had a single room. Then, looking at her computer screen, she smiled and said, "Perfect timing. They're bringing him up now." Neither Rex nor Martha was in any mood to go just sit in a chair in Charlie's room anyway. They were pacing, especially Rex, a super-pacer who wore paths in carpets! Their eyes were glued to the elevator doors, waiting for a glimpse of their boy.

Finally, one of the doors opened and there was Charlie, on a gurney with Nurse Emma Grace wheeling him. He lifted his head slightly, alert enough to be scanning, looking for, and hoping to see exactly what he saw. He locked eyes with his mom and then dad. They got on the sides of the gurney, Rex holding Charlie's right hand, Martha holding his left, slowly rolling down to Room 301. Two other nurses came to assist getting Charlie transferred from the gurney and properly positioned in the adjustable bed. Charlie smiled some and interacted with them in soft, whispered tones, still floating on the edges of la-la land. When the nurses left, they flanked his bed. Martha kissed him all over his cheeks. His head was partially bandaged, and the part that wasn't was covered by a funky hospital bandana.

Rex held Charlie's hand as he asked, "How ya feeling, kid?"

"Don't worry 'bout me, Dad; I'm as happy as a dog with two tails," Charlie said, eyes half-mast.

Rex laughed nervously. "I see your whacky sense of humor hasn't left you; that joke was a little weak, though."

Martha kissed Charlie again. "We love you, son. Dr. Sievers says you're doing well. You don't have to talk much now; just rest. Visiting hours are over in about fifteen minutes. We'll stay until then and be back tomorrow morning. Remember, your buzzer is right here; anytime you need something, just push the button. They'll be checking on you regularly throughout the night too."

A soft knock interrupted them. "Knock, knock," said a deep, familiar male voice. "It's Timothy Ramage and Rebecca Scully. Is it okay to come in?"

Rex sprung from his seat and pulled back the privacy curtain. "Of course! Timothy, Rebecca, thank you for coming!"

The Rammer pivoted on his left foot, sort of a half-pivot dance move, and turned to face Charlie, focusing intently on him. "Charlie Collier, you are a warrior. You are destined for greatness. I am president of your fan club, young man, and I look forward to doing great things with you. Big T had to be in Boston for his niece's wedding or he'd be here too. He asked Ms. Scully and me to give you his love."

Charlie's eyes were now more open; he'd perked up just a tad. "That's really nice, Mr. Ramage. Thank you."

"And if Ms. Scully will get out from behind me, I think she may have something for you."

Rebecca Scully stepped around Timothy, stood over Charlie, looked down into his eyes, and with a big smile, reached into the right pocket of her black leather coat and pulled out *the thinking ball!* Rex, Martha, and The Rammer watched Charlie's eyes widen and gleam as he gazed at the old ball with the stitch missing. Rebecca Scully tossed the ball back and forth from one hand to the other, something she'd done thousands of times.

"Charlie, you know some of the history of this ball," Rebecca said. "By now, you know it's magical. I want you to keep the magic for a while. It has never been out of my possession, but I know I'm supposed to loan it to you to help your recovery. Keep it with you; hold it, toss it, and talk to it. You'll know when it's time to give it back. You're the best, Charlie. You *are* a warrior, and we'll see you at the ballpark soon!"

"Wow!" was the only word Charlie could muster. Through his grogginess, he felt the love for him in that room.

"Hospital visiting hours are now over," was announced over a loudspeaker. The foursome left Charlie's room together. Before they left, Rex and Martha thanked the visitors for coming with long, warm hugs.

★ CHAPTER 26 ★

PRESEASON
in Daytona

It was a perfect day—palm trees, a slight breeze, 80 degrees, low humidity, and brilliant sunshine! Setting up spring training facilities for a new franchise was a ballbuster, but GM Kurt Grimmer had made it happen. The Knights would be headquartered in Daytona and use the facilities of two local colleges, Daytona State College and Stetson University. Each had a baseball program and had agreed to share its ballpark and practice fields. The college coaches were eager to have their charges rub elbows with the pros. It wasn't an ideal situation for a major league club, but it wasn't awful.

Players were running wind sprints in the outfield and along foul territory. Most had been "given" to the Knights from other teams, as the league rules stipulated when a new team was formed. A few had been free agents, and the Knights invited some players to camp who had been overlooked in the draft but whose scouts thought they were "gamers," hustling players, or foreign players not scouted much. In a surprising series of acquisitions, they'd added seven Japanese play-ers from the Nippon Professional League. The Knights were assigned to the National League and the other new franchise, The Raleigh Raiders, would be in the American League.

Manager Larry Wenzel, GM Kurt Grimmer, and Head of Minor League Development Butch Dory were standing on the outfield grass just behind second base observing the players. Butch was telling Larry and Kurt about the youngest player in camp, a speed demon named Florio Ford, only eighteen and from the Dominican Republic. The older players, meaning everyone else, had already nicknamed him Race Car because of his last name. Butch was gushing about the kid and saying how well he'd fit into Project Baseball when Kurt's phone buzzed. Seeing Big T's photo on his screen, Kurt turned it so the other two could see and said, "The man himself."

"Howdy, Boss. It's a beautiful day in Daytona!" said Kurt, answering.

A pause was followed by Kurt saying, "Whaaaat? No, I haven't seen the news or been online this morning."

Butch pulled at his silver goatee, wondering what was on the news that would cause Kurt to say "whaaaat?" like that. Larry also turned his attention from watching the players to the phone call.

Kurt was still listening. Then he said, "Uh-huh, uh-huh, okay. So we shouldn't worry? How should we handle it?" Another pause. "Okay, I'll let them know that's how we'll respond. See you in a couple of days. Later, Gator!"

Kurt put his phone back in his pocket. "Guys, we have a leak. Big T says there was a segment on TMZ about Charlie, our meeting at

Wintergreen, and some details about Project Baseball. It could have been one of the servers there, overhearing things. It could be that a TMZ 'plant' was staying at the resort and finding ways to get info. Those creeps can be creative. They could have found an agenda in the trash, paid off a server to eavesdrop, who knows? I doubt one of *our* people would leak."

Butch was still tugging on his goatee. "So, what does this mean, and how pissed is Big T?"

"Oh, he's not pissed at all. He thinks it will be a good thing if we handle it right. He wants us to defer any questions about it to Tim Ramage, and otherwise, refuse to comment. He said it could be a public relations bonanza if the MLB channel and the print media pick up the story. So, that's it. That's what he said, and it makes sense to me. It'll be interesting to watch the TMZ segment when we're off the field. We could watch on our phones now, but let's focus on the players…keep our priorities straight."

Larry Wenzel, who had been nodding his head in agreement about the PR bonanza, added, "This will make Rex and his marketing team very happy. It'll create buzz and add fuel to ticket sales. When you think about it, the whole story of Charlie, Boy Wonder, architect of a plan to change Major League Baseball while battling brain cancer… it's an irresistible story, the stuff movies are made of."

* * *

Two days later, Pilot Larry Fickel made his usual smooth-as-silk landing as *The Glider* gently kissed pavement at Daytona Beach International Airport. A few minutes later, Timothy Ramage, Rebecca Scully, and Big T McCraw disembarked. They caught a ten-minute Uber ride to Stetson University in Deland and the Knights' training facility, where the Knights had an afternoon exhibition game against the Braves. The driver, a talkative college student named Zach, maneuvered through traffic like a Daytona 500 pro, crossing S. Woodland Blvd on E. Euclid and turning right into the parking lot of Melching Field at Conrad Park, home of The Stetson Hatters. Immediately, they saw a gaggle of reporters and camera crews in the parking lot closest to the gate behind home plate. Big T leaned forward in the front seat, surveying the scene. "I reckon this'll be fun!" Rebecca giggled from behind the driver and put her face between the two front seats. "Big T, look at all that free publicity, just waiting for you!" The Rammer clapped his meaty hands and said, "The world is watching; the story is unfolding. Go get 'em, Big Fella!" With that, Zach, the yakety Uber driver, pulled to the curb and the three of them got out.

It took about 3.1 seconds for Big T to be recognized. Then the gaggle moved toward him like a swarm of bees to nectar. The red light of the cameras came on and questions were flying. The Rammer and Ms. Scully eased their way to the side to watch the spectacle while they waited for their celebrity friend. Big T deftly deflected questions for twenty minutes, many of which were about the whiz kid and his "secret plan," which the reporters even asked about by name, "Project Baseball." They also wanted to know about Charlie's medical condition. Big T revealed nothing about that, only saying, "He's a great young man," "just fourteen," and "his privacy will be respected."

"Since y'all are gathered here," Big T added, "it's a great time to announce that the Knights have started a foundation to help kids with cancer. It will be called Charlie's Kids Foundation. The team will donate five-thousand dollars for every Knights victory. We'll be setting aside a section of seats for kids battling cancer and seeking corporate partners. One-hundred percent of the money raised will go to the kids and their families."

When Big T said, "One last question," someone shouted, "Who were the people in the car with you?"

Rather than reply, Big T walked over to where The Rammer and Ms. Scully were standing, turned to the gaggle, and said, "This is Timothy Ramage, the Knights' newly appointed executive VP, and his assistant, Rebecca Scully. We're headed in now to watch a baseball game. Thank y'all! We'll talk again soon."

★ **CHAPTER 27** ★

Changes

The morning sunshine reflected off the refrigerator's chrome handle and hit Rex square in the eyes, so he moved over next to Martha rather than across from her. It was a rare morning when the two of them could sit and enjoy breakfast unhurried. They needed this.

David Bowie's song "Changes" was coming from the small plug-in radio sitting on the black granite countertop. Rex had cooked up his specialty again, *Scrambled Eggs Delight*, as he dubbed it. He always scrambled the eggs with scallions or basil, Tillamook sharp cheddar, cherry tomatoes, mushrooms, and sunflower seeds, or whatever else he had to throw in. Today's version included a special treat—a cameo appearance of thick, hickory-smoked bacon from a local farm.

"That song really hits home right now," Martha sighed as she touched her heart.

"Yeah," Rex nodded. "It feels like everything around us is changing and we're in a sea of swirling eddies. Charlie's cancer and almost losing him on the operating table made clearer what's important and what isn't. We just have to manage the changes as they come and pray for divine guidance. We have a top-notch team of doctors and physical therapy people, but what a *change* for Charlie. Thank God his mind is *un*changed, but I do worry about the psychological damage from the balance issues. We've avoided the conversation, but he may not be able to play baseball again, or any sports. How will that affect his dream of playing pro?"

Martha had a thoughtful look on her face. "Charlie might somehow turn this into a positive. Maybe he'll own a baseball team one day. That really sounds odd, doesn't it? To say brain cancer might be turned into a positive, and to think we almost lost him."

"That's unthinkable. None of it should surprise us, not with our boy. Maybe he *will* own a team, or he may be the next big baseball agent, the next Scott Boras," Rex chuckled as a piece of bacon slid off his plate to the floor. Gandolfini, hanging close by to wait for food, quickly consumed the droppage. "I think Charlie will figure out a way to be in baseball throughout his life. He's already made history with his Project Baseball. Heck, look what just happened with TMZ talking about him, and there were reporters swarming Big T to ask about him. It's crazy already."

"Yeah, that's great, Rexy," said Martha, "but back to the *here and now*. We need to keep Charlie's mind active since his physical activity is limited. He's walking with a little more steadiness now, but he'll need the cane for the foreseeable future; hopefully, not forever. Too bad it's between semesters now. He did tell me yesterday that he's looking into some online graduate programs that Vanderbilt offers. As it is now, he's studying online already, on his own, statistics and history. I understand his interest in history, but why anyone would study statistics for fun is beyond me."

Rex rubbed his chin. "I'm not so sure he'll need the cane long term; he's so determined to run again."

Rex cleared the pile of papers on the countertop and popped a hazelnut K-cup into the Keurig. "What's on Charlie's agenda today?"

Before Martha could answer, they heard Charlie slowly descending the stairs, not two or three steps at a time like usual.

"What's up, bud?" asked Rex when his son came into view.

"Me. *I'm* up, Dad. I smelled the slices of hog simmering in the skillet. It got me out of bed. Good morning, Momma Bear!"

Martha scooped some bacon and eggs onto a plate and popped two slices of Dave's Killer Bread into the toaster. In a couple of minutes, Charlie was chowing down like a big dog while the real big dog waited underfoot, hoping for more scraps.

Rex tapped Charlie playfully on the hospital bandana he still wore to look cool. "How's your noggin today, son?"

"Well, my brain is experiencing technical difficulties. I need to adjust the knobs a little so I can walk normally and run again. I miss sprinting. I wish I could *just sprint*. Jonah says anything is possible if I work hard." Jonah was Charlie's new physical therapist. The two had quickly bonded given Charlie's can-do attitude.

"Charlie," Martha asked, "what do you think about the team starting a Charlie's Kids Foundation?"

"It's great, Mom. Cancer's a scary thing and the money can help the families so they can just focus on beating it. I like that the kids will be able to sit together in a special section. They'll have everyone in the ballpark cheering for them. Think how that will make them feel. It will encourage them, which causes physiological changes in the body to help them beat the disease. It's kind of weird having my name on it because I'm a kid myself."

Martha smiled lovingly at her boy. "I think Charlie's Kids Foundation will be around when you're old and gray, son."

Rex's phone went off—a different ring tone than normal. He swiped and answered, "Uncle Frank! You're on Skype! Welcome to the twenty-first century!" Rex pulled Martha in and stood behind Charlie so they all could see and be seen. Frank was sitting in their usual corner booth by the window at Berwyn Café. He was tickled with himself for using Skype, but trying not to show it.

"Well, I had to call my favorite nephew on my first Skype call. Howdy, Martha and Charlie! You know how Maddy here likes to eavesdrop on conversations. She heard me ask someone what Skype is, so she got all hopped up to get me on it. I'm not sure why this crazy redhead girl has fun messing with me, but she does. I can't believe she talked me into doing this Skyping business."

Maddy stepped proudly into camera range with her winning smile, pointing at Uncle Frank and giving a two-thumbs-up approval. She put her face close to the camera and said, "Hiya, Charlie and everybody else! We miss you around here. Charlie, next time you're in town, get one of the geezers to bring you by. Catch ya later; we're getting busy. Gotta make some *moolah!*" After Maddy got out of eavesdropping range, Frank teased, "I think Maddy *likes* you, Charlie."

"How old is Maddy, anyway?" Charlie asked.

"Seventeen, I think."

Rex quickly changed the subject. "How are *you* doing, Uncle Frank?"

"Better than I have a right to be. If I leave this earth tomorrow, it's been a heck of a ride. And we have Knights baseball to look forward to! You gonna score your favorite uncle some Opening Day tickets?"

"You bet, Uncle Frank! How many do you want?"

"Two, please. Thank you kindly!" Then Frank addressed his great-nephew. "Charlie, I've been keeping tabs on your progress and praying for a full, fast recovery. I'll see you on Opening Day. Good to see your mug; keep that old man of yours out of trouble. I guess I'll sign off now, if I can figure out how to do that. Aren't y'all proud of me being a Skyper? Is that what you call a person who Skypes? I'm kind of techy, huh?"

"Yeah, you're techy all right. Just push the End Call button, Uncle Frank." Rex laughed. But Uncle Frank had already figured out how to end the call before Rex was halfway through the sentence.

A minute later, Charlie's phone chimed. Alfred was calling on Face-time.

"*Al-fred!*"

"*Sus-ter!*"

"Hey, Sus! I got permission to come down to see you in Nashville sometime, so let me know if that would work and when."

"Yee-haw! That's fantastic news! Okay, maybe you can come for Opening Day weekend. What do you think, Dad? Can we get Alfred tickets?"

"Of course. We'll get Alfred up to the Owners Suite with us; how about that, Alfred?"

"Now, *I* get to say *yee-haw!*" Alfred yee-hawed like a cowboy at a rodeo.

Rex suggested Alfred have his mom contact Mrs. Collier to coordinate everything. "Yes, sir, Mr. Collier. I'm on it!"

To make the perfect trifecta of a day, after Uncle Frank and Alfred's calls, the doorbell rang. Standing on their porch was Big T McCraw! Even though they knew him, they were still star-struck.

It turned out Big T had been in the neighborhood and had a prompting to stop and say hello. He'd never been to their humble home, so it was quite the shock for them. Big T hoped they didn't think him rude to surprise them. They all sat in the living room drinking sweet tea, in the Southern tradition, while catching him up on the latest with Charlie.

After a while, Big T said, "Hey, Charlie, I know you can't run yet, but can you stand still and play catch? If I throw the ball right back to you, chest high, would be able to play catch?"

"Yes, I think so. Are *you* asking *me* to play catch, Mr. McCraw?"

"If it's all right with your mom and dad, I think we have some time before dusk. I have my glove in the car. It's always with me. I used to take it with me on the road back when I was touring. A few of the roadies, my bass player and drummer, were decent players. We could have put together a pretty good semi-pro team."

Martha looked a little reticent and did her mom thing. "Please be careful."

It was glorious. It was the right thing at the right time. How did Big T know? He and Charlie were in their own world, smiling, talking, and just throwing a baseball for twenty minutes while Rex and Martha joyfully watched from the window. True enough...Big T was like a good batting practice pitcher. He was laying them in there and Charlie didn't have to move, just flip his glove up, catch, and leisurely toss it back. He couldn't stop grinning. Neither could Big T. When it got too dark, they called it quits. Big T thanked the Colliers for letting him just drop in and said, "By the way, look for the invite in your mailbox with directions, but I want y'all to join me at my log cabin on Saturday night before Opening Day. We're having a barbeque, Tennessee-style, to celebrate! See y'all soon!"

And he was gone. The Colliers all looked at each other as if to say, "Did that really happen? Was music legend and MLB team owner Big T McCraw hanging out at *our* house?" It felt surreal.

★ CHAPTER 28 ★

BIG T'S
Log Cabin

The Rammer and Ms. Scully purposely showed up early for the shin-dig at Big T's. They were hoping to visit with him before the others arrived. They knew it was borderline rude, but they decided to take their chances.

Once they turned off State Road 19, it got real country, real fast.

"Man, he lives out in the boonies, RS."

Timothy had taken to calling Ms. Scully "RS" because "Rebecca" is three syllables and she didn't like "Bec" or "Becca."

"Yeah, *Jimothy*," she replied. "This does feel like the sticks. But just as long as we don't see some toothless dude playing banjo, I'll be okay."

"Jimothy" had become her nickname for him because when he signed his name, his T looked like a J. "I think this is the entrance; turn right here."

As the car swung around, they laid eyes upon the biggest entrance to a "log cabin" there could possibly be—two giant thirty-foot-tall oak baseball bats with the knob end in the air and the barrel end anchored in the ground. Across the top of the two baseball bats was a sizable wooden beam to support a full-sized dugout bolted onto the beam. Three words were carved into the facing of the dugout: *Big T's Team.*

"Jimothy, stop! We *have* to get a picture of this."

They both got out and just stood there gawking at it, feeling small.

"All right, RS; let's go," said Timothy after Rebecca got her photo. "We want to get some time with him."

The second jaw dropper was the three-quarter-mile, cobblestone driveway lined by stately oaks, with a picturesque lake on the left and a horse stable on the right. The music industry had been very, very good to Mr. McCraw. At the end of the long driveway, there it sat, the "log cabin." It had logs all right—big logs, *lots* of big logs. Maybe 20,000 square feet of them! As they slowed to a crawl, gawking again, a young man waved to them and signaled to park next to what looked to be an old Mercedes sports car. "This probably is one of his cars," Timothy said. "I know he collects old cars. Look at that! It's a '59 Mercedes SL *Gullwing*. I only know because my pal Dave Pride used to own one and regrets selling it. His wife says she'll shoot him if he buys another one. They're super-hard to find, and you'd spend upwards of a million bucks to own one today."

The young man, who'd signaled them to park, sprinted over and greeted them. "Howdy, folks! I'm Eddie, and I'm helping Mr. McCraw today. I'm here to get you where you're going, which is probably the BBQ party?"

"Thank you, Eddie. I'm Timothy Ramage; this is Rebecca Scully. Yes, we're here for the party, as the Gretchen Wilson song says. We're with the Knights."

"Oh, I know all about y'all. Well, not *all* about, but Mr. McCraw gave me the scouting report on our guests tonight. You are the executive VP, and you, Ms. Scully, are serving as his assistant. Mr. McCraw is excited to have y'all here. He told me that. He was so excited that he wanted to take it down a notch, so I reckon y'all can find him fishing down at the lake."

"We drove by the lake and didn't see anyone there," said Timothy.

"No, he'd be at the *other* lake, the one off the back side of the property," Eddie said, pointing in the opposite direction. "I heard him say something about wanting to catch three or four catfish. Our chef, Bubba Idell, has a special catfish side dish he'd like to prepare for the group, so Mr. McCraw said he'd go catch the ingredients. Y'all can walk around there. I'm sure he'll be glad to see ya."

"Thanks, Eddie," The Rammer and RS replied at the same time.

As soon as they were out of earshot, Rebecca whispered, "Jimothy, that was *hilarious!* The man's a mega country music star, owns a Major League Baseball team, and he just went to catch catfish for our dinner!" She had to stifle the giggles from fear of detouring too far into The Silly Zone.

"Well, I'll tell ya what," Timothy replied, chuckling, "I've known him for a few years now, and I'm not surprised by anything he does. But I'll tell you something else; he'd be the same if he didn't have money or fame. He's not as much of an extrovert as everyone thinks. And his wife stays completely out of the limelight. I've met her once; her name's Kate, and she's real sweet. Only difference for them with his fame and fortune is they can afford things, like baseball teams, and they can be more generous. They do a lot of charitable things, but he won't talk about it. Word gets out, though."

They continued around to where Eddie had pointed and saw the other lake and two men fishing. One was Big T, but who was the other?

The men were sitting side by side on paint buckets turned upside down, flipping their fishing lines into the water. Big T, being the bigger man, sat on the bigger bucket. He was on the right and the other man on the left, which was good because Big T was right-handed and the other man was a lefty. Their lines came close to touching when they cast out at the same time. It would have been safer to be farther apart, but they appeared to be enjoying a lively conversation.

Timothy and RS continued down the gentle slope to the lake, dodging the ubiquitous goose droppings with every treacherous step. It had rained overnight, so the slope was slick, prompting her to say, "I hope I don't fall on my ass and land in goose poop." Timothy added, "And I hope *I* don't kick the ever-loving goose crap out of the unlucky bird *bastard* that gets in range of my size twelves. I did play collegiate soccer."

"Be nice, Jimothy; be nice. The way you said *bastard* was with a vengeance."

Feeling no need to receive a fish hook to the face from the fishermen's backswings, they circled to the side of Big T, who hadn't yet seen them. Now the other man's features came into view, but he wasn't familiar to them. He was smiling and nodding at whatever Big T was saying. When they were ten feet away, Big T spied them out of his periphery and jumped from his upturned bucket so fast that he kicked it over. "Rammmmer! Ms. Sculllllly!" He reeled in his line, set down the fishin' pole, and stretched his strong arms toward them for a hug. At 6' 6", he had the usual leaning down to do. He had his fishin' garb on—old jeans (rolled up at the bottom), a black T-shirt bearing a picture of Johnny Cash, old black hi-top Chuck Taylors, and a straw hat with a wide brim to block the sun. His gray curly locks—his most striking feature besides his height—just brushed his shoulders.

The Rammer was not a touchy-feely dude, so he was somewhat uncomfortable with the hugging, even with his friend Big T. He used to refuse to hug at all, but he'd gotten better. That he had recently initiated a group hug was a good sign that maybe he was loosening up. Later, he confided to Ms. Scully, "If my younger self had seen that, he'd *kill* me."

The other man, about Rebecca's height with a rugged face and warm smile, stuck out his hand. "I'm Smokey Fields; pleased to meet you!"

"I'm Timothy Ramage, and this is Rebecca Scully."

"Well, I'm thrilled to meet you both. Rebecca, I hear you're related to Vin."

"Yes, I am! He's a distant cousin!"

"Well, butter my butt and call me a biscuit! I listened to him thousands of times. Hope you don't mind me multi-tasking. Me and Big T, we're just getting' some catfish for supper. We have some bluegill too. Do you have a preference?"

"Either one, Mr. Fields; I like them both," Rebecca said.

"Please, y'all call me Smokey. Now, I'm gonna take these three fat catfish we caught," he said, holding up the string of catfish, "and head on up yonder to the kitchen to get these appetizer ingredients in Chef Bubba's hands. Y'all can talk and catch up." Smokey tiptoed through the treacherous goose tulips and up the grassy slope to the main house.

Timothy and Rebecca now had the opportunity they had hoped for—some alone time with Big T.

The big man stretched his hands skyward, eyes closed. "Warm sunshine, vitamin D, that feels *so* good." He inhaled audibly and deeply through his nose, then exhaled through his mouth. "Ahhhhh. And how are y'all doing? I'm so glad you're here at my little hangout."

Rebecca looked at Timothy, expecting him to say something, and he obliged.

"We're doing great, and we feel we owe you some news. Ms. Scully and I have, um, become an item. I hired her last June as my assistant, and a friendship grew from working together, and then more developed, organically and unexpectedly." He paused. Rebecca smiled. "Yes, unexpectedly."

"Well, that's wonderful, y'all!" said Big T. "I figured that out at Wintergreen; maybe I saw it before you did."

"Well, that's when we started wondering too," Rebecca said as she glanced at Timothy for affirmation.

The Rammer laughed. "I do remember the day at Wintergreen when you changed clothes and came back after lunch in your skirt and boots. You put on some makeup, too."

Rebecca giggled and blushed, busted.

"We wanted to be sure you're okay with your employees dating," said Timothy. "I can assure you I'll do my best to keep Ms. Scully from being too demonstrative with her affections for me. She usually can't keep her hands off me in public."

"Shut up, Jimothy!" exclaimed Rebecca. "Don't give me that crap, you lounge lizard!"

Big T laughed. "You *sound* like an item! Look, you two, I don't give a rat's patootie if you date except to the extent that I'm happy for you, but it's nice of you to tell me. Just no drama, mind you. Let's head up toward the house and I'll show you around."

The resort-sized house looked like it should be on the cover of *Log Cabin Magazine*. They ascended thirteen steps to the wraparound deck on the second floor where a lovely, shapely, redhead greeted them. "Hi. I'm Kate McCraw. Welcome to our ranch! Tommy and I are so excited you're here today. It's great to see you again, Timothy, and to meet *you*, Rebecca!" Big T stood a good foot taller than Kate and leaned down to kiss her as she stretched upward. They met in the middle.

Kate McCraw was the kind of woman who wants, above all else, to create fun experiences for people. Born and raised on a farm five miles as the crow flies from downtown Nashville, Kate had met Big T through music. She'd been a backup singer for the Country Bumpkin Avant Garde Band, a local group that played weddings, senior proms, and had twice opened for Big T concerts. Big T had told Timothy that Kate battled social anxiety, but once people were gathered, she was masterful at making sure everyone had what they needed and was having fun. He described Kate as the shiny object people gravitated to first while he was the acquired taste. When fans didn't recognize him, he enjoyed the anonymity, especially when they traveled to other countries. Kate's long, thick mane of auburn-colored hair had always turned heads. Today, it was thickly braided with a single braid all the way down her back.

"Would y'all like me to show you around?" Kate asked. "I think Tommy needs to change before the crowd starts arriving."

Sounding like husbands all across America, Big T feigned misunderstanding, throwing his hands up in the air. "*What?* What's wrong with this?"

"The jeans and Chucks are okay; Chucks are cool again, but drop the straw hat and the Man in Black shirt." It didn't sound like a command. Kate's Julia Roberts' smile and sweet tone had a way of making you just want to do whatever she said.

"Okay, baby; the straw hat was coming off anyway. I'm gonna wear my Knights ball cap, though! And I'll wear a Knights jersey, too, *over* the shirt. You know I like to honor Johnny."

Kate turned to Timothy and Rebecca. "This used to be Johnny Cash's house. Johnny and June built it; they bought the property and tore down an old farmhouse that was on its way down anyway. We bought it with one owner in between, but Johnny and June were friends of ours. Everybody knows everybody down here in Nashville. C'mon; lemme give you the grand tour." She led them around a back staircase and to one of the wings. "Down this hall, we have Tommy's recording studio, this door right here," she said, pushing it open. Inside, they saw platinum records on the walls, lots of recording equipment, and a soundproof room. "Johnny and June had this built; we just upgraded some of the technology." They stood in the doorway of the studio in awe and followed Kate down the hall to the next room. "And here's Tommy's pool room. He likes to challenge his pool-playing pals to a 'World Series,' the best of seven games. I rarely come in here. As you can see, it's more than a game room. Tommy has some of his favorite memorabilia here."

Rebecca couldn't resist asking, "Do you ever call him Big T, or is it always Tommy?"

"Heavens, no! He's always been Tommy to me; not Tom, Thomas, and especially not Big T! He's not so big to me. He's more like a lovable little boy. I *get* that everybody else sees him as this larger-than-life figure, but to me, he's my lovable, wonderful Tommy. He's a softie."

Rebecca glanced at Timothy, then back at Kate. "I can relate. This guy's nickname is Rammer, but he's a marshmallow."

"Not true," The Rammer quipped.

"What's not true? Your nickname isn't Rammer?"

"It's not true I'm a marshmallow."

"*Riiiight,*" RS replied, and they all had a chuckle.

They moseyed to the back staircase again and ventured down another hallway. "Here's our living quarters; this room is our gathering spot when friends and family are over, usually watching a game or movie. We love the view from here, looking out to the woods and over the valley, with downtown Nashville just a little off to the right there. We call this our family room."

"The floor-to-ceiling windows are so cool, aren't they, Jimothy?"

"Agree; what a view! It's gorgeous. I'd love to see it when the leaves are changing." The Rammer gently tapped the glass. "Hmm, that's thick. My dad worked for a glass company and I used to go on calls with him. Never saw a window with that kind of glass; it's substantial."

Kate laughed. "Nobody ever made that observation, before. You have a good eye for glass, I guess. Yes, that's bulletproof glass. Johnny had it installed at June's request after John Lennon was shot. She thought some other nut out there might play copycat, and she became worried about someone hiding in the woods and shooting into the house. Plus, people hunt out there. All the windows facing the woods are bulletproof."

Leaving the family room, Kate opened the next door and chilly air came out. "Johnny and June had this climate-controlled room built for her furs; June loved her furs. As you can see, I only have one, which was given to me, but we keep it in here and occasionally put other things in here that do well being colder. We're almost done with the tour, this part anyway. Let's go down to the barbeque area. We have great weather today, so guests will be flowing in and out. Oh, I have one more room to show you." There didn't appear to be another room down this hallway. Kate led them back to the family room, where she touched a wall; the wall turned to reveal a secret room. "This is our Safe Room. This is where we would go if we had a home invasion. Johnny and June also worried about kidnapping attempts. In this room, there's food and water, as well as a telephone that cannot be disconnected if the power is cut. Bad guys wouldn't be able to mess with us in here. Tommy and I don't worry about that; it's just part of the history of our little log cabin."

The three of them made their way back to the wraparound porch where they reunited with Big T, now appropriately attired in Knights gear. They followed the aroma of smoking meat to the barbeque area. The horseshoe pit was conveniently built next to the smoker so people could pass time while tending the meat.

Big T and Smokey each had an area in the pit from which to work. The competition was on, as always, when the old friends got together with their grills. Smokey wore a gray apron with "Smokey 'Dork King' Fields" written on it in white cursive lettering. Atop his head was a black baseball style cap that said "Dork Award Winner." On the left side of the cap was a picture of a duck smoking a cigar, and on the right side, a pig smoking a cigar. Ms. Scully zeroed in on the cap right away and laughed. "Jimothy, you have to have a *dork* cap like that." Directing her attention to Smokey, she said, "That's a funny cap. Is that what you're cooking here today—your secret dork recipe?"

"You bet, Missy! When you put duck with pork, you get dork, and that's one special treat! Their unique properties, blended together with Smokey's seasonings, make for a savory delight unequaled in culinary history and superior to anything Big T could ever dream up using some danged animal called yak! Who the hell eats yak? Yak means talk where I come from."

Big T protested, "Go ahead and talk while I debut my bi-yak burger that'll open up a can of whoop-ass on you—half bison, half yak, prized Himalayan yak. It'll kick your dork burger's piggish, web-footed behind! I get only the best bison and yak, the upper one-quarter of 1 percent—the bison and yak equivalent of elite athletes. The best of the best!"

Kate rolled her eyes. "You guys are both big dorks. Guests are *arriving*; we better get up there. Let's go, boys."

The party would go well past dark. All the dork and biyak burgers were consumed, and most of the twenty or so pizzas delivered, courtesy of Smokey Sam's Prodigious Pies, were wolfed down. The crowd was an eclectic mix—politicians, music industry friends, Knights players, employees and their families, neighbors, and Nashville business leaders all blended together. It was especially pleasing to Big T that Charlie had come. He had hoped to have an opportunity to pour encouragement into the young man. He pulled Charlie aside to have alone time. Charlie walked slowly with his cane. They walked to the stable where Big T introduced Charlie to his horse, Knight Winner. It was an excuse to have a private conversation with Charlie.

"Charlie," Big T began, "I'm glad you're here. This is where I come when I need to clear my head or just think. Sometimes I bounce my ideas off of KW, my short name for Knight Winner. He just listens and neighs occasionally." Big T looked Charlie directly in his eyes. "Charlie, where's your head on your recovery progress? You've got the hitch in your giddy-up and you're working hard with the physical therapy, but I want to know how you're doing up here." He tapped his temple. "How are you doing? Feeling up? Down?"

"It changes," said Charlie. "Most of the time, I believe I can fully recover. Other times, there's a guy inside my head with a megaphone telling me to give up and accept my fate. I shout him down and tell him he has no home inside my head. He goes away and then comes back. Rinse and repeat; this scene plays over and over." Charlie paused, choking up. "What really bugs me is that I can't run gracefully anymore. I don't mean to be too boastful, but people used to say

I had a beautiful running stride. Not anymore. The way my legs bang together, I could put cymbals on the insides of my knees and keep a rhythm. My physical therapist says it's only temporary, though—that I'll get better."

"Well," said Big T, "if you keep working as hard as you are, I believe you'll fully recover, maybe even be better because of it. Have you heard of a runner named Glenn Cunningham?"

"No. Why?"

"Because there are similarities between your story and his; you both faced tragedy. He battled back; so will you. Would you like to hear the story? It might help with the megaphone man."

"Yes, please. Tell me."

Big T grabbed two of the folding chairs that were leaning against the wall, since the stable doubled as a storage unit. "Sit, please." They sat facing each other. Charlie leaned forward on his elbows while Big T draped himself over his backward-turned chair.

"Glenn Cunningham loved to run," Big T began, "but when he was seven, his legs were burned severely in an accidental explosion that killed his brother. Doctors said he would never walk again, let alone run, and they recommended amputation. Fortunately, his mother was not a lady who was going to accept that answer. Nor was young Glenn. Mrs. Cunningham massaged his legs every morning and at bedtime. She prayed for him, encouraged him, and repeated over and over that he would walk and run again. It took over a year, but he walked. He kept walking, and every day his mother massaged his legs. Because of her efforts and Glenn's determination, he was out-running high school boys by the time he was twelve. He set records in high school, in college, and in the Olympics. Glenn Cunningham, the boy the doctors said would never walk and should have his legs amputated, set the world record in the mile! His world record stood for three years before it was broken. It wasn't a pretty sight when he ran; he didn't have a graceful gait; he labored, but his incredible endurance set him apart. He was called The Kansas Ironman.

"You remind me of Glenn Cunningham in some ways, Charlie. Did I mention that he had the highest academic record in his class at Kansas? He was smart, like you. He was determined, like you. He had great support, like you. You can go as far as you can dream, Charlie, if your belief level is high enough like Glenn Cunningham's was, and if you put in hard work for extended periods of time, against all obstacles, amazing things will happen throughout your life. I did a book report on Glenn Cunningham in the sixth grade. That's a pivotal time in a boy's life, and the story had a big impact on me. Still does. It warms my heart to share it with you. Always believe you can achieve what others may say is unimaginable."

"I love that story," Charlie replied. "I had no idea. I've never heard of Glenn Cunningham. When you were talking about his mom massaging his legs and believing in him, that made me think about my mom. She'd do that for me."

"Yes, she would, Charlie. It's good that you see that. Did you want to talk about anything else?"

"Well, sir, I just want to say that Glenn Cunningham's recovery made me think about Charlie's Kids Foundation and that we'll help lots of kids recover. I'll do some research to learn more about Glenn Cunningham. This has been a day I'll always remember."

"Me, too, Charlie. And it's not even over. Let's get back to the party before they wonder what happened to us."

When they reunited with the group, Charlie had the look of a man, yes, a man, of destiny. He seemed an inch taller; Thomas McCraw had that effect on people.

Some of Nashville's music world brought their instruments and took to jamming near the BBQ area. After a while, Big T commandeered the mic and led the partiers in a rousing rendition of "Take Me Out to the Ballgame." He thanked everyone for supporting the Knights and promised to build the team into an organization that Nashville, Tennessee, and all of baseball would be proud of. After finishing his remarks, he said, "One more thing…we forgot to vote on the best bar- beque. Where's Smokey? Smokey Fields, c'mere." Smokey ambled over. Big T continued, "Everybody who thinks Smokey's Dork Burger is the best, yell and scream now."

"Wait a minute!" Kurt Grimmer yelled. "You have to recuse yourself; you're a contestant." Kurt walked over and took the mic. Then he positioned himself between Smokey and Big T. "I'm going to hold my hand over Smokey's head, and y'all cheer if you think his dork burger is the best. Then I'll hold my hand over Big T's head if I can reach that high, and you'll cheer for him if you think his bi-yak burger was the best. Whoever gets the loudest cheer wins!"

Kurt implored the crowd to scream for their favorite. There was no clear winner the first or second time. The cheers grew louder with each attempt, but it was too close to call. After the third and final try, Kurt pointed to the nearby drummer. "I'm gonna need a drum roll," he said, then addressed the party-goers again. "After monitoring the cheers with the seismograph app on my phone and listening with my own ears, I declare this BBQ cook-off…" (drum roll) *"a draw!"*

"Boooo!" Both sides booed. When the boos ended, someone shouted, "Well, kiss my sister!" and everybody had a laugh.

Big T high-fived Smokey and grabbed the mic one last time. "Thanks again, everybody. Three days until Opening Day! *Play ball!* Let's all shout it together, on three. One, two, three." The crowd screamed, "Play ball!"

Timothy and Rebecca walked hand in hand to their car. "What an amazing experience, Jimothy. I *love* Big T and Kate! They're so normal. No, I don't mean normal; maybe saying 'down to earth' is better. Who wants to be normal anyway? Whatever normal is." Rebecca stopped abruptly as she was getting into the passenger side. "We're not normal; we're a couple of whackos, right?"

"Yeah, we're whackos who don't appear to be whackos. That's the key. We're incognito whackos," he replied, as they both shut their doors and he started the engine.

As they passed under the thirty-foot-tall oak bats and the dugout again, Rebecca asked the unspoken question lingering for both of them. "So, Mr. Rammer, since we're kinda official now, what does it mean? What's next?"

"For us? The team?"

"Both."

"Here's how I see it, RS. I'm a SoCal boy, so I think of surfing. I see us riding a huge wave, personally and professionally—the kind the average Joe Bag of Donuts wants to ride but is too scared to try! As the great philosopher Smokey Fields said, 'Butter my butt and call me a biscuit!'"

The former soccer goalie *kicked* the accelerator and fishtailed back onto State Road 19.

CHAPTER 29

Opening Day Eve

The "Berwyn Boys," Dustin and Frank, were flying in for the big game with Charlie's best pal Alfred in tow. Rex had gone to the airport to pick them up. Meanwhile, Martha was scurrying to get the house ready while Gandolfini cast his big Al Jolson eyes intently on his silver chow bowl. Charlie was listening to a personal development podcast on enhancing human performance until Martha called him to duty.

"Charlie, would you just help me some with straightening up? If you feed Fini first, that'd be good. He won't stop staring at that bowl till something's in it. Then, please empty the trash cans and put in new liners. That would help. We have to get this joint ready for company."

"This *joint*? Is this a prison, a speakeasy, or a place with marijuana cigarettes?"

"*Mi hijo es un comediante!*" Martha replied with hands on hips.

"I know what you just said. Yes, I *am* a comedian. And sometimes I amuse my own self."

"My *own* self? Good grammar there, Mr. Rhetoric! And you're busting on *my* linguistics?"

"I picked up 'my own self' from Mister D; he said it a couple of times at the café. I think it's funny. It's in my lexicon now."

Martha gave an eye-roll and was about to retort when her phone chimed the special Rex chime.

"It's your man again, Mom. He's pursuing you, you know."

"Hey, Rexy," Martha answered. "Okay…uh-huh…you bet…I'll tell him. Keep me updated…. Okay, baby. Love you."

Martha disconnected the call and then told Charlie, "Your dad got to the airport early, but said their flight's now coming in late. That puts them touching down about five, so it'll be close to seven by the time they get here. Maybe we can time it so we have Smokey Sam's pizzas ready for them. They'll probably be hungry. I'll text him and suggest that. I'll go and pick it up."

"That sounds like a plan, Mom," Charlie replied. "I'm going up to my room. There are some articles I need to read. I'll save my energy for the pizza."

* * *

A few hours later, Rex pulled into the driveway before Martha was back with the pizza pies. Uncle Frank, Dustin, and Alfred exited the car with their luggage. Charlie opened the front door and yelled, "Alfred!" Alfred dropped his overnight bag, ran to Charlie, and hugged him.

Frank spread his arms as wide as they would go, and Dustin followed suit. "Hey, what about your uncle Frank and Mister D?" Frank asked. "Are we like three-day-old bread or something?"

"Sorry, Uncle Frank and Mister D! You're not like old bread. Before I break down and *rye*...I'll say, *I loaf you too.*"

Rex could only shake his head, bemused. The brain cancer hadn't put a dent in his boy's quickness in the fine art of punning. Rex led the all-testosterone group into the house, announcing that Martha should be home with pizza soon.

"Charlie, you and Alfred can hang out upstairs if you want," said Rex. "I'll call you when Mom's back with the pizza. You'll probably hear her come in anyway. You guys come down and get your pizza and drinks."

"Okey, dokey, Dad! What say you, Mr. Bailey?" Charlie asked Alfred.

"Mr. Bailey?" Alfred replied. "I like the sound of that. Nobody ever called me Mr. Bailey before.... Sure, Sus, let's hang in your room like we used to in Maryland. Can we look at your card collection?"

Once upstairs, the best friends sat on the floor. Charlie laid the 1984 Topps Set, the almost-complete set, before them.

"Sus," said Alfred, "I'm so sorry about your operation and that you had to have it. It must have been scary, huh?"

"It was scary at first," Charlie replied, "but in the end, it wasn't. I haven't told anyone except my mom and dad, but you're my best friend so you should know. When I was being operated on, my heart stopped due to a reaction to the anesthesia. It stopped for under a minute, they say. In that time, I felt myself float over my body and I saw the medical team working on me. It wasn't scary at all; it felt glorious, and there was a bright light embracing me. I know I saw a glimpse of heaven. Heaven is real. I used to think and hope it was real, but now I know."

"Wow, Sus. Thanks for telling me that. I've heard of people having experiences like that."

"Wanna see my scar?"

"Okay."

Charlie took off his Knights cap and turned so Alfred could see the scar at the base of his head.

"Ouch. How are you doing? I saw that you caught yourself on the stairs. Will you be able to play baseball again?"

"I'm not sure. Now I couldn't. My balance is messed up. You see how slow I'm walking. I hate using this stupid cane, but if I want to walk faster, I've got to. It's maddening that I can't run anymore. I wish I could sprint around the bases. I'm hopeful. Hey, that's Mom's car. She's home, which means our pizzas are home. Food is here! Let's go!" Charlie opened the door and moved gingerly down the stairs. Alfred followed along. "Hey, Mom, can Alfred and I eat upstairs? We're looking at baseball cards."

"Sure, son. Hi, Alfred! So good to see you and have you here for Opening Day! Isn't this exciting?"

"Yes, ma'am, Mrs. Collier! It's like a dream to be here in Nashville. I've only been to four states. And I miss not having Sus in Maryland!"

Martha gave Alfred her sweet motherly smile. "You boys go ahead and take your pizza and napkins up. I'll bring your drinks in a minute."

"Don't get your pizza on the baseball cards; they're valuable," Rex said. "Eat your pizza first, and then wash and dry your hands."

"Yes, sir! Good reminder, Dad. That actually happened once. I got grease on a Ryne Sandberg rookie card."

A few minutes later, Martha delivered two mugs of A&W Root Beer filled with ice to Charlie's room. "Here are your drinks, boys." Then Martha turned to Charlie and said, "*And* Mr. Charles Collier, why is that pile of clothes on the floor?"

"It's gravity, Mom."

"Then please reverse the gravitational pull so they float into your dresser."

"I'm on that mission, Mom. I'm currently reading a book about anti-gravity, and *it's hard to put down!* Thanks for the pizza!"

Once the boys' hunger monsters were satisfied, and they had washed their hands, they focused on the '84 Topps collection and which cards Charlie was missing. Of the 792 cards in the entire set, Charlie possessed 789. "I'm missing three cards: Cal Ripken #490, Don Mattingly rookie card #8, and Darryl Strawberry rookie card #182."

"Maybe the next time you're in Maryland," said Alfred, "you can check at Mr. Bill's Card Store. He might have them. Actually, I'll check for you when I go home. If Mr. Bill doesn't have them, I'll ask him to ask his son Loren. Loren started his own card store in California. He's only nineteen and has his own card store. That guy's my hero!"

"That's cool," said Charlie. "Loren knows a lot about baseball *and* collecting. He's a huge Vin Scully fan, always talking about him. Maybe someday he can meet Ms. Scully…Rebecca Scully. She's Vin's distant cousin, and she's sort of a friend of mine. She's an adult about my parents' age. She's the assistant to the Executive VP of the Knights, Mr. Ramage. I think they're boyfriend/girlfriend too. Mr. Ramage and Ms. Scully, I mean. They're really nice. He seems gruff, but he's not, and she helped me when I was giving my presentation and again after the operation when she let me use her lucky baseball. She calls it her 'thinking ball.' It does seem to have magical powers." Charlie picked up the old ball sans three stitches and continued. "She said I could keep it and that I'd know when the time came to give it back. She's never given the ball to anyone else before, so it was kind of a big deal, and I do believe the thinking ball has helped me."

Alfred, intrigued but puzzled, said, "That's cool!" and they both refocused on the Topps '84 set for a while before they switched to video games.

The adults talked in the living room until it was time to turn in. Sleep would come slowly for all, as if they were kids on Christmas Eve. Tomorrow would be memorable—their minds were tingling.

CHAPTER 30

Opening Day

Everything around the new ballpark was awash in baseball nostalgia, from the architecture to the intricate work on the railings and seats. It had been an impressive private/public partnership. For Nashville, having a major league franchise said to the rest of the nation, "Hey, America, we're not just country music; we're a *big-time city! How do you like us now?*"

Knights Park at Riverfront, as it was officially named, was constructed in eighteen months on land adjacent to Cumberland Park in downtown Nashville. The players couldn't get on the field until the opener due to a drainage issue. They arrived in bunches between 8 and 9 a.m., wanting maximum time to get a feel for the field, its angles, and how the ball would carom off the twenty-nine-foot-high right and left field walls. Definitely a "pitcher's park," it would take a heck of a poke to hit home runs there—335 feet down the right field line with that twenty-nine-foot wall, then 373-feet to right center where the wall tapered down to nineteen-feet. Straightaway center 410 feet with an eleven-foot wall. Left center measured the same as right center,

373 feet with the nineteen-foot wall. The distance down the left field line mirrored the right field line, 335 feet with a twenty-nine-foot wall. Big T had pushed everyone involved in planning to give him a big ballpark that would lend itself to "small ball." And that was before Project Baseball had been birthed. As it turned out, you couldn't have designed a better ballpark than this one if you wanted to shock the baseball world; it was custom-built for the Project Baseball playbook!

Red Smithberger, baseball writer of twenty-seven years for *The Tennessean*, was on the field near the Knights' dugout, interviewing Manager Larry Wenzel. Larry was pointing to the two big walls in left and right field. Smithberger had written some columns about the unique dimensions of Knights Park. He postulated that the team might, in the inaugural season, break records for doubles and triples with all the balls careening off the big walls in left and right. Smithberger dubbed the park "Double Fenway."

The gates wouldn't be open to the public for a few more hours, but already, a swarm of locust-like media was jockeying for position to get their Pulitzer-winning photo or big scoop interview. They had come from all over the world, but especially Japan, since the Knights were carrying seven Japanese players on their roster. Head of Scouting Wally Rupp had done a brilliant job bringing in players from Japan who would fit Project Baseball's playbook. They played *small ball* in Japan to begin with, and the Knights' management believed these seven players were especially skilled in the fine art of *small ball*. And there were more in the pipeline. Wally had also recommended pitching coach Mitch Mackenroth. He had met Mitch while scouting the Japan League. Mitch had been the English-speaking pitching coach for the Yakult Swallows.

Dustin, Frank, Martha, Charlie, and Alfred arrived at nine-thirty. Rex had secured them all seats in the Owners Suite, which had a capacity of forty-five. Big T told his celebrity and political friends not to be mad because they weren't invited to the Owners Suite; instead, he wanted his executive team and their families and friends to have the experience. Rex did put them all in box seats around the home dugout to lessen their disappointment. The celebrities understood, but the politicians, not so much. Big T assigned The Rammer to be in charge of the guest list—he was the guy who would most enjoy stiff-arming the pleading, pathetic, political beggars, mostly underlings, who were begging on behalf of their bosses so they could be the shining stars in their bosses' gimme, gimme, gimme eyes.

The Owners Suite had once been described by Smithberger as "Cowboy Swank meets Medieval Chic." Standing guard at the door was a fully armored knight holding an eight-foot spear. Unlike any other Owners Suite in professional sports, the interior featured a vaulted ceiling and locally sourced wood with black iron accents throughout. One wall had a mural of rodeo events, and a second wall had three medieval weapons—a crossbow, sword, and battle axe. A third wall featured a series of photographs featuring the baseball history of Nashville, including a photograph of Nashville native son Mookie Betts hoisting his 2009 Tennessee state championship high school trophy. The Owners Suite was every bit as unique, and in many ways similar, to Big T's log cabin. Despite the cowboy/medieval theme, every modern accoutrement was there. One thing was for sure—there was not another Owners Suite anywhere in professional sports that looked like this one. Then again, there had never been a *team* like the Nashville Knights.

Dustin, Charlie, and Alfred stood by the armored knight and watched as the Knights started infield practice. What a treat to watch big leaguers take infield practice. The way they flipped the ball around so gracefully and accurately was mesmerizing to Charlie. Normally, fans don't get to watch infield practice because it occurs before the gates open. This was the first time Charlie had seen it.

"Wow, Mister D! Look at how silky smooth they are on the double play; it looks effortless when they do it."

"I haven't seen this in years," Dustin replied. "When we were kids, the gates opened earlier, and it was always a thrill to watch infield. Somewhere along the line, all the teams stopped letting fans watch. I don't get that. In some ways, this is more fun than watching batting practice."

"It's so much fun to watch. Maybe Mr. McCraw will let fans in earlier, if MLB lets him; maybe they have a rule against it."

Charlie pointed to one of the players. "Who's the guy playing short-stop? He's so fast with the exchanges on the double play, and his feet are so quick. He reminds me of Omar Vizquel, except he looks Japanese."

"That's one of the Knights' biggest coups from what I have been reading online," said Dustin. He's been the top shortstop in Japan, playing for the Tokyo Yomiuri Giants. He's a power hitter who'll steal bases, bunt, or do whatever it takes, and he can play any outfield position. He rarely strikes out; he's a switch hitter, too. He has one of the best baseball names ever—Yoshi Nakahoma. I can hear the play-by-play guy now…another homer by Nakahoooooooma!"

Alfred cracked up and said Nakahoooooma three times. "I love the sound of that!"

"I like that, Mister D! That's funny!" said Charlie. "That's the guy my dad was telling me about. I think my dad's using him in some television commercials to promote season ticket sales. Nakahoma seems like exactly the kind of player suited to Project Baseball. See the guy shagging flies in right center? That's Florio Ford. My dad said he's just eighteen, from the DR. His nickname is Race Car. He has world class speed, another good fit with Project Baseball. They think he'll be the first Knights superstar, and it could happen right away!"

"Doggone right," Big T bellowed, walking up to meet Dustin. "Race Car can run! We got ourselves a good one there!" He stuck out his big right paw in Dustin's direction. "Howdy; I'm Big T McCraw. I just met Frank and was talking with him and Charlie and Alfred. They tell me you're one of the guys involved in the early conversations about Charlie's theories at that café in Maryland. In a way, you're part of the history of the team, Dustin. Welcome to Nashville. If there's anything I can do to make your visit more pleasant, let me know. I mean that."

Dustin stretched his face with a huge grin, surprised by the attention he was getting from the iconic music superstar and MLB owner Big T McCraw. "Thanks, Big T! I don't need anything. Being here is enough. I've been to All-Star games and opening days before, but I've never felt excitement like today. This ballpark is as pretty as any, and I love the dimensions! Thank you for letting Rex invite us."

By now, the visiting Dodgers had come out for batting practice and the stands were half full. Butch Dory and Wally Rupp showed up with their families, so most of the executives had arrived, except for Timothy Ramage and his assistant Rebecca Scully. Kurt Grimmer and Larry Wenzel, as GM and manager respectively, were in the clubhouse with the players.

Big T excused himself from the conversation and motioned Charlie and Alfred over. He whispered to them, "You guys come with me. Charlie, your dad knows you're with me. I have a surprise for you two ballplayers. Let's go."

The boys followed Big T to a private elevator. It had an extra button that wasn't in the other elevator. Big T pushed the button that read "CLUBHOUSE"!

Alfred's eyes widened and his lips curled up. When he exhaled, it sounded like "Whoa." Charlie cocked his head quizzically toward Big T, and his lips curled upward too; not a full smile because it didn't seem real yet, but the elevator *was moving*!

When the door opened, they saw a medieval sword pointing them straight ahead to the clubhouse. A fully armored knight, the team's official mascot, stood guard in front of the doors. Big T passed the knight and strode through the double doors, saying, "C'mon, slowpokes!"

The doors to a whole new world opened right there, in that moment, the *first time* Charlie Collier walked into a major league clubhouse.

Immediately, they saw Kurt and Larry, standing near the double doors, going over pre-game prep. Both stopped to give Charlie a handshake and hug, this being their first time seeing him since the operation, which everyone knew about, and their way of showing Charlie that they cared. Kurt and Larry were huggers. Big T got in on the act.

"Hugs all around. Why not? A day can't get much bigger than this!"

The players were in various stages of switching from their warmup jerseys into their gamers. The boys hung by Big T's side, off in some crazy baseball fantasy where they were in a big league clubhouse on Opening Day of the inaugural season. That would be totally nuts, something that would never happen—except when it did.

Big T stopped at the locker of R. Casanova. "Hey, Raul, how you doing, kid?"

"Doing good, boss; doing good."

"I'd like you to meet a couple of my friends, Charlie Collier and Alfred Bailey. They're young ballplayers, and we all know Charlie is the brains behind our Project Baseball philosophy. Alfred plays catcher, too; do you have any big league advice for him?"

Raul looked at Alfred and offered, "Number one: Block, block, block! Number two: Be smart, be smart, be smart. I said that three times so you'll remember. My granddaddy, Paul Casanova, was a catcher, and he told me to practice blocking every day. Have someone throw balls in the dirt all around you. Learn to block 'em and keep 'em in front of you, like a hockey goalie. That gives your pitcher one less thing to worry about. Number two advice is 'Be smart.' Being the catcher is like being the quarterback in football. You have to know what everybody else has to do on every play, every pitch. Then you're like an orchestra leader making sure everyone is in sync. You have to be the smartest and the toughest guy on the field to be a great catcher. Block and be smart. There you go, kid. Nice meeting you boys!"

"Now, Charlie," said Big T, leading the boys away after they thanked

Raul for his advice, "let's go find one of our pitchers to give *you* advice. I know; we'll go talk with Daniel Daneker. They call him 'Dancing Danny,' not because he dances, but because his knuckleball dances. He's another young'un, turns nineteen in July, and he is the second youngest guy, next to Race Car. Nobody even knew about this kid, but our head scout, Wally Rupp strikes again. Apparently, a friend of a friend told someone, who told Wally, that this kid was getting tutored by R. A. Dickey. Dickey is one of the top ten knucklers ever and a native of Nashville; he still lives here. Turns out, Danny was pretty much an average high school pitcher, pitching for a school three miles from where we're standing, but when he met R. A., R. A. volunteered to teach him the knuckler. This was going into his senior season, and he wasn't on *anybody's* radar. He was the number-three pitcher on an average high school team; decent, but no MLB or draft potential. Enter R. A. Dickey. *Now,* Danny not only throws a wickedly dancing knuckler, but he throws it at three different speeds. When he's got it going on, and that ball's dancing, he makes anybody look silly swatting at it.

"Hey, Dancin' Danny!" Big T called, as they approached him, "I'd like you to meet a couple of my friends, Charlie Collier and Alfred Bailey."

Danny, sitting on the bench in front of his locker, stood up and extended his hand to Charlie. He looked like he should *still* be in high school. "Pleased to meet you, Charlie. So glad to hear that the operation went well! We all know the story of Project Baseball; it's been drilled into our brains since day one of spring training, and we know it was your creation. Thanks, man; we players are real excited to play this style. I'm a weird knuckleballer; we're the quirky weirdos of baseball, maybe like field goal kickers in football—not real players, so some say! But karma smacks sluggers who scoff at the thought of a guy floating an erratic butterfly for him to swat at. R. A. Dickey dished out a lot of karma and had 1,477 strikeouts in his big league career. My goal is to surpass my mentor."

Charlie surprised himself by blurting out, "I'd love to talk about the knuckleball someday."

"Tell ya what, Charlie! Let's do better. Let's meet up and we'll play some catch. Alfred, you too! We'll see if you can catch some of my floaters. Maybe I'll teach Charlie how I throw it. Mr. McCraw can set it up, and I'll be there. Nice to meet you, guys; enjoy the game, and I look forward to playing catch."

Larry Wenzel came over and spoke to Charlie. "Charlie, please follow me. I have something to give you—a jersey. I have one for you and all of the players, too." Larry led Charlie over to the front of the locker room where the players could see them. He tapped five times in rapid succession on a locker with a bat to get their attention, the baseball equivalent of tinging a wine glass with a spoon.

"Hey, guys, listen up!"

Big T and Kurt Grimmer came to the front and flanked Larry. Charlie stood dutifully at Larry's side, as instructed. Alfred, with his face lit up like a lottery winner's, took a seat on the bench next to his new friend, Raul Casanova.

Once everyone was paying attention, Larry paused, letting the antici-pation build. It was a technique he'd picked up when he was a member of Toastmasters.

"Gentlemen, we're going to go out there today and play our brand of baseball, right out of here: Project Baseball." He waved his copy. "We have an unbelievably cool ballpark that will reward our style of play. Whether we win or lose today, it's historic. I want all of you to appreciate the experience. We have 162 games to play and then playoffs. We'll remain steady, we'll stick to our plan, and we'll shock the world." Larry put his arm around Charlie. "Mr. Charlie Collier is the architect of Project Baseball." The Japanese players, who were huddled close together listening to their translator, looked at Charlie with eyes of respect. "A few of you may not know the whole story. Project Baseball came about when Charlie had a hypothesis that the overuse of analytics in baseball was pulling down performance, not enhancing it. He presented it to his statistics professor and, eventually, to our management team at our winter planning session. This young man is not only smart; he's a cancer survivor, so he's tough too."

Charlie was looking at the floor, avoiding eye contact with everyone, except for a quick glance at Alfred.

"Charlie, we are dedicating this inaugural season to you. You've not only created our unique plan for winning, but you've inspired us through your personal battle as a cancer survivor. We know you're not able to play baseball yourself now, and we heard that what you miss most is being able to *just sprint*. So, we had these under-jerseys made up for the players to wear all season."

Big T handed Larry a box. Larry pulled out a jersey, holding it up so everyone could see the words on the front: JUST SPRINT! When Larry turned the shirt around, everyone could read *Charlie* on the back. Larry handed the jersey to Charlie, whose eyes, unable to hold any more water, allowed some tears to trickle down his cheeks.

"We're gonna sprint for you, Charlie. We're gonna hustle, and this will remind us to do so all season long. Here you go, guys; come and grab two apiece."

The Japanese players were seated together off to the left of Charlie and the others. Two of them stood and started clapping; then the other five and their translator joined in, and a few seconds later, every player in the locker room was giving Charlie a standing ovation. Someone started the chant, "Charlie, Charlie, Charlie!" It was a goose-bumpy moment for the ages!

Larry yelled, "Bring it in, guys!" He held out his hand; the players put their hands in and on top of Larry's for a rousing, "One, Two, Three… Go Knights!"

Big T led Charlie over to Alfred. "Time for us to bounce upstairs, fellas," he said in a tone that, if one didn't know better, made it seem like what had just happened was an everyday occurrence. Charlie and Alfred were still in a dream-like state of bliss; they didn't even remember getting back on the elevator. All of a sudden, they were back in the suite, and the first people they saw were Timothy Ramage and Rebecca Scully, who had just arrived.

Charlie broke out of his daze when he saw Rebecca. "Ms. Scully! I was hoping you'd be here. This is Alfred, my best friend from Maryland."

"Well, hello, Alfred! It's a pleasure to meet you!" Rebecca replied.

Alfred stuck out his hand and gave her hand an enthusiastic shake. "Nice to meet you too, Ms. Scully."

"Oops, Mr. Ramage," said Charlie, "I'm sorry; I didn't mean to ignore you. This is my best friend, Alfred. I got too excited seeing Ms. Scully and thinking about the *thinking ball*. Ms. Scully, it's time. You said I'd know when to give your ball back. I have it in my backpack. Hold on just a sec." Charlie grabbed his backpack from under the table.

Alfred gave Timothy a vigorous handshake, prompting The Rammer to say, "Now, *that's* a handshake! You must be a catcher."

"How'd you know that? Did Charlie tell you?"

"Nope, just guessed. Most of the catchers I've known shake the be-jeebers out of me like that."

Ms. Scully snickered, shaking her head. "Nice vocab, Jimothy! What-ever bejeebers are." He ignored her, except for the slightest downturn of his lips.

Charlie popped back up, grinning ear to ear with his silvery smile, and held up the thinking ball. "It's time, Ms. Scully. I love this ball, and now I know why *you* love it so much. Thank you for allowing me to borrow it. It helped me recover and gave me comfort. I must have flipped it from one hand to the other a thousand times, maybe two thousand."

Ms. Scully beamed and hugged Charlie. "I'm so happy for you, Char-lie—so happy you're doing well. If you ever need it again, just ask."

The game was about to start. Big T had already left to go onto the field for the National Anthem. Red, white, and blue bunting hung all around the ballpark on a flawless Tennessee Sunday of 80 degrees, with one lonely white cloud against the sky, the same color as Rex's first car, a robin's egg blue VW. It was a perfect day for the first game. There's nothing like a first—the first time you ride a bike, hit a homer, or kiss a girl—but best of all had to be the first game ever for the Nashville Knights! The excitement in the air could only be described as electric, in the same rarified air with the biggest concerts or sporting events. It wasn't an average Opening Day, that was for sure.

The medieval mascot, dubbed Sir Scorealot, was on top of the Knights' dugout, strutting back and forth, waving his giant foam sword, imploring the crowd to be even louder. Sir Scorealot had been one of Rex's marketing brainstorms. He wore a long, black, chain mail cloak, called a hauberk, which hung to his knees, with thousands of metal rings attached for protection. Under the hauberk was a padded silver undergarment. Both arms were covered by silvery metal. Sir Scorealot's legs had heavy black stockings that blended with his black boots. His black robe, or medieval surcoat, was emblazoned with a silver "N" in medieval script. The headgear covered from the top of his eyebrows to the base of his skull, with a pointy peak and a foot-long black plume. You'd think all that garb would limit Sir Scorealot's mobility and that he'd be inflexible, but you'd be wrong. He busted out some surprising dance moves, including cartwheels, without his sword, of course. He thrilled young fans when he let them hold his sword and their picture went up on the Jumbo Screen to be seen throughout the ballpark, indeed all across America since the game was nationally televised and the only one on. All the other teams would open on Monday.

Everyone in Big T's suite and all around the new ballpark was abuzz with excitement. The individual electricity, multiplied so many times over, must have rattled something metallic, producing a seemingly ever-present buzz. Pure, undiluted excitement was in the air. Players were being introduced, with the Knights lining up on the home side along the first base line, and the visiting Dodgers along the third. The crowd *roared* for the Knights and gave polite applause for the Dodgers. Some Dodgers fans were in attendance, wearing Dodgers Blue and making sure their presence was at least noticed.

The Knights wore their "home whites," white uniforms with black trim, old school, early-twentieth century. The white pantaloons extended just below the knees, where they met the silver stockings, covered mostly by black stirrups. Knights players had signed a contract to wear the old-style stirrups and black cleats; it was part of the deal— the branding, the marketing, the money-making, all tied ultimately to paying the players' salaries. The silver medieval axe was stitched into the sides of the stirrups. The medieval theme flowed through to the cap, which was the old pillbox style (popularized by the '70s Pirates), black with a medieval-style silver N on it, and three silver lines horizontally circling the cap. Lynda Bilo, Rex's marketing intern, who had grown up a Pirates fan, suggested the Knights mimic the style of the old Pittsburgh uniform. Its hipster-looking kind of cap caught on with the young Nashville crowd, who were not necessarily into baseball. Looking into the stands, there was a sea of the black caps, worn by approximately 80 percent of the crowd. Between real fans and the Nashville hipsters, the caps had been scarfed up faster than the supplier could deliver them, or even more would have been atop the Tennessee noggins. One section of seats down the left field line was filled with Charlie's Kids, and stood out because they were not wearing black Knights hats. Instead, they all had white hats with the letters CKF (Charlie's Kid Foundation) on them.

The wave of noise was nearing crescendo as the public address announcer, who was holding a microphone behind home plate and facing center field, bellowed:

"Ladies and gentlemen, please remove your hats and honor America by standing and turning your attention to the flag.

"*Introducing*...to sing our *first ever National Anthem* at Knights Park at Riverfront, fifteen-time Grammy Award Winner and *owner* of *your* NASHVILLE KNIGHTS, *Mr. Thomas "Big T" McCraaaaw!*"

The crowd went wild before quieting down to focus on the Stars and Stripes.

Big T stood before the microphone on the stand and removed his Knights ballcap. He paused for a full five seconds, looking around; he seemed to be savoring the moment, wanting to memorize every nuance of it. He tugged on the bottom of his Knights jersey and smoothed it out against his black jeans. Then he hit the first note... perfectly. Big T outdid himself, singing the anthem better than he ever had before, singing from the depth of his soul and bringing forth his love for his country. His voice was a beautiful, gravelly/velvet mix, more than worthy of the moment. There were goosebumps all around Knights Park and in living rooms across America.

The Knights fell behind 2-0 in the bottom of the third inning when the Dodgers had four straight hits off of Knights starting pitcher Asito Hirisoto, who struggled with control, walking four in the first three innings, the antithesis of the Project Baseball principle of limiting walks. Pitching coach Mitch Mackenroth noticed a mechanical issue with Asito's delivery and made a mound visit, after which Asito's control improved. If it weren't for Race Car aka Florio Ford making two sensational plays, the Knights would have been down at least 5-0. The Knights came back and scored two runs with a triple off the left center field wall and a sac fly in the sixth to tie the score. It remained tied until the ninth when the Dodgers scored one run on back-to-back doubles by Brennan Mayfield and Michael Mirisch, the "M Brothers."

The bottom of the ninth brought drama, giving the fans their money's worth. Race Car led off with a walk, after fouling off five pitches with a 3-2 count. Straight from the Project Baseball handbook, he used his speed to steal second base, and beyond that, he was distracting the pitcher's focus from the hitter. As Wally Rupp said, back at Wintergreen, speed dis*rupts*! Race Car took a big lead off of second, the shortstop and second baseman darting back and forth toward second, playing cat and mouse, trying to keep Race Car close to the base so he wouldn't swipe third too. The batter, Raul Casanova, dug in. A patient hitter, Casanova didn't offer at the first two pitches from the Dodgers' big lefty, both low and away. The right-hand hitting Raul stepped out of the batter's box and peered down at his third base coach, who was going through the signs. Raul tapped the side of his batting helmet, indicating he had gotten the sign, and dug in again. The next pitch was up and in, *way* up and in, *chin music up and in!* Raul hit the deck, flat on his back in the dirt. He got up, didn't even look at the pitcher, and dug in harder, with a vengeance, like he wanted to hit the ball into the Cumberland River! The next pitch was a blazing fast ball you could hear more than see. Raul bunted! A thing of beauty, pushed off to the right side, past the big lefty who fell off to the third base side of the mound, the ball rolled toward the second baseman, but not far enough for him to make the play, and too far for the first baseman to get it…the perfect no-man's land between first, second, and the pitcher. There is no defense for a well-placed bunt. Raul was on first and Race Car idled into third base! Raul asked for time and consulted with first base coach Jim Gunderson.

The cat-and-mouse game was on again, with Race Car taking his lead and dancing off third, making the pitcher jittery. Raul took a long lead off first too. Catchers are notoriously slow runners, due to all the squatting they do, but Raul was an exception, which had been a significant factor in signing him. The Dodgers' lefty was trying to watch Raul on first, but he was more concerned with Race Car on third. He should have focused more on the batter because pinch hitter Daito Saito *hammered* the next pitch between the center and right fielder, and it was *game over!* Race Car strolled home while lanky Raul flew around the bases. Third base coach Kevin Owens had his windmill going, waving Raul home. He scored standing up, and his teammates mobbed him at the plate! Thunderous, long-lasting applause rained down from the baseball-starved Tennesseans, some of whom had figured they'd never live long enough to see Major League Baseball in Nashville. The crowd wouldn't stop cheering until somebody pushed Saito back onto the field for a curtain call. Up in the Owners Suite, there was delirium, sheer delirium!

The players stayed in the locker room for twenty minutes before opening it up to the press. Manager Wenzel made himself available for questions and answered them patiently. Meanwhile, Rex gathered up Daito Saito and his translator, along with Florio "Race Car" Ford, to meet with reporters. Opening Day had been a marketing man's dream, and Rex was beaming.

It was just one win, out of 162 games, but man, it felt great!

★ CHAPTER 31 ★

ALL-STAR
Weekend

If the All-Star game couldn't be played in Nashville, then DC was the next best thing for the Colliers. The three months since Opening Day had zoomed by like a Nolan Ryan fastball. The Knights finished the first half in first place, a game ahead of the Braves, with the Nationals two games behind. Five Knights made the National League squad: Dancin' Danny Daneker, Florio Ford, Daito Saito, Raul Casanova, and Yoshi Nakahoma. Dancin' Danny brought an 8-1 record and a league leading ERA of 1.08; Race Car Ford had forty-three base heists, and the other three were pounding the baseball. Saito was leading the league in triples with 11 and Casanova was leading in doubles with twenty-seven. Nakahoma was living up to his name with twenty-one "Nakas," what they called his home runs in Japan, seventeen of which came on the road. The dimensions of Knights Park held down his home run totals just like they did with opposing sluggers. Some skills that set Nakahoma apart were his ability to bunt, hit behind the runner, or choke up and protect the plate, whatever the situation called for. He'd only whiffed seven times going into the All-Star break, and he was close behind his teammates in doubles and triples. Clearly, the team was constructed to fit the dimensions of the ballpark and the rules of Project Baseball.

It all circled back to the Albert Einstein quote The Rammer had dropped on them that first day at Wintergreen: "You have to learn the rules of the game, and then you have to play better than anyone else."

For the first half of the season, the Knights adhered well to the Project Baseball rules of the game, and they did play better than anyone else. The plan was working, and the sports world was taking note. A photo of the Knights' five All-Stars was on the cover of the *All-Star Official Program*, and Big T was featured on the latest cover of *Sports Illustrated* holding a baseball in one hand and a guitar in the other. The team had become a darling of America, an upstart, the underdogs, led by an aging, iconic country music star and using a strategy devised by a now almost-fifteen-year-old who had survived brain cancer. In a country full of political divide, the Nashville Knights had the best feel-good story in the news in a long time. People who weren't even baseball fans were beginning to know the name Charlie Collier and the names of some of the top Knights. Various media outlets were clamoring to get interviews with Charlie, but Rex, Martha, Big T, and the team shielded him. All requests went through Rex, who fended off almost all of them, save a couple of charity events. They had requests for Charlie to appear on *The Tonight Show*, *Good Morning America*, and the MLB network. Charlie didn't want to do any of them, except for the MLB Network, but that would come later. For now, he was just trying to be a kid and work his physical therapy so he could sprint again. He found motivation in the doctors telling him it was unlikely he'd be able to sprint—that pricked his stubborn side, launching his mission to work harder and prove them wrong.

The Colliers stayed at Uncle Frank's over the three days of All-Star festivities. Being back in Maryland was comforting and familiar. They would actually stay five nights, arriving Thursday evening and leaving Tuesday morning after the Monday night game. Big T, the five All-Stars, and the other executives also got into town Thursday night.

Fortuitously, the schedule would allow for a coffee meet-up at the Berwyn Café at 9 a.m. Friday with Uncle Frank, Dustin, Charlie, and Alfred.

Alfred was peeking out the window when Rex pulled the rental van into the Bailey driveway. Uncle Frank was riding shotgun, with Charlie occupying the backseat. He'd had his head up between the front seats, yammering excitedly since they had gotten in the car. Mr. and Mrs. Bailey came out with Alfred and walked over to the van. Mr. Bailey, the perfect gentleman, thanked Rex for inviting Alfred to go along.

Alfred jumped in the backseat. "Sus-ter!" he shouted and gave Charlie an exploding fist bump.

"Al-fred!" shouted Charlie. "It occurred to me that you don't have a nickname. Why is that?"

"I dunno," Alfred said. "Nothing ever stuck. My dad calls me Boomer, but it's because I farted so loud when I was little. He says I'd fart so loud it sounded like it should be coming from a 250-pound man; then people would turn and see me, a forty-five-pound, five-year-old boy grinning at 'em. The story he likes best is when it happened in a crowded elevator and everybody gave him the stink eye for my stinker!"

"That's hilarious—little Alfred's fart fireworks! Ah, man, that's a funny image. Farting in an elevator, now that's *wrong on many levels*!" Charlie paused to laugh at his own joke, then continued. "People don't have to know you acquired your nickname because you were *tooting* your own horn. That'll be our secret! Boomer *is* a perfectly good baseball nickname, especially for a slugger like you. When you shout 'Suster,' I can shout back 'Boom-er'! You wouldn't be nickname-less any more. Boomer Bailey has a nice ring to it, too—alliteration."

"Okay, Sus; let's try it. I'll be *Boomer Bailey*. If I don't like it after a while, I can remove the nickname, okay?"

"Deal! You gonna tell your dad the nickname he gave you is being revitalized?"

"Yeah, I'll tell him. He'll laugh. He laughs a lot more now that he doesn't drink and we've been going to church—the Saturday night service. My dad's happy again. Mom's happier, too."

"Yay! That's *great*, Boomer! You look pretty happy your *own* self!"

Alfred "Boomer" Bailey smiled.

Rex turned left onto Berwyn Road from Route 1 and passed Holy Redeemer Church and School on the right. He slowed just to take in this sacred ground that he'd walked thousands of times growing up. Rex went into tour guide mode, all for Alfred, and himself maybe, because everybody else in the van had either lived through it or, in Charlie's case, heard the story a few hundred times.

"There's the blacktop where two generations honed their hoops skills, with today's young'uns making the third generation. Over there was Ray's Variety Store, run by Mr. Ray. It was the place where we kids stopped on the way home from school and bought candy or an ice cream sandwich. Sometimes, we'd get those terrible sandwiches from The Macke Company—rubber hamburgers. Put 'em in Mr. Ray's microwave and you had yourself a meal! You remember those terrible sandwiches, Uncle Frank?"

"I didn't think they were that bad, but I'd eat anything back then. The Macke beef barbeque sandwich was pretty good. I have a *refined* palate now. Speaking of bad food, nothing was worse than those Little Death Burgers from The Little Tavern, '*10 cents apiece or buy 'em by the bag.*'"

"Yeah, they were across the street from the dorms, making money off broke college students with cast iron stomachs. Location, location, location."

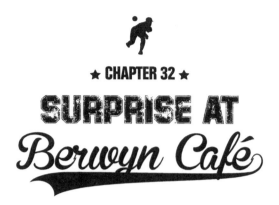

★ CHAPTER 32 ★

SURPRISE AT
Berwyn Café

Rex parked on Berwyn Road in front of The Beautiful Day Trading Company, an iconic old hippie store, just fifty feet from the Berwyn Café, on the same side of the street. The men and boys got out. The café didn't look too crowded; the seven-thirty rush had passed and the corner booth was open. Rex made a beeline for Maddy and whispered something to her. Maddy rarely whispered, and loudly said, "No way, that's not happening; you're funny though, Mr. Collier."

Dustin walked in then, said his howdy-dos, and slid into the seat by the window.

Maddy brought menus, even though the café's offerings hadn't changed for the past year and everybody except Alfred knew the menu by heart.

"What have you been up to, Maddy?" Dustin asked.

"Well, yesterday I finished recording 'Slow 'n Easy on a Beautiful Day' in the studio. Now I have to figure out how to get it out there so people can hear it; that's the hard part."

Dustin ordered his usual chocolate frappe, Frank had his water with lemon and toasted poppy seed bagel, and Rex got his sixteen-ounce Americano and a toasted sesame bagel. Alfred ordered a chocolate frappe, and always-vanilla Charlie got his vanilla frappe.

Maddy winked at Charlie and said, "Charlie, one day I'm gonna prank you with a white chocolate frappe and tell you it's vanilla; that'd freak you out, wouldn't it, Mr. Creature-of-Habit?"

"Maddy, two things: One, you can't prank me if you tell me in advance, and two, you *know* the only *creatures of habit* around here are the nuns across the street at Holy Redeemer."

"Ooh, Charlie, that was good; *quick too!* Are you gonna be punny all morning to *entertain* me?"

Six months ago, Charlie might have blushed, but now he was enjoying the attention, and tip-toeing to the edge of flirtation with the spunky redhead, two and a half years his senior.

"That would be a *dream* for you," he replied boldly, totally out of character for the humble and somewhat shy Charlie Collier.

Everybody else watched as Charlie and Maddy matched wits.

"I don't know about it being a *dream*, but you *are* punny. Speaking of dreams, last night I had a weird one; you were in it, Charlie. We were in orange kayaks. Yours said *Island Boy* on it, and mine said *Island Princess* in black letters. We paddled the kayaks into the bay, and the water was all orange. The kayaks were orange and the water was orange. Isn't that weird? Then I woke up and realized it was all just a—" Maddy stopped mid-sentence, ripped a page from her notepad, and wrote in big letters: *Fanta Sea!* "It was just a Fanta Sea, Charlie!"

Maddy the punster laughed, turned on her heels, and sashayed triumphantly to the kitchen. Charlie had a funny look on his face—the look of knowing he'd just been bested and was surprised to enjoy it so much.

The last remaining table cleared out and they had the place to themselves. The guys chewed the fat in general, and then talk turned to the Knights and how amazing their first half performance had been.

Maddy brought the drinks and bagels. Then she pulled up a chair to the end of the booth, facing the street so she'd see anybody coming in while they were still outside. She'd made herself a fancy latte, with a swirly design floating on top.

A minute later, Maddy went slack-jawed at whatever or whoever she was gazing at through the front plate glass window. "Oh, my God!"

When she said that, everyone turned to look outside to see if she'd seen Bigfoot or something. It wasn't a sasquatch, but it *was* Big T McCraw! Big T was walking toward the Berwyn Café, and he wasn't alone!

Maddy kept saying, "Oh, my God" over and over. She trembled, like people used to do with Elvis or the Beatles.

Maddy glanced sideways at Rex. "You weren't making it up."

Alfred pointed. "That's Raul Casanova, the Knights' catcher!"

Charlie yelled, "And Dancin' Danny Daneker!"

Big T, Raul, and Dancin' Danny paused on the sidewalk before coming in, giving Rex a chance to tell how it had happened. He was grinning ear-to-ear. "Man, it was hard to keep this one secret, but Big T wanted to come here, to the café, because he says it's part of the lore, the history of our franchise, and we need to recognize it as such. Even though it's in Maryland and the team is in Tennessee, the foundation upon which the team is built has roots in this region, and in this very café. Big T was going to come by himself, but everybody is staying at The Marriott, so Big T texted me this morning that he saw Raul and Danny in the hotel coffee shop and asked if they wanted to come along. I wanted it to be a surprise. Was I successful?"

"You could knock me over with a feather," Frank said.

"When we're older," Dustin said, "I mean *really* old, and we talk about all the things that happened at and around The Field, this day will be right up there at the top of the list."

Over the next two hours, the Berwyn Boys told Big T, Raul, and Danny all about growing up there, before the townhouses, when life was like the best baseball movie ever, *The Sandlot*. Big T told everyone that growing up in Oklahoma, they had a version of the Berwyn field, where the kids met up to play baseball all summer long. A few other customers came in and shockingly didn't recognize Big T, which was good.

Dustin managed to work into the conversation that their favorite barista, Maddy, wrote *and* sang her own songs and had recorded her newest one yesterday. Big T couldn't resist and asked her the big question, "So, Miss Maddy, would you sing a verse or two of your new song? What is it called?"

"It's called 'Slow 'n Easy on a Beautiful Day.'"

"Nice title."

"Mr. McCraw," Maddy said, "I'm so nervous even meeting you. I'm usually not like this; ask them. I'm too nervous to sing it now. Would it be okay if I show you on my phone? A video of me singing it?"

"Sure, Maddy! Let's take a look and a listen!"

Maddy pulled up the video on her phone, turned up the volume, and handed the phone to Big T. He paid close attention as he watched and listened to her sweet tone. When it was over, he looked directly into Maddy's eyes and said, "You're good. Keep working on your craft and please keep me current on your new songs. Keep writing. You can send me the YouTube versions. At some point, if you're good enough and keep working at it, I may be able to get some music people in Nashville to have a listen. Keep it country; don't go hip hop on me."

"Thank you, Mr. McCraw! Thank you, thank you, thank you!" And she gave him a hug, then pulled back. "I guess I should have asked first."

"Then ask!"

"Can I have a hug?"

"Of course!"

Maddy jumped in for another.

Rex and Raul were engaged in discussing the fine art of catching. Rex had caught in the minors for five years and played with some guys who had coached Raul—small world. They were talking technique and footwork. At one point, Raul got out of the booth and went into a catcher's squat to demonstrate his footwork when a runner is trying to steal second.

Big T finished off his egg sausage breakfast sandwich and coffee, and then he asked if he could get Charlie and Alfred's opinions on Major League Baseball from a kid's perspective. Specifically, he asked about the role model issue—how players might be better role models for youth. Big T probed some to get Alfred talking and the probing bore fruit.

"In our baseball games, we shake hands with the opposing team after the game. In the Big Leagues, each team shakes hands with themselves. That's not right; it sets a bad example. Why can't they shake hands with their opponents to show respect and honor the game? Even MMA fighters shake hands and hug after trying to knock each other's heads off."

"Yeah," Charlie agreed. "What a great signal that would send out. It shows respect, and without an opponent, none of us would have a game, so why not shake hands to thank them?"

Big T fell back against the back of his chair. "I've never thought about that, in all these years. Thank you, Alfred! That's a very intriguing thought. I'm going to cogitate on that. That would be another idea for the good of the game coming from this little coffee shop in Maryland. What's the name of this town again?"

"Berwyn," said Frank, Dustin, and Rex, proudly and all at once.

Big T gave a big, "DUH…. It says Berwyn Café. Guess we are in Berwyn. I'm a hick from Oklahoma; what do I know? What other good things come from Berwyn? Some good ball players?"

"Have you ever heard of Bill Werber?" Frank asked.

"Can't say as I have," Big T replied.

"Look him up; he played twelve seasons in the big leagues with the Red Sox, Reds, and Yankees; lifetime batting average of .271 with seventy-eight home runs; played third, shortstop, and left. He grew up in the house on the corner of Potomac Avenue and Berwyn Road, next to The Field. Before he passed away in 2009 at the age of ninety-nine, Werber was the last living teammate of The Babe."

"Bill Werber, great story. I'm gonna look him up. I like Berwyn, and there's one more thing I'd like to do with you boys before we head back to the Marriott. How about we play some catch? Raul and Danny told me y'all said you wanted to play catch someday when y'all talked on Opening Day. I reckon there's no time like now! We have our gloves, and I know you have yours because Rex made sure of that. I hear there's a small, grassy playground on the other side of the school that isn't a baseball diamond, but is big enough to play catch. Maybe Bill Werber even played there."

Big T paid everybody's tab and left Maddy a $100 tip before leading the group outside where they retrieved their gloves and started walking the 150 yards or so to the playground. Raul walked beside his fellow catcher, Alfred, and asked if he'd been working on blocking balls in the dirt. Alfred said yes, but he was fibbing.

They all walked across the Holy Redeemer parking lot, across Quebec Street, to the park. There were big, heavy green picnic tables—the kind it would take four burly men to pick up, a fenced-in tennis court, a set of monkey bars, two see-saws, and a patch of grass about fifty by twenty-five yards. The park was empty except for two dog-walkers. This small grassy area had been used by the little kids in the neighborhood who later graduated to playing with the big boys on The Field. The grassy area was big enough to play catch, as long as Raul and Danny didn't play major league long-toss.

On the way over, Dustin griped that he hadn't yet heard a pun from Charlie today. "What kind of puns would you like, Mister D? I have categories; I've told you some of my baseball ones, but I have brain puns, too, since I'm a brain cancer survivor. That might sound morbid, but I like to laugh at cancer. What does a brain do if it sees a friend across the street? *Brainwave!*

"Here's one more…why didn't the brain take a bath?"

"I'm not sure," said Dustin. "Maybe because the brain*waves* were washing over the tub?"

"Hmm, not a bad guess. Pretty close, Mister D, but the answer is: *It didn't want to be brainwashed!*"

Big T put his phone down on one of the 900-pound picnic tables. "Okay, guys. I gotta give you The Talk. Before we start, I want to lay down the rules. We're all gonna stretch and warm up first. Raul and Danny are used to doing that, but I want everybody to stretch together before we start slinging the ball around. And, Charlie and Alfred, you guys take it slow until we get loose. I know the deal; it's a thrill to play catch with a real major leaguer, and it's natural to want to show him you can wing it, too. That's fine; you can wing it at the end when you're good and warmed up. Okay? No injuries due to not being smart. Alfred, you're still in your season, right?"

"Yes, sir."

"So, you don't want to tweak your arm trying to throw as hard as Raul," said Big T. Then he turned to everyone and said, "Okay, so let's stretch, and then y'all play some catch. Charlie and Alfred, watch how Raul and Danny get loose. Do what they do. It's the Knights' way!"

Frank and Dustin felt like they were in one of those major league fantasy camps where fans pay to play with former players. Who would have thought two MLB All-Stars and a team owner would be on this "field" in sleepy little Berwyn? Frank looked at Dustin and said, "This is Twilight Zone freaky. What's next? We go back to the cafe and have coffee with Mike Trout and Mookie Betts?"

Dustin laughed. "Maybe Satchel Paige will come back from the other side too! He could show us how he throws his 'hurry-up' pitch!"

Raul and Danny warmed up together and started to toss the ball back and forth. Danny said, "We'll loosen up first with each other; then we'll switch off and throw with you guys."

Alfred and Charlie started to toss with each other. Dustin, Frank, and Rex played three-way catch. Big T sipped from the Dr. Pepper he had brought from the café and took a seat on one of the big picnic tables to watch his flock play catch.

After a while, the big leaguers stopped and motioned for the boys. Raul started tossing with Alfred from about fifteen feet away, backing up a step with each toss. Dancin' Danny was showing Charlie his knuckleball grip, explaining that he gripped with his fingertips, not his knuckles. He went over the mechanics of the pitch, maintaining a stiff wrist, and releasing the ball from contact points at the same time.

Then he told Charlie to give it a try, but Danny wouldn't throw Charlie his knuckleball; it just danced too much for anyone but an experienced catcher—too risky. Charlie struggled with throwing it because everybody struggles with throwing a knuckleball, but he was hooked on learning the quirkiest of all pitches from the guy who learned it from R. A. Dickey. Charlie did get a couple of "wobblers," for which Dancin' Danny gave him "atta boys." After throwing for about fifteen minutes, Big T said, "We gotta call it quits, fellas. It's been a blast, but we really have to get back to the Marriott for the festivities."

The boys didn't want the game of catch ever to end; they'd been in baseball heaven, playing catch with *real* big leaguers, *All-Stars*, no less! Alfred walked in lockstep with Raul, feeling like a big leaguer himself. Charlie did the same with Dancin' Danny, like they were just a couple of pitchers strolling to the bullpen, with Charlie working on his knuckleball grip as they walked. When they got back to their cars to go their separate ways, Rex, Frank, and Dustin each thanked Big T and the two players profusely. Frank told Raul, "Raul, you remind me of your granddaddy Paul. I saw him when he caught for the Washington Senators, back in the '70s. He was a fan favorite and the public address announcer would say, 'Now batting, Paul Casa*nooooooooova*!' Fans loved the intro and joined in every time he came to the plate. You have a zest and joy for the game like he did. You might appreciate this story—I remember waiting outside the ballpark to get autographs when I was a little kid. It was 1969 when Ted Williams managed the Senators, and after a game, your grandpa and Frank "Hondo" Howard were walking out of the ballpark with Ted right behind them. I got all three of their autographs and still have them."

"That's a great story," Raul replied. "I loved Hondo; he was my favorite player other than Grandpa and my dad. I remember going to Pompano Beach where the Senators had their spring training, and I got my picture taken with Hondo. Those were good times. They had a batboy named Mike Charbo; he took a liking to me and let me be his assistant for a few games. I still get Christmas cards from him. I've been playing baseball since I was in a diaper. I had no choice between my grandpa and daddy. But now I choose it because it's still fun. It's a kids' game, and I get paid to play it; that's the unreal part. Thanks for telling me about seeing my grandpa play and getting his autograph; I remember him preaching to me 'bout throwing behind the runner at first. His teammates and friends called him Cazzie; nobody called him Paul except announcers. He passed away in 2017 in Miami. I miss him; he was a kind man. I learned a lot from him, about catching and life."

Rex was pulling away from the curb when Dustin beeped his horn from across the street and signaled Rex to roll down his window. Dustin cupped his hands to his face and yelled, "Tell Frank that Mookie and Mike had coffee while we were playing catch! We just missed them. They sneaked in, then left out the back door."

It was wonderful for Rex and the other guys with DC ties to be back in town for the All-Star game. The first half had been a dream for MLB with the excitement of two new teams. The Raleigh franchise, in the American League, was three games over .500, in third place in the tough AL East, but the Knights, who had finished eleven games over .500, were the biggest story in the sports world.

Later that afternoon, Rex dropped Charlie and Alfred at Mr. Bill's Card Store. Mr. Bill greeted the boys with "Hi, ballplayers!" He always called kids "ballplayers." He was quirky and friendly like that. Around the corner from the back room came Loren, who was visiting from Orange

County, California, where he now owned a card store too.

Loren, remembering their names, said, "How ya doing, Charlie and Alfred? You guys looking for anything specific, or you just wanna talk some baseball today?"

"What's up, Loren?" Alfred said, feeling stupid that he couldn't come up with a more original greeting. Loren didn't help by saying, "The sky—the sky is up."

Charlie got down to business. "I'm looking to complete my 1984 Topps set, and I'm three cards short."

"Which cards do you need, my card-collecting pal?"

"Darryl Strawberry rookie card, Don Mattingly rookie card, and Cal Ripken."

"Okay, Cards #182, #8, and #490, in the order you gave them. We have two of them here and could get the third. We don't currently have the Ripken 490; this close to Baltimore, they sell quickly. We could get it, though, right, Dad?" Mr. Bill nodded.

Charlie marveled at Loren's quick mind—how he remembered their names and also knew the numbers of Topps 1984 baseball cards off the top of his head! "Wow! How'd you get so knowledgeable?"

Loren pointed his thumb in the direction of Mr. Bill and said, "Him— Dear Ol' Dad! Dad and Vin Scully passed it on to me. I'm just passing it through to the next generation. Scully was the greatest storyteller ever in baseball, and I listened to him tell hundreds of stories. How I remember numbers is beyond me. I just do."

"I get it, Loren. I have a brain that remembers numbers too."

Mr. Bill went into the back while Loren told the boys about his store in Orange County and how it was a little different from this store. Mr. Bill came back with two cards in protective sleeves that he placed on the counter. Darryl Strawberry #182 and Don Mattingly #8, face up on the glass, looking at the boys.

Mr. Bill cleared his throat. "Twenty dollars for both of them. They're worth at least that much each, but you boys have been here before, plus I like you. And Charlie, we know your story; everybody does; it's all over ESPN and everywhere. Loren and I didn't want to make a fuss, but it's an honor and a privilege to give you a great deal. We *love* what joy your Project Baseball has brought back to the game. *In fact*, this is my gift to you. Take these cards and we'll get you the Ripken #490 too. You'll have to pay for that one, but I'll give you a good deal."

"Wow! Thanks, Mr. Bill!"

The boys said their goodbyes and hurried back to Alfred's, where they would hang out like back in the old days when Charlie still lived in Maryland. Rex picked him up a little later, and they went back to Uncle Frank's. There was still this little thing called an All-Star game to be played tomorrow.

★ CHAPTER 33 ★

The Game

Everybody got up early at Uncle Frank's house and wolfed down waffles so they could catch the early train to the game. Uncle Frank made the waffles while Charlie started the morning with a joke. "What did the syrup say to the waffle?"

"I'm sliding all over you?" Rex guessed.

"Nope. I love you a waffle lot."

"Groaner!"

"Those are the best, Dad."

Uncle Frank drove to the College Park Metro Station, on the Green Line, and parked in all-day parking. When they got out of their car, they heard a familiar voice yell, "You're late!" It was Dustin, standing by the turnstiles, obviously pleased that he had beat them there. He had picked up Alfred on the way too.

"Boomer!"

"Suster!"

Rex made sure they all had enough on their fare cards and they got through the turnstiles. After only a ten-minute wait, the train approached, almost silently—a miracle of modern life. They boarded the near-empty car; College Park was the second stop on the Green Line, the first being the town of Greenbelt. After stopping at the W. Hyattsville, Fort Totten, and Georgia Avenue-Petworth stations, the car was getting full. By the time they arrived at the Navy Yard station, people were hanging off of every strap and pole. They exited there and were immediately thrust into the revelry in the streets surrounding the ballpark. There were food concession stands; vendors selling team gear, All-Star Programs, and bottles of water; a face painting booth; a dunk the clown booth; and all kinds of All-Star clothing from hats to infant outfits. Music blared through unseen speakers. Alfred and Charlie saw the radar gun booth and asked to play. The gates wouldn't open for another twenty minutes, so they got in line and paid their money. Each person got five throws. The heavy-set man with even heavier eyelids, and a full, dyed black beard, repeated to each thrower, "Go slow with the first two; then increase a little each time with the next three."

Alfred's final three throws were seventy-two, seventy-three, and seventy-seven. The old Charlie would have disregarded advice and just let 'er rip right away, but the wiser Charlie, the one who knew he was not invincible, didn't throw very hard. For one thing, he couldn't do the crow-hop like Alfred or an outfielder throwing to home plate to get momentum. He didn't have the balance anymore. The good news was that while he couldn't *sprint* yet, he *was* up to a fast jog. *Plus*, a knuckleballer, which he now considered himself, didn't have to register a certain number on the radar gun. Even so, he threw sixty-six, sixty-nine, and seventy-one just standing still.

Alfred said, "I want to throw eighty-five on the gun by the time I'm seventeen. If I do that, I might have a shot at playing baseball past high school."

"That's a great goal! I have two goals. To master the knuckleball and to *sprint* by the time I'm sixteen…. I'll be fifteen at the end of July, so I have a year and two weeks. I know I can't *master* the knuckleball—nobody masters it—but I will get good at it. I can pitch again in the sixteen- to eighteen-year-old select league in Nashville, if my balance keeps getting better. They also have lots of American Legion teams, like in Maryland."

The gates opened and the best friends gave each other a celebratory, exploding fist bump.

Rex led the group around to the Home Plate Gate on Potomac Ave. S.E. and handed the five tickets to what had to be the oldest ticket-taker in the league. His nametag said "Herman Yoder." Mr. Yoder resembled Yoda, looked to be 105, had possibly seen Walter Johnson pitch, and had a face as full of crinkly joy as Santa Claus'.

"Enjoy the game, men!"

Charlie and Alfred's chests swelled to be included in "men."

Big T had a suite for the game, so they were in the *tall cotton*, as they say in Oklahoma. Big T had given the Nationals' owner a suite for the Knights' opener, the only game on the schedule to kick off the season. Worldwide attention was on this game because of the seven Japanese players, and it being the first Midsummer Classic for the Nashville franchise. The two toughest tickets to get were the Knights' opener and the All-Star game. So the owners just traded.

Walking along the concourse, they saw Red Smithberger, the sportswriter from *The Tennessean*, walking by himself. Red saw Charlie and Rex, and altered his route to come their way. He looked happy to see someone from Nashville. "Howdy, Rex! Howdy, Charlie!"

"Hi, Red! Ain't baseball great? And *we* get paid to be this close to it."

"Yeah, the only thing better would be to be out there ourselves."

Red paused, threw his shoulders back, lifted his head upward, closed his eyes, and breathed in a deep breath through his nostrils.

"Bacon in the air! Ahh, the sweet aroma of *bacon-flavored popcorn* wafting by our sniffers, so apropos. Every ballpark is known for some type of food…Boog's barbeque in Baltimore, Dodger Dogs in LA, North Side Twist in Chicago…. *Bacon-flavored popcorn* is a perfectly good one for DC. They put pork on everything inside the Beltway!"

"You're makin' me hungry, Red!"

Red shook hands with Alfred, Frank, and Dustin. Again, Alfred felt like one of the "men."

As they were about to go to the elevator, a good-looking, seventy-ish Native American man wearing a U.S. Marine Corps hat walked toward them with respectful body language and spoke to Charlie in a soft, kind, but gritty voice. "Are you Charlie Collier?"

Charlie looked politely at the man.

"Yes, sir, I am."

"My name is William. I am from the Lakota Nation; grew up on the rez. We listened to baseball on transistor radios. I hope to get to Nashville this summer to see the Knights, my favorite team. My son works for the Oakland As and gets me great seats sometimes when I visit him, but I want to see a game in Nashville. I'm sorry. I talk too much when it comes to baseball. I just want to ask if you'd sign my baseball. I've been following everything about the Knights ever since I heard about your Project Baseball. I predict it will occupy a spot in baseball history. Would you please sign my ball?"

Charlie's first thought was that this was a prank or he was daydreaming. Somebody wanted *his* autograph? Alfred was just grinning, eyes wide in disbelief that a full-grown man was asking his pal Charlie for an autograph. Rex, Frank, and Dustin stood back, observing the surprising scene.

Charlie took the Sharpie from William and signed, "Charlie Collier" across the big sweet spot on the baseball, then handed back the pen and ball.

"Thank you, Charlie! Could I ask one more favor? Would you put *PB* somewhere by your name and today's date?'"

Charlie made the requested addition.

"Thank you, Charlie! You're making baseball better and more watchable. First place, baby, and doing it the *PB* way! It's fun to watch the bunts, hits behind the runner, and stolen bases. Not to mention just putting the ball in play instead of so many whiffs. See, I told you. I talk too much! Thank you! And thank you, gentlemen; I guess you must be Dad and the bodyguards. We didn't officially meet because I just started talking. Anyway, thanks everybody. Peace, Semper Fi, and Play Ball!"

William walked off as they waited for the elevator.

Rex, Charlie, and Alfred made it up to Big T's suite before any other autograph seekers stalked them. Dustin and Frank went to their seats behind the NL dugout. Players were all over the field, stretching and throwing while being watched by cameras, reporters, and fans. Dustin and Frank stopped by to say hi to Frank's long-time friend Brent Polkes and his wife Cheryl.

The scene in Big T's suite was a mix of music people and the baseball world. It wasn't quite the *Star Wars* bar, but it *was* a crazy scene. Red Smithberger was making the rounds talking with the Knights' executives, working on a supplement to *The Tennessean* highlighting Project Baseball, and its creator, Charlie Collier. One of Tennessee's US Senators stopped in, looking for babies or asses to kiss; finding no babies and no one willing to publicly have their ass kissed, he left quickly.

Charlie and Alfred found themselves standing alone while the adults were conversing all around them. That was fine because it gave them some time to talk among themselves about how cool and crazy this all was, like a fantasy, *a baseball fantasy*. Then, directly in their field of vision was the door to the suite, and when it opened, the fantasy continued. It was *Maddy!* And her father, Mike!

Charlie and Maddy saw each other at the same time. Charlie just stared with his silvery smile. Maddy, her dad in tow, weaved her way past everyone to get to Charlie. "Charlie! Can you believe we're here?"

Maddy hugged Charlie; it was spontaneous. Her hair brushed against his face, and he liked the girly scent of whatever she was wearing. Maddy was the hugg-*er*, Charlie the hugg-*ee*.

"Hi, Mr. Dullum!"

"Hi, Charlie! Hi, Alfred!" said Maddy's dad. "Yeah, this is quite a shock. Big T sent us two tickets in the mail at the café, right out of the blue. He included a note and said he enjoyed talking with Maddy about her music. Where is Mr. McCraw? We want to thank him."

Just then, Big T came back into the suite, and he weaved the same path past the celebrities. He went right over to Maddy and Mike, stuck out his big right hand, and said, "Thanks for being here!"

"No, thank *you*!"

"It's my pleasure. I enjoyed meeting your lovely daughter Maddy at the café and listening to her song, 'Slow 'n Easy on a Beautiful Day.' What ya working on now, Ms. Country Singer/Songwriter?"

"I can't believe you even remember the title! This one is different from 'Slow 'n Easy'; it's more a fun song, along the lines of Kenny Chesney, Brad Paisley, or Jimmy Buffett. It's called, 'If You Bring the Razzle, I'll Bring the Dazzle.' My dad helped me with the melody; he's a musician too. It's a fun, goofy song."

"I do play some guitar," said Mike, "but I identify as a baseball player; once a baseball player, always a baseball player."

"I know what you mean, Mike," Big T said. "We *seamheads*—that's how we define ourselves—will always be baseball players. I don't think of myself first as a singer/songwriter, no matter how many platinum records they toss at me. I'm a baseball player first, even though I never played pro ball. Let me give you my cell number, Maddy, and you can send me a recording of 'You Bring the Razzle, I'll Bring the Dazzle.' I'm excited to hear it. You've got a memorable title."

"Yeah, the refrain, 'If you bring the razzle, I'll bring the dazzle,' is repeated several times in the song. People tell me it stays in their heads."

"I'll give you my take after I hear the song. Let me write my cell number down so you can send *your songs* to me…a phone number on a napkin; that's never happened before." He laughed.

"Wow! Thank you *so* much!"

Maddy entered Big T's number into her cell with shaky fingers and promised not to give it out to anyone. She couldn't believe her good fortune—that a music *legend* had just given her his phone number!

Meanwhile, Charlie and Alfred found the best perch in the suite from which to watch the game. Maddy and her dad came over to join them, which pleased Charlie. A local Fire Department captain sang a beautiful rendition of the National Anthem and the game was on. It started as a pitcher's duel, with no score after two innings of play. The American League scored three runs in the third inning and another two runs in the fourth. At the end of the fourth inning, the public address announcer said, "At the end of four innings of play, our score is the American League five, the National League nothing."

Up in the suite, Kate leaned over to Big T. "Did you hear what he just said?"

"What? The score?"

"Yes, he said five to *nothing*!" That doesn't sound nice; our guys already know they're losing; he didn't have to say *nothing*; that might make them feel bad."

Big T just shook his head at his beautiful Kate, who always strove to make others feel better, but clearly did not have a competitive bone in her body.

"My sweet Kate, if they hear five to *nothing* and it bothers them, maybe they'll get their asses in gear and focus more so they won't have *nothing* in another inning or two!"

Kate just smiled; they'd had discussions like this before.

The National League came back and scored four in the bottom of the fifth with Knights Daito Saito and Yoshi Nakahoma teaming up for the first two runs. Saito led off with a checked-swing hit over the first baseman's head that hit the foul line and rolled into foul territory. He ended up standing on second base with a double. Richard McCowen grounded out to second, moving Saito up to third. Then Nakahoma *crushed* a pretty good curve ball for a two-run "Naka"! Pinch-hitting specialist Hubie Stockhausen came up next and drew a walk, which brought the league leader in hits, Brian Madden, to the plate. He took the first two pitches for balls, waiting on a pitch he could hit. The third pitch was the one. Madden hit it for the second home run of the inning, adding two runs and bringing the NL to within one run of the lead. The next two hitters were retired and the score after five innings was 5-4, AL in front.

Big T put his arm around Kate. "Now, baby, do you *feel* better? They don't have *nothing* anymore."

"Yes, I do feel better, and they feel better, too!"

He let out a hearty laugh and said, "I sure love my girlee!"

"Love you more," she cooed, snuggling against his shoulder.

Charlie got a text from Jimmy Ryan, who was at the game with his brother Pat, Billy Holiday, Taylor Tobias, Steve Dudrow, and Marty Hoover. Marty's dad, Gary, had gotten tickets down the right field line in the third row, and brought six of the guys from the team. Charlie and Alfred met them on the concourse for a quick hello between the sixth and seventh innings.

In the top of the seventh, the American League got a two-out rally going and had runners on first and third when Raul Casanova did exactly what his granddaddy Paul preached to him—throw behind the runner. Raul snapped a rocket of a throw to the first baseman, without getting out of his crouch, and caught the runner flat-footed. By the time he recognized what was happening, it was too late; the tag had been slapped on him. Raul had a little celebratory strut, fist pump with his catcher's mask. His granddaddy was smilin' somewhere!

The National League manager had been saving Danny Daneker for the later innings and brought him in to pitch the eighth. Danny's knuckleball was *dancing* all over the place. He struck out the first two batters he faced, who swung wildly at the floaters, and recorded the final out on a weakly-hit dribbler to the first baseman. In the bottom of the eighth, the NL bats came alive. Raul Casanova led off the inning with a hard-earned walk, fouling off three pitches with a 3-2 count, before taking ball four, low and outside.

Race Car Ford, who, at eighteen was the youngest All-Star, had not yet entered the game; he now came in to pinch run for Raul. Everyone in the ballpark knew Race Car was put in the game at this moment for one reason: to steal. Race Car looked ready and eager. The pitcher and catcher didn't look ready or eager—they looked nervous and uneasy—and they asked the umpire for time to talk. The infielders came in to join the conversation, which was, no doubt, about how to keep Race Car from stealing. He went on the first pitch. It was a pitch-out, but he beat the throw anyway! Who steals on a pitch-out? Speed dis*rupts!*

Race Car took a huge lead off second. The pitching coach asked the umpire for time; time was granted, and the pitching coach walked to the mound to talk strategy with the pitcher. They looked nervous and uneasy, *again*. Speed dis*rupts!*

Florio had his eye on third. If he could advance to third, a sacrifice fly or passed ball would tie the game! He went on the third pitch and made it with room to spare. The next two hitters popped up and struck out. Two outs, and up steps Race Car's teammate, Daito Saito, who entered the game in the fifth when he doubled and scored on Naka-homa's home run, or "Naka."

Daito, hitting from the right side, had a fabulous first half in part because he was not predictable. He was sometimes very patient; other times, he'd "ambush" the first pitch when the pitcher thought he wouldn't be swinging. He'd been patient on his first trip to the plate and ended up doubling on a checked-swing.

Daito peered down at the third base coach, hand-signaling him to go through the signs again. He did, and Daito stepped back into the batter's box, digging in, deep in the box. He was ready. He was in *ambush mode* and hunting a fastball on the outer half.

There it was! When the ball hit the sweet spot perfectly, you hardly felt it. It was a beautiful thing when it happened, and it had just happened! Daito and everybody else watched as the ball rocketed off his bat toward and then over the right-center field wall. The outfielder took one step back and that was it; it got out in a hurry and the National League pulled ahead 6-5 as they went into the final frame.

The NL manager decided to send Dancin' Danny out to close out the game, since he'd done so well in the eighth, and his knuckler appeared to be unhittable. That proved to be the case as he struck out the side to end the game—a game in which all five Knights players had made significant contributions and Daito Saito was named MVP. In a season where the Nashville Knights have been the talk of baseball, it was fitting that the All-Star game would be their story too.

After the game, Red Smithberger was in the locker room feverishly scribbling on a yellow legal pad. He was old-school like that. He went from player-to-player, getting quotes. The title of his column the next day was "The Genius Who Saved Baseball." In it, he dissected the All-Star game, with a lens on the individual Knights players, and how they had won the game for the National League. Then, he pointed out that these players probably wouldn't even be in the major leagues if not for Project Baseball and its creator, Charlie Collier. Smithberger made the case that the teen genius was saving the national pastime.

★ CHAPTER 34 ★

Media Frenzy

Sixteen months later....

Most people would be happy to make the World Series for the second year in a row and force a game seven against the mighty American League champs. Big T McCraw and his Knights weren't most people, though. They had expected not only to make it to the World Series, but to win it. Making it as far as they had was only surprising to others. Losing in game seven had left a lasting sting. Now, here they were again, for the second year in a row, tied three games to three in the World Series, with game seven to be played in Nashville tomorrow.

Project Baseball had done for the Knights exactly what Charlie and the team had envisioned. They had won 119 games in their first year, breaking the MLB record for most wins in a season. Over the offseason, the Knights were approached by every free agent pitcher of note. Charlie had predicted that number-one starting pitchers would clamor to join the Knights' staff to get the chance to pitch every fourth day, and not be held to crazy pitch count limits. Consequently, the Knights picked up three ace starters to add to Dancin' Danny Daneker, which gave them the most formidable starters in the game. They added southpaws Anderson Boulet from the Royals and Adam Owens from the Mariners. Then they picked up another steal from Japan, their top change-up pitcher of all-time, thirty-seven-year-old right-hander Soji "So-Slow" Watanabe. An interesting fact was that none of them could throw over 95 mph; instead, each was masterful at changing speeds, and collectively, having the lowest base-on-balls ratio in the league. That was strategy straight from the Project Baseball playbook.

The Knights' skipper, Larry Wenzel, pushed the right buttons all season long, and the players were one, big happy family. Of course, winning 119 games makes for a lot of happiness, but it was more than that. They were having fun! It had been an exciting season throughout *all* of baseball. Baseball was cool again, and it had become fashionable with young people. Charlie and his story had captured the nation. Segments had aired on ESPN and other networks about Project Baseball and its teenage whiz kid. That Charlie was a reluctant interviewee, and being protected by the team and his parents, only served to bring more attention to him as an oddity, rather than a wholesome, now sixteen-year-old boy. It was easy to view him as an oddity because of all he had already accomplished in his short life, including surviving brain cancer. Even in the past year, he'd managed to earn an MBA online from highly regarded Babson College in Massachusetts.

Charlie could now run "good enough"—not a full sprint like his pre-cancer self, but fast enough that he had played American Legion baseball in Nashville over the summer, excelling as his team's top pitcher. Between a growth spurt and hard work in the gym, Charlie was now a lean, muscular 6' 1" and 180 pounds. A couple of big league scouts took note of him at one of his games when they were scouting a slugging third baseman on the opposing team. Charlie struck out the stud slugger three times and got him out on a weak grounder the other time. The scouts didn't realize, until they spoke to Charlie's Legion coach Richard Pyle after the game, that the pitcher was *the* Charlie Collier, the whiz kid creator of Project Baseball.

Try as Charlie might to avoid attention, the team had experienced relentless media pressure to hear from Charlie himself, especially during the World Series. He'd captured the hearts of sports and non-sports fans alike. The public and the press wanted more—more Charlie—and the more he was shielded, the more reporters pressed to land an interview. Most of the requests were directed to Timothy Ramage, where they ran into the curmudgeonly brick wall, except when Big T McCraw called for an exception.

To relieve the pressure, Big T scheduled a press conference for himself and the Knights' "brain trust," composed of Charlie Collier, GM Kurt Grimmer, and skipper Larry Wenzel. Big T knew the public wanted to hear more about the Knights from all four of them, but the keen interest was on Charlie, who was everybody's darling. The Knights' play-by-play announcer, Jon Grobins, called it Charlie-mania, and likened it to the beginnings of Fernando-mania, which older Dodgers fans would remember. Surrounding Charlie with Kurt, Larry, and himself was Big T's way of protecting Charlie so he didn't have to face the press alone.

Knights Park at Riverfront, the pride of Nashville, has a beautiful press room with comfy seating for about eighty reporters. This day, at least 100 reporters were crowded into the room with the overflow standing wherever they could. Looking "'cowboy fine'" in his pressed dark blue jeans, Rios of Mercedes smooth ostrich boots with goat leather tops, light blue San Juan Western shirt, and a silver Stetson with a thin black hatband atop his head, Big T led his group onto the platform. He took the far left seat at the table, with Charlie, Larry, and Kurt to his right. He took off the Stetson and laid it before him, fluffing out his silver curly locks. The reporters had been briefed by Marketing Director Rex Collier just moments before that Big T would make a statement first, then open it up for questions.

The Nashville icon smoothed out his shirt, took a sip of his signature Dr. Pepper, and adjusted his silver cross necklace.

"Welcome to Nashville, you baseball lovers, you! I was gonna make some opening remarks, but let's just open it up for questions. Raise your hand, and if I point to you, Ms. Scully will walk the microphone over. Most of you don't know her; she's an executive assistant with our team, and Vin Scully's distant cousin. When you ask your question, let us know which of us the question is for and which organization you're from."

Hands shot up and Big T pointed to a reporter in the third row.

"Gary Gubisch, *Hollywood Tribune*," said the reporter once Ms. Scully brought him the microphone. "My question is for Charlie. Charlie, how has your life changed with all this Charlie-mania? Are you able to be a normal teenager?"

Charlie spoke directly into the mic. "I'm 99.7 percent sure I'm within three standard deviations from the mean, which means I'm technically in the normal category. You might recognize that as the bell curve. I *do* have my learner's permit now; that's pretty normal. As far as the mania thing, I don't pay attention to the news much, by choice. I prioritize. Pride goeth before the fall."

Big T pointed to one of the standing reporters.

"Julie Clark, *Seattle Times*," she said. "My question is also for Charlie. Charlie, you might not be watching all the Charlie-mania, but you're becoming a heartthrob for lots of girls. I heard that you have a girlfriend; is that true?"

"That would be fake news, ma'am." (The panel stifled their grins.)

The reporter pressed on in an annoying tone, walking right up to the line of being too personal with a minor. "Are you dating?"

Charlie answered quickly, before Big T had time to run interference and cut the reporter off at the pass. "I have three main focuses beyond faith and family—playing baseball, getting my driver's license, and taking flying lessons. I'm too busy to date. Besides, the only perk of being with me would be that I laugh at my own jokes, so she wouldn't have to." That made the whole room smile—another of Charlie's gifts.

Big T beamed at seeing his young protégé handle the press like a seasoned pro. He pointed to a reporter in the front row for the next question.

"Gary Sommers, *Pittsburgh Post*," said the reporter. "My question is also for Charlie. How did you originally come up with the idea for Project Baseball?"

"That's an interesting question. It was over a couple of years, as I watched the overuse of analytics make games nearly unwatchable. I got madder and madder. All that play-by-play announcers seem to talk about was and still is *pitch count, launch angles, exit velocity, and spin rate*. Who cares if the ball spins 2,689 times on the way to the plate, as I heard a play-by-play guy say recently? When I had a project due for my statistics professor, I decided to prove that analytics has decreased a team's chance of winning due to the loss of instinctual play. A more colloquial way—more fun way—to say it is analytics is a pile of hogwash. So I made my case, backed it up with data, and can you believe my professor gave me a C–?" Charlie looked directly at the camera with the red light on and gave a little wave, "Hi, Professor Jacobs!"

Everyone laughed!

Big T chose another questioner from the middle of the pack.

"Vince St. John, *ESPN*. Charlie, you mentioned playing baseball yourself. Can you tell us a little more about that?"

"I love playing baseball more than anything," Charlie replied. "I pitch, and I'm just trying to take it as far as I can. I'm mostly a knuckleball pitcher; Dancin' Danny tutors me. It's hard because I can't play for a high school or college since I don't attend one. I play in the best summer leagues I can find. I'm hoping next summer to pitch in a college-age wood bat league. There's a team in Maryland, The Germantown Black Rox, whose owner, Buddy Gibson, invited me to try out. I'm being asked too many questions. I'm not the deal here. I hope you have some for Mr. McCraw, Mr. Grimmer, and Mr. Wenzel."

"You beat me to the punch, Charlie," Big T spoke into the mic. "Let's hear some questions for Larry and Kurt."

Big T pointed to another standee, a familiar one.

"Red Smithberger, *The Tennessean*," said the reporter. "This question is for everyone not named Charlie." The line got some laughs. "Would you each tell us something we don't likely know about the team and your journey over the last two years?"

They all looked at each other, like, *Who wants to take that one?*

After a few seconds, GM Kurt Grimmer broke the silence. "You may not know that the team put unique clauses in players' contracts to pay them specific sums for executing what is emphasized in Project Baseball. As one example, we pay $5,000 extra, on top of salary, for every successful bunt. We built in other incentives too, like paying $3,000 every time a player has ten straight at-bats without striking out. Pitchers are paid $3,500 whenever they pitch nine consecutive innings, which can be in different games, and walk fewer than three in that nine-inning stretch. Those aren't the only incentives, just some examples."

Larry Wenzel leaned forward on his elbows with arms folded and pushed his glasses higher on the bridge of his nose. "You know, there's been an awful lot written and reported on about our team, so most of our story has been out there already. But there is an aspect people don't know, and that's the behind-the-scenes decisiveness that the big guy with the cowboy clothes brings. Before we ever took the field for the first time, he made the executive decision to follow the strategies developed by a teenager. Who else would have done that? He could have taken little bits and pieces of the plan and tested it out, gone slow with it. Instead, he decided to go all in, and here we are, playing the seventh game of the World Series for the second year in a row. Had he not been so bold, we couldn't have done it. Something else we can all be proud of is that Big T had the idea to establish

Charlie's Kids Foundation. Over two million dollars has already been raised and the foundation is having a big impact already. Some things are even bigger than baseball. The community is blessed to have an owner like Big T McCraw."

"That's kind of you to say, Larry," Big T replied. "You were steady at the helm all season, and last year too. All in all, we have a great team, not just the players, and yes, we want to do good work in the community too. Timothy Ramage, Butch Dory, and Wally Rupp aren't up here taking questions, but their contributions have been enormous too. And Charlie, your story has been the breath of fresh air the game needed. It's been a great ride and we have Game 7 tomorrow."

"Who's starting for you tomorrow?" a reporter shouted.

"I'll defer to Larry Wenzel for that answer," Big T replied.

Larry played it coy. "It'll be Dancin' Danny or Anderson Boulet. We'll see whose stuff looks the best in warm-ups and make a game time decision. That keeps our opponents guessing, not knowing if they're facing a righty or lefty, a knuckleballer or a curveball artist."

Big T picked up his Stetson as a getting-ready-to-leave signal. "Thank y'all for being here. I think we'll end it here and go prepare for one of the biggest days in Nashville history."

He stood up and positioned his Stetson perfectly. Charlie, Larry, and Kurt stood too, and they all exited stage left, as reporter Julie Clark screeched, "When will we see Charlie again?"

They ignored the question.

Walking down the hall, back to the clubhouse, Charlie said aloud,

"Wow; what's up with asking me about girlfriends? I didn't expect that."

Kurt laughed. "Not easy being a heartthrob, huh?"

"The only thing I can figure was that Clark reporter lady saw Maddy hugging me at the All-Star game. She's got a loud voice too—Julie Clark, I mean."

Kurt chuckled. "You know, you're right. I remember seeing her come into the suite for a few minutes. You're always being watched, Charlie!"

Big T looked at Charlie. "Get used to it, rookie!"

★ CHAPTER 35 ★

Game 7

Boomer Bailey was bummed he couldn't go to Nashville for the World Series. The next best thing was watching with five of his teammates (and Charlie's former teammates) at Marty Hoover's house on a super-high definition Samsung 75" Q90R television.

"Hey, guys," said Boomer, "can we listen to the Knights' radio play-by-play guy Jon Grobins? I've been doing that all season and he's good, way better than the blather of Joe Buck and Bob Costas. Can we mute the sound on the TV and listen to the radio on my tablet? His play-by-play makes you feel like you're there. He talks about Charlie sometimes too."

Marty muted the TV, and Mr. and Mrs. Hoover came in with chicken wings and plates for everyone. On the billboard-sized TV screen, Larry Wenzel and the Yankee manager, Howard Mackert, were meeting with the home plate umpire, going over ground rules. The players were ready, fans in the ballpark were ready, and people in living rooms all over America were ready.

And then it happened.

Larry Wenzel went berserk, throwing his hat on home plate and going nostril-to-nostril with the umpire, screaming, red in the face. He stomped, kicked dirt, making a cloud of swirling dust, and then looked up at the sky for guidance. Alfred said what everyone was thinking: *What's this about? The game hasn't even started yet.* He turned up the volume on his tablet so they could hear what the play-by-play guy was saying:

> **Grobins:** I'm not sure what's going on down there. Knights Skipper Larry Wenzel is beside himself at the ground rules meeting! He's in home plate umpire Jeff Wendstat's face! Wow, this is a shock! Okay, now the skipper's walking away, heading to the dugout. Oops, now he's turned around again, walking back toward Wendstat, screaming even louder! Yankee manager Mackert is getting out of the way, moving closer to his on-deck circle, putting space between him and the potential Mixed Martial Arts action. If Larry's not careful, he's gonna get tossed before the National Anthem! Oh, boy. This is not good. Assistant Coach Kevin Owens is doing his best to restrain him. I've never seen anything like this before a game started. It looks like er, he may be, um…. Okay, I may have figured out what it's about. The skipper now appears to be demonstrating a batter leaning into a pitch. In Game 5, when Wendstat was behind the plate, a couple of the Yankees made no effort to avoid getting hit, yet were awarded first base. This is especially tempting against the low-speed knuckleball since the batters have no risk of injury. I think maybe Larry is ques-

tioning that and telling him to watch for it. I don't know what was said to make it get so out of hand, but the skipper would probably be gone already if this weren't Game 7. Blue's giving him a lot of leash, and he's taking all of it. There you go; it looks like Larry has had his say, didn't get tossed, and is now heading to the dugout, to the cheers of the Knights' faithful!

The boys—Alfred, Marty, Steve Dudrow, Jimmy, and Pat Ryan—were staring in disbelief. Alfred said, "I met Larry Wenzel, and he seemed so mellow; you know, he's a minister too."

Mrs. Hoover had her own interpretation, "Well, it looks like the minister is possessed and doing an exorcism on himself."

Pat said, "I noticed he was wearing a cross when he walked out." Younger brother Jimmy added, "And he grabbed it to his chest, probably praying to keep his cool."

"Let's not make this about religion. It's baseball. This is baseball, the World Series," Marty stated.

"Baseball *is* religion," Mr. Hoover countered.

"Well, then, let's thank God for baseball," Mrs. Hoover rightly said, putting it to rest.

Back in Nashville, a decorated war hero walked to the microphone behind home plate to thunderous applause and sang the National Anthem from the heart. Tears of patriotism welled up among the 67,000 in the ballpark, and in living rooms across America. As the singer extended the final note on impressive lungpower, the Blue Angels roared overhead, tipping their wings in tribute to America.

In College Park, in the Hoovers' family room, everyone stood, hands over hearts. When it was over, Mr. Hoover said, "God bless America." Boomer Bailey shouted, "Play ball!"

Larry Wenzel had kept the Yankees guessing on who his starter would be as long as possible. He had Dancin' Danny and Anderson Boulet throwing leisurely in the bullpen, even though he already knew his starter would be Boulet. The best lefty to come out of Louisiana since Ron Guidry, Boulet has a devastating curveball, sneaky fastball, and an occasional old school pitch he called an in-shoot.

> **Grobins:** The Cagey Cajun, southpaw Anderson Boulet, from Broussard, Louisiana, goes into his windup, and Game 7 is underway. Strike one to the Yankee leadoff hitter George Hollis, a fastball on the outside corner. Boulet doesn't play around out there on the mound. He pitches like he has a plane to catch. The big lefty drops down sidearm with the in-shoot, swing, and a miss! Hollis steps out, adjusts himself, and digs back in, buying time and trying to slow down the big lefty's pace. Boulet looks in for the sign from Casanova, shakes one off, now nods in agreement. He kicks and delivers…. Oh, my! Strike three on the Louisiana Loop, Boulet's knee-buckling curve ball! Unhittable, a nasty pitch! That ball started at eye level and dropped to the knees like it fell off a table. Some of the old-timers used to call that pitch a 'drop.' Hollis is left standing at the plate, bat on his shoulder, staring at nothing, not believing what he just saw. Finally, he walks back to the dugout, saying something to the next hitter as he walks by. Boulet calls that pitch the Louisiana Loop because it curves so much it almost loops back around like a wiffle ball. If you're

listening on the radio and not seeing the break, think Clayton Kershaw's curve ball, only better. If his curve ball's this good today, we should see lots of Yankee hitters muttering to themselves. The Pin Stripers are fortunate to still be in the series. Their three wins all came at Yankee Stadium with their short fences; their five home runs would be routine outs here. The Yankees have yet to prove they can adapt and play the style of baseball that Knights Park at Riverfront was built for. Double Fenway might be their undoing.

Back in the Owners Suite, the Knights' executives and their families were all mingling comfortably with some of the Nashville music crowd…Joe Bob Dupree, Haley McClanahan, Big Daddy Putnam, and T-Man Wiley.

Rex, Martha, and Charlie were sitting with Smokey Fields and his granddaughter Sam. Charlie was in baseball heaven. Who wouldn't be when their team was in Game 7 of the World Series? It was more than baseball, though. Since moving to Nashville two years ago, Charlie had developed a love of country music, so he was in country music heaven, too, being around all the stars. Timothy Ramage and Rebecca Scully came over to join them.

The Rammer whispered, "Can you believe all the stars here? I met Haley McClanahan last year; she remembered my name, she's so sweet."

Rebecca, like she often does, offered a loving but sarcastic counter. "So, somebody remembers your name and they're sweet? Haley really *is* sweet, but you like anybody who remembers you, Jimothy."

"Thank you, *Your Royal Snarkiness*. Kind of you to notice; glad you're so *interested* in me."

"Yes, Jimothy, I am interested in you. As law enforcement would say, you are a *person of interest.*"

"Am I the most interesting person in the room?"

Rex answered that question. "Well, Timothy, not anymore; perhaps the most interesting man in the room just sneaked in and nobody noticed."

"Who's that, Rexy?" Martha asked.

Rex nodded toward the corner. "Over there with his back to us, in the black hat, talking to Big Daddy and T-Man Wiley." As the smallish, older man in the black hat turned a bit, they saw his profile. From the side view, he was unmistakable—the greatest songwriter ever, Bob Dylan. Smokey's jaw dropped, "Oh, my God! Bob Dylan *is here!*" Rebecca Scully stunned them all by saying, "Who's Bob Dylan?"

Dead silence. Finally, Timothy cocked his head, and scrunching his face like he felt pain, said, "What did you say"?

"Who's Bob Dylan?" she repeated with a hint of a smile, as if realizing the joke might be on her.

Rex took a deep breath, exhaling audibly. "Dylan is the Babe Ruth of songwriting…The Sultan of Song, The Colossus of Prose, The Great Bamlingo!"

Recovering, Scully murmured, "I think I've heard of him."

"We'll talk later. You're in for a treat to learn his music," Timothy said with a kindness he reserved for Rebecca.

Then Dylan looked in their direction and gave a small wave; at least it looked like it might have been a wave. He lifted his hand slightly upward along with the subtlest nod. Like his lyrics, his wave, if it was one, was subject to interpretation. Rebecca, Timothy, and Smokey saw the same thing. Timothy and Smokey did *not* interpret it as a wave, but Rebecca *did*, and waved back at him. Simultaneously, Big T appeared behind them. "Louie, come on over here for a sec!" Big T, standing behind them, had been the one "Dylan" had waved to. As the man approached, it became clear he was merely a look-alike. "Thanks for coming by, Louie. Great to see you; been a while. Let me introduce you to my friends, the Colliers—Rex, Martha, and Charlie. And Timothy Ramage and Rebecca Scully. Meet Louie Goldstein, financial planner for half the stars in Nashville." Louie smiled and nodded politely to each of them, knowing whom they had mistaken him for. "Happens all the time," he said. "I've even had people threaten to beat me up for not signing autographs; they don't always believe I'm not him." Rebecca somehow didn't feel quite as silly.

Back at the Hoovers, they were cheering every pitch and listening to Grobins' play-by-play. The game went into the bottom of the fourth, deadlocked at zero. The Knights had managed only two hits: a bunt single and a double. Anderson Boulet, the cagey Cajun, retired the first nine Yankees, striking out five. Mrs. Hoover brought out more wings, while Mr. Hoover popped open a can of Natty Boh beer—a Maryland tradition. The fourth was a big inning, as the Knights put four runs on the scoreboard with two bunt singles, a sacrifice bunt, a double, and a triple. The team had practiced bunting every day—100 bunts a day—like basketball teams practice free throws, and it had paid off again. They were bunting with precision. The mighty Yankees looked frustrated, unable to defend against the strategy. Boulet continued his dominance in the fifth, walking one, but not yet allowing a hit. A run-saving, diving catch in left by September call-up Derek Thielen, a local kid from Sweet Water, Tennessee, made the third out.

As the game moved on, the mood at the Hoovers' house was getting tense and giddy with anticipation. The Knights were close to being World Champions—just four more innings. Alfred's phone pinged; it was Charlie texting, telling him about the scene in the Owners Suite. Just when Alfred read the text out loud, the television cameras zeroed in on the Owners Suite. Mr. Hoover turned up the volume on the TV to hear what the announcers were saying. Joe Buck was talking about the mix of baseball and music people, and he mentioned the stars by name as the camera scanned the suite. When the camera zoomed onto the youngest face in the suite—Charlie's—Bob Costas made a rare interesting comment: "That young man, who just got his driver's license, is the youngest MLB executive, ever." Everyone at the Hoovers erupted in applause, whooping and hollering at seeing their pal Charlie on TV. Costas said Charlie reminded him of a modern-day Joe Nuxhall, who at fifteen, had been the youngest player ever to play in a major league game. That was in 1944, during World War II. "We're watching history," Costas said. "Nobody could have imagined a teenager would change the game of baseball like young Charlie Collier has."

The Yankees scored a run in the sixth on back-to-back doubles by Mike Farmer and Rob Mirrione, making the score 4-1. Mirrione, acquired mid-season from Tampa Bay, had been the Yankees' hottest hitter in the second half. Anderson Boulet was still baffling batters with his *Louisiana Loop* curveball, catching two more hitters looking.

Grobins: Ladies and gentlemen, Anderson Boulet has the best curveball this announcer has ever seen. The dang thing looks like it's about to hit 'em in the head and ends up at the knees on the outside corner. And if they adjust and lean that way, he surprises them with that nasty in-shoot. As we head toward the seventh inning with the Knights up 4-1, we'll avoid the commercial break and welcome into the booth Mr. Red Smithberger, baseball writer for *The Tennessean*. Welcome, Red!

Red: Thanks, Jon! What a thrilling time to be a baseball fan, especially a Knights fan!

Grobins: Red, you've watched the Knights all season, like I have. What are your thoughts about this team, and why have they been so successful on the field and at the box office?

Red: It comes down to two people, Charlie Collier and Big T McCraw. You and I know Charlie a bit, so we see what an unassuming, in some ways normal, kid he is, but we also know he created Project Baseball, and it is a masterpiece. A masterpiece we're seeing played out right here in the World Series. The game itself is becoming more beautiful as some other teams strive to copy Charlie's strategies, so we owe the kid a great debt. Games are more fun to watch now. Look at the beautiful bunting in this game. And I credit Big T McCraw because he was bold, decisive, and went all-in, betting on a then-fourteen-year-old genius whiz kid. And we can't forget, the kid beat brain cancer!

The whooping and hollering got even louder at the Hoovers' as they listened to Red Smithberger and Grobins talk about their pal and former teammate.

The pre-game Larry Wenzel tirade was just a warmup for the seventh inning. The cagey Cajun, Anderson Boulet, had another 1-2-3 inning with a lot of help on defense in the top of the inning. Right fielder Larry Hardy and first baseman Ryan Greenen each made spectacular plays, robbing Yankees George Hollis and Tyler "Clutch" Martindale of extra base hits.

> **Grobins:** Okay, baseball people, here we go! The Knights would love nothing more than to pad their lead right here. They'll send Yoshi Nakahoma to the plate. He'll face the great Yankee closer Justin Kase. The Yankees are going all out by bringing in their closer this early. The hard-throwing right-hander hasn't been scored upon in his last twenty-seven innings. Nakahoma is 2 for 3 today with a bunt single and a double. He stands in the very back of the batter's box and digs at the white chalk. The Yankee righty goes into his wind-up and Yoshi takes for strike one. Yoshi didn't like the call and steps out, shaking his head, saying something to umpire Jeff Wendstat, who motions for Yoshi to get in the box and hit. Yoshi digs in again, a little closer to the plate this time. Kase peers in for his sign, nods, kicks, and delivers, and Nakahoma fouls it straight back with a vicious swing! Oh, my! He just missed that one. That runs the count to two balls, two strikes for the leadoff man here in the bottom of the seventh with the Knights leading 4 to 1. If you're just joining us, it's been a well-played game and the electricity of the moment is as great as any I've ever experienced in the world of sport. Nakahoma is looking down at the third base coach, who is going through his signs.

There appears to be some confusion, so Coach Kevin Owens goes through them again. Yoshi nods, restraps his gloves, and steps back into the box. Kase toes the rubber and goes into his windup as Yoshi steps out again. Kase delivers the pitch anyway, way high. Strike three called! Jeff Wendstat just rung up Yoshi on a pitch head-high; he must not have granted time and then stepped out of the box, which would be an automatic strike. Oh, my! Here comes Larry Wenzel running out of the dugout, flailing his arms like he's having a seizure. The skipper and Wendstat are in each other's faces again, and Kevin Owens is playing bouncer again, trying to pull Larry away. First base umpire and crew chief, Mike Nance, steps between the two like a referee stepping between fighters. Larry seems to be losing some steam and turns to walk away. Never mind; now he's going after him again. He's got more rant in him; his mouth is going a mile a minute. Let's see if we can pick up anything from the microphone behind home plate. Larry is jabbing his finger in Wendstat's face and shouting something. "And you're pigeon-toed too!" (Lots of laughter.) That's got to go down as one of the weirdest things a manager ever shouted at an umpire. In case you couldn't hear that out there in radio land, skipper Larry Wenzel lost the argument, but as he left, he jabbed his finger in Wendstat's face and yelled, "And you're pigeon-toed too!" Well, that was entertaining; now back to baseball. Ryan Greenen, Knights first baseman, steps to the plate. Greenen is a switch-hitter who likes to slap the ball the other way when hitting from the left side.

Back at the Hoovers', they watched as Greenen laid a perfectly placed drag bunt down the third base line that died where nobody had a play. He promptly stole second, Raul Casanova popped out, and Daito Saito walked, which brought Florio "Race Car" Ford to the plate with two outs and runners on first and second.

> **Grobins:** Race Car Ford has been an amazing story, all year long. The youngest player in the league and an MVP candidate in just his second year, Florio set all-time marks for doubles, triples, and stolen bases while still a teenager. You gotta love the name too, and the story behind it. He changed his name from Florio Rodriquez to Florio Ford as a tribute to his stepdad, Herman Ford, who raised him. The Yankee defense is expecting a bunt. The first and third basemen are way up on the grass, playing very close-in, double-dog daring Florio to bunt. Florio shortens up on the bat to bunt, but pulls back. Ball one! Justin Kase looks in for his sign, kicks, and delivers. Ball two! Race Car was showing bunt again, and the corner infielders were still creeping in, double-dog daring him. Race Car steps out of the box and looks down toward third base coach Kevin Owens longer than usual. He's getting back in the box, looking cool and composed, especially for a recently turned twenty-year-old. The Yankee right-hander, Kase, kicks and delivers. Race Car swings and connects, sending a rocket into deep center; it hits high off the wall at 410 feet. Race Car is off to the races; Greenen and Saito are coming into score! Race Car is rounding second and the ball has careened off the big wall and taken a weird ricochet, bouncing back past the outfielders toward the infield. Race Car isn't stopping; he's rounding third, headed for home, looking at an inside-the-park home run! Kevin Owens has his left arm flying wildly, windmill style, waving Florio home! It's not even close; Florio

slides, but could have scored standing! A three run, inside-the park home run! Wow, he looked like an Olympic sprinter and almost caught up with Saito! You can't hear in this ballpark! Oh, my! I'll shut up and let you listen!

Grobins, being a real pro and taking a page from Vin Scully's book, knew not to talk too much at moments like this, but to let the moment and the crowd speak for itself. That's what Scully did when he called Hank Aaron's 715th home run in 1974 and Kirk Gibson's walk-off home run in the 1988 World Series.

When Race Car scored, the boys were jumping up and down like five-year-olds who have to pee. So was Mr. Hoover! And at Knights Park, the ovation wouldn't stop until Florio was shoved back onto the field by teammates for a curtain call. Nashville fans could *taste* it now.

Grobins: Sixty-seven thousand fans in Knights Park and millions at home are witnessing a big moment in baseball history. Anything can happen in the final two innings, but if the upstart Knights can hold on and topple the mighty Yankees, it will indeed be a David defeats Goliath story, David being Young Charlie Collier. But we have another hitter for the Knights rubbing some pine tar on his bat as he walks to the plate. It's the scrappy second baseman Harry Braxton, who will battle like a pit bull to get on base, no matter what the score or situation. Braxton sets up in the front of the batter's box and crowds the plate. Braxton likes to look at a pitch or two usually and will only swing early in the at-bat if the pitch is in the zone he's focusing on. Braxton asks for time and it's granted. He steps out, thinking, trying to figure out which pitch Kase will throw him. Kase and his catcher have decided, Kase rocks, and fires a fastball on the outer half, thigh-high. Oh! Braxton hits a line drive right at Kase, who snares it in complete self-defense! That was almost tragic. Kase barely got his glove in front of his face in time. That was scary. Braxton clearly was looking for that pitch and couldn't have hit it any harder. At the end of seven innings of play in Game 7, our score is your Nashville Knights 7 and the New York Yankees 1.

In the Owners Suite, it was getting giddy. The combination of music personalities and baseball people made for an interesting, fun mix. Sir Scorealot came to the suite and escorted Haley McClanahan to the rail. Together, they hung over the rail and started the chant, "Let's Go, Knights!" The crowd, seeing Haley and the metal mascot, picked it up. Big Daddy Putnam joined them, and the crowd took it up another level. Big T asked his executives, including Charlie, to follow him down to the clubhouse to watch the ending from there and celebrate with the players.

The eighth inning was epic. The Yankees would send John Kelly, Frank Reed, and Patrick Kack to the plate against the big lefty who'd been mowing them down all afternoon.

> **Grobins:** The Knights are six outs away! Here we go, boys and girls; could this be any more exciting? The Knights have written a story nobody would have believed two years ago. Anderson Boulet throws his last warmup pitch and ducks as Raul fires the ball down to second. Yankees leadoff hitter John Kelly steps in and does some rearranging of the dirt in the batter's box and now appears ready. The quick-pitching Boulet is always ready, and he paints the outside corner. Strike one! Kelly asks for time and rearranges dirt again. The Yankees are

trying to slow Anderson down and disrupt his pace. They're desperate to find something that works; not much has for them today. Kelly is ready now; Boulet rocks and fires—a fastball, way inside—Kelly bails but accidentally makes contact; a bloop, oh my; just over first baseman Ryan Greenen's reach. Kelly is on with the luckiest single you'll ever see! And he's coming out of the game for a pinch-runner. Russ Sims is coming in to run for John Kelly. Kelly runs like he's got a load of bricks in his britches. Sims brings speed; they're hoping to avoid the double play. Frank Reed comes to the plate. Reed has been held hitless today, but he is always dangerous. He crowds the plate more than anyone in baseball and leads the league in getting hit. The cagey Cajun peers in for the sign, nods, and delivers—and he hits him! What did I just say? He didn't even lean in this time; it barely brushed his jersey, but there he goes, trotting down to first base. And now pitching coach Mitch Mackenroth is making a visit to the mound. The Yankees have two men on and nobody out. Mackenroth wants to see how the big lefty's feeling. It was a quick visit. Whatever Anderson said satisfied his coach. The Yankees are sending another pinch-runner for Frank Reed, who's faster than Kelly, but not by much. Phil Bolsta is coming in to run for Reed. The Yankees have their fastest runners aboard. That brings up Mike Thaxton, always a long ball threat, even in this park. Thaxton digs in near the front of the box. Boulet is ready and delivers. Ball one! Casanova fakes a throw to first and fires the ball back to his pitcher. Sims is taking a big lead off second as Boulet toes the rubber. Anderson spins around counter-clockwise, driving Sims back to second. He focuses on Thaxton again, stretches, and delivers. Strike one!

Shortstop Nakahoma and second baseman Braxton are at double-play depth, hoping for a ground ball. Anderson goes into his stretch, glances at Sims on second, and delivers; the double steal is on; runners break; Thaxton hits a line drive up the middle; Braxton dives, snares it, lands on second, doubling up Sims, and turns to tag the stunned Phil Bolsta, who thought he was stealing second, for the third out. A triple play—unassisted! This place is going crazy! Are you kidding me? A triple play in the World Series? And the score after seven and one-half innings of play—your Nashville Knights 7, the mighty New York Yankees 1. We need to hear from our sponsor and pay some bills. We'll be right back.

Big T, Charlie, and the executive team were hooting and hollering as they watched the triple play on the big screen in the locker room. Three attendants, also hooting and hollering, were setting up for a post-game victory celebration. Dozens of bottles of champagne were lined up on two plastic-covered tables. Charlie commented to Big T, "I'm not sure about setting out champagne early; might that jinx us?"

Big T laughed. "It's visualizing, Charlie. We're visualizing victory. Have you always been so superstitious?"

"I wouldn't say I'm *super*stitious. I'm just a little stitious."

"Well, my young friend, I think we'll be celebrating within the hour, and it has zippo to do with luck or superstition and everything to do with *your* Project Baseball! One more at-bat for them and we'll be World Series champs!"

Grobins: During the break, we learned that Harry Braxton's unassisted triple play is only the second in post-season MLB history. The first was by second baseman Bill Wambsganss of the Cleveland Indians in Game 5 of the 1920 World Series. An unassisted triple play is the rarest of the rare, even more so than perfect games. The stars seem to be shining on the Knights today. Yankee skipper Howard Mackert is bringing Tom Cressman in to pitch, and he'll face Steve Shaw, Larry Hardy, and Derek Thielen. Mackert is a hard-throwing right-hander who lives and dies with the fastball. Shaw's a contact hitter with occasional power to the gap. Cressman is ready to go and looks in for his first pitch. He rocks and delivers; Shaw popped it up toward third into foul ground. McPhillips is almost out of room, but he reaches into the stands with his long arm to snag the first out. Everybody's on their feet now; they'll be standing for the duration. Larry Hardy walks to the plate. Larry made a stellar play in right field last inning, showing off his Gold Glove award credentials. Hardy is ready, Cressman is ready, and here comes the pitch. Ball one, low and away. Cressman's peak years were with the Mariners, but he can still bring the heat enough that Mackert trusts him here. Cressman rocks and fires, low and away again, ball two. Hardy steps out, says something to the umpire, and digs in again. The Yankee righty looks in, gets his sign, and delivers. Hardy hits a drive to left-center. Tyler Martindale makes a diving catch; he can sure cover a lot of ground. That looked like a sure double, at least. Two outs, and Tennessee native Derek Thielen comes to the plate. Thielen was expected to be an impact player next year, but he did so well at Triple A that they couldn't keep him there. He's proven to be all they say he is. Thielen steps in and holds his bat out toward the pitcher before readying it on his shoulder. Cressman has his sign and delivers. Thielen turns on it and crushes one toward left field, but Tyler Martindale didn't even have to move. Three up, three down, as we head to the top of the ninth. Your Nashville Knights are three outs away from winning the World Series!

All eyes were on the Knights' dugout as the crowd stood and watched for Anderson Boulet to emerge and take the mound for the ninth inning. The roar probably could be heard three states away. Anderson walked slowly to the mound as he always did, stepping over the chalk marking the first base line to avoid bad luck. When he stepped over the line, the ovation reached a crescendo. The Louisiana lefty would be going for his seventh complete game win for the season and his twenty-sixth win overall. Soji "So-Slow" Watanabe, the Knights' change-up artist, got up and started throwing in the bullpen, but it looked like Anderson Boulet was going to finish the game.

> **Grobins:** Anderson Boulet has been masterful all afternoon, limiting the mighty Pinstripers to two hits, walking one, and striking out thirteen through eight innings. In twenty-five years, when history looks back on great moments in baseball, this will be at the top of the list—the improbable story of young Charlie Collier and music icon Big T McCraw, an upstart in baseball, who has brought this new franchise to the brink of a World Series title in their second year of existence! The Yankees will send up Chris Aubertin, Randy McPhillips, and Freddy Huffins as they hope for a miracle. Right-hand hitting Aubertin steps in and takes a fast ball up and in for ball one from Anderson Boulet. Casanova fires the ball back to Boulet and he's ready to go again. Strike one, fast ball on the black, at the knees. Aubertin doesn't agree; looks back at the umpire. He steps out and restraps his batting gloves, now digs in, crowding the

plate. Boulet has his sign, kicks, and delivers. Strike two, the Louisiana Loop. Aubertin was paralyzed by that pitch. That might have been the best curve ball he's thrown all day. The crowd is feeling it now. They're all on their feet. The noise level is deafening as the Knights' faithful fans cheer for a strikeout! Boulet looks in, gets his sign, rocks, and fires…swing and a miss, strike three! That was his wicked in-shoot that ran away from Aubertin. He couldn't have reached that with a telephone pole! The Yankees are down to their last two outs.

Up steps Yankee third baseman Randy McPhillips. McPhillips has had an off year, but he's a veteran, clutch performer. They need more than clutch; they need a miracle. Soji Watanabe isn't even throwing in the bullpen. All the bullpen pitchers are hanging on the fence, waiting to rush the field. Knights catcher Raul Casanova signals the outfield to take a few steps back for McPhillips.

Anderson Boulet toes the left side of the pitching rubber against the left-hand hitting McPhillips, the tallest third baseman in baseball. Boulet gets the sign, kicks, and delivers; strike one on a fast version of the Louisiana Loop. That ball seemed to start behind the hitter before breaking down and into umpire Jeff Wendstat's strike zone. Boulet, working quickly, kicks and fires again. Strike two! Another Louisiana Loop, this one with more speed, his fastest version. McPhillips is in a big hole now, no balls, two strikes. Boulet takes a moment to rearrange some dirt on the mound and peers in for the sign from Casanova. The decibel level is peaking again. Boulet might throw a 90-mph curve ball, he's so amped up! Anderson winds, kicks, and fires! Swing and a miss. Strike three! It wasn't a 90-mph curve ball; it was his slow Louisiana Loop, a change-up with wiffle ball movement. McPhillips was fooled and your Nashville Knights are one out away from making history!

Sir Scorealot is dancing like a wild man on top of the dugout, and it's not just him—67,091 people are all out of their seats, dancing or jumping like the wild Knights fans they are! Anderson Boulet takes a moment behind the mound to rub the ball, with his back to home plate. In the enormity of this moment, he looks to the sky, nods, and walks back up the backside of the mound. He'll be facing Freddy Huffins, who grew up in Brooklyn, and lives every boy's dream of playing for the team he grew up rooting for. Now, he stands as the Yankees' last chance. Huffins is a free swinger; he starts hacking away when he leaves the dugout. Huffins, a switch hitter, will be hitting from the right side against the big lefty. Boulet toes the pitching rubber, this time on the right side. The crafty Cajun fires… Huffins swings, a dribbler; first baseman Ryan Greenen gets to it. It's a footrace to first. Greenen sprints to first. Huffins is out!

The Knights Win It All! The Knights Win It All! The Knights Win It All!

Anderson Boulet throws his glove straight up in the air and Raul Casanova jumps into his arms! Ryan Greenen is clutching the final out ball as if his life depended on it. The players are dog-piling on the infield grass behind the mound. Charlie Collier and Big T McCraw are down there joining the fray too. Let's listen to the crowd….

At the Hoovers' house, the boys had been standing on the couch and chairs for the final out. They had their own dog pile on the floor in front of the television, squealing in delight. They watched their teammate Charlie on television surrounded by a sea of reporters, shielded by Big T. This was a day they would never forget. The celebration was just beginning. Nashville was about to have its biggest party ever.

★ CHAPTER 36 ★

The Celebration

The scene was chaotic bliss, players running every which way looking for another teammate or coach to hug. No one was leaving the
ballpark, and no one was sitting. The huge guitar-shaped jumbo
screen beyond the center field wall flashed *Nashville Knights World
Champions!* Sir Scorealot was riding around on the outfield grass on a
white stallion, thrusting his giant sword into the air. The grounds crew
quickly set up an awards presentation platform behind the mound,
and MLB dignitaries ascended the three steps. The bow-tied reporter,
Ken Rosenthal, would serve as emcee. MLB Commissioner Roscoe P.
Dittsberry was ready to present the championship trophy, which stood
half as tall as Rosenthal. Big T, GM Kurt Grimmer, and Manager Larry
Wenzel were on the platform while Charlie remained on the field just
in front of the platform with his dad, Timothy Ramage, Wally Rupp,
and Butch Dory.

> **Rosenthal:** Ladies and gentlemen, it is with great pleasure that
> I introduce the commissioner of baseball, Mr. Roscoe P. Ditts-

berry, to present the trophy.

Commissioner Dittsberry: Thank you, Kenny. Having been involved in our grand game for the past fifty years, I can say I have never witnessed anything like what the Nashville Knights have accomplished in their first two years of existence. It is unprecedented. To the Knights' owner, Tommy Big T McCraw, players, and everyone associated with this amazing story, congratulations! Some say you've made baseball cool again. Of course, we know baseball has always been cool, but because of what your amazing team has done, Major League Baseball is having a growth spurt we haven't seen in decades. All of baseball is grateful to you. So, Mr. Thomas "Big T" McCraw, would you please step up to accept this trophy?

I present to you, Thomas McCraw, the championship trophy!

Big T hoisted the huge trophy and did three overhead presses, to the cheers of the standing-room-only crowd.

Big T: Thank you, Mr. Dittsberry! So many people made this happen. We were like a bunch of worker ants, every employee of the Knights, every single one, has worked like crazy for the last two years to follow our dream of playing old school baseball and entertaining fans. And we all pulled together like ants—no bickering, no fighting, everyone contributing their part, and working for the common good of the organization. I never intended to talk about ants, but I'm just saying it was a team effort involving hundreds of people, many of whom are non-players, behind-the-scenes people who contributed mightily. Thank you for the trophy, but most of all...thank you,

Nashville. *Thank you, Knights fans!* The Knights love and appreciate you!

Rosenthal: We also have an MVP trophy to award. I'm looking around on the stage and someone is missing. Does anyone know where we might find Anderson Boulet?

Boulet was just a few steps to the side of the platform with Harry Braxton, Raul Casanova, and Derek Thielen. The three of them shouted, "Here he is!" and shoved him toward the stairs. As comfortable as Boulet was on the mound, he was equally uncomfortable accepting praise, and God forbid, public speaking. He was about to deal with both.

Rosenthal: Mr. Anderson Boulet, you pitched two magnificent games in the World Series and you are this year's World Series MVP! Please accept this trophy from Major League Baseball and the keys to your brand-new Chevrolet Corvette, courtesy of Chevrolet! How are you feeling right now?

Boulet: *Laissez les bons temp rouler! Laissez les bons temp rouler!*

Rosenthal: Maybe you can translate for the non-French speakers?

Boulet: Let the good times roll!

Rosenthal: What were you thinking in the ninth inning when you walked to the mound and got the loudest ovation this reporter has ever heard?

Boulet: I was thinking about my dad who could have pitched in the big leagues. He was the best pitcher of his generation to come out of Southwest Louisiana, but he had to work the shrimp boats to feed us. He couldn't risk riding the minor league buses; he had to make money.

Rosenthal: Well, Mr. Most Valuable Player, you have made your family proud, and you have given a performance for the ages today! Congratulations!

Boulet: Thank you, Ken. May I say one more thing? The real MVP is Charlie Collier!

Upon hearing those words, a chant began, faintly at first, but then it grew louder. "Charlie, Charlie, Charlie! Charlie, Charlie, Charlie!" Rosenthal had seen Charlie in the crowd standing near the platform and waved him up. Charlie hesitated, not knowing what to do. His dad tapped his shoulder, silently communicating, *Go up there, son.* The reluctant hero walked up the steps to stand next to Rosenthal, who at 5' 4" came up to Charlie's nose, now that he'd sprouted to more than six feet tall.

Rosenthal: Well, you've done it now, young man. Three years ago, at age fourteen, you wrote a paper for a graduate-level statistics course alleging that analytics is hogwash, and we understand your professor was underwhelmed. You presented your old-school, anti-analytics plan to the Knights, they adopted it, and the result is *this*. (He swept his arm toward the sea of delirious fans.) What do you make of it all?

Charlie: I don't know what to make of it, Mr. Rosenthal. I want to thank God and my parents first. I just feel such joy now. I'm happy for everyone who loves baseball. I think the Knights' brand of baseball has made baseball better. I'm just happy to be a part of it.

Daito Saito and Yoshi Nakahoma sneaked behind Charlie, one on each side. Suddenly, they each ducked down, grabbed a leg, and hoisted Charlie up on their shoulders. The crowd went wild, shouting "MVP!" to Charlie. He took off his Knights ball cap and waved to the frenzied crowd. Embarrassed, he implored the players to put him down, and when they did, he went back to stand with *Dad and the Bodyguards*.

CHAPTER 37

Victory Parade

It was a picture-perfect day for a parade and the biggest celebration Nashville had ever seen. It was the best weather since that glorious final game two weeks before. Estimates were that more than one million people lined the parade route starting at Union and 1st Ave. N., continuing along 1st Ave. N., turning right on Broadway and ending at Rosa Parks Boulevard, where a grandstand was set up for a ceremony. Charlie got to ride with Big T, Kurt Grimmer, and Larry Wenzel in the lead car. He caused more of a fuss than the players. Chants of "Charlie, Charlie, Charlie" hailed the hero as the parade inched along, stopping every half-block, letting players interact with fans. Sir Scorealot led the parade on his white stallion, thrusting his sword and slinging small Frisbees with "*Knights—World Champs*" written on them from his saddlebags to the kids along the way. Kids caught them and then ran alongside the cars, getting the players, coaches, Big T, and Charlie to autograph them.

The parade turned right onto Broadway at The Hard Rock Café, where the crowds were even larger. The mayor and other dignitaries waited at the end of the route in Humefogg High School's parking lot where a bunting-draped podium had been erected. Fans held signs, and kids were on parents' shoulders, straining to catch a good view of their new sports heroes. As the procession approached the high school parking lot, the gathered crowd roared, almost as loud as the decibel level inside Knights Park for Game 7. As the cars pulled alongside the podium, players made their way through the line of security and ascended the stairs to the platform. Dancin' Danny, who was actually a terrible dancer off the field, was dancing. Raul Casanova was one big grin, like a happy bear who had found a jar of honey. Big T, flanked by Kurt Grimmer and Larry Wenzel, carried the trophy onstage where he thrust it overhead to the delight of the crowd. Nashville Mayor Clayton "Camera Ready" Carr walked to the lectern and adjusted the microphone to accommodate his diminutive frame. "Ladies and gentlemen, I present to you the Nashville Knights, World Champions of Baseball!" The applause lasted a good two minutes, and the mayor milked it, standing there grinning for the cameras, as if the applause were for him.

> **Mayor Carr:** Today is a great day in the history of our beautiful city, one of the greatest days ever. A few years ago, who would have dreamed we'd even have a team, and now we are World Champions! It is my honor and privilege to give a lifetime key to Music City, USA to musician and visionary Thomas "Big T" McCraw! Big T, can you please come take this heavy key to the city off my hands?

Big T took two steps and took hold of one end of the four-foot-long key to the city, in the shape of a guitar, with the words *Nashville Knights* scripted across the body of the guitar. The mayor held onto his end, posing for the cameras. Big T handed the key back to the mayor and stood before the microphone to address the crowd.

> **Big T:** Thank you, everyone. Thank you. I'm a songwriter, but this is one time when words can't really express the gratitude I have—that all of us who work for the Knights have for *you*, our fans. We love you! We couldn't have done it without you! Two years ago, when we were just getting started, I promised our General Manager Kurt Grimmer that when we won the World Series, I'd write a song about our team. Kurt plays some ukulele, and we made a deal that we'd do a duet, him on uke, me on guitar. How about we debut that song right now? Would that be okay?

The crowd roared.

> **Big T:** I'll take that as a yes! Kurt, get up here with your uke. We will also be joined by our director of minor league development, Mr. Butch Dory, on blues guitar and my old friend Smokey Fields on bass. C'mon up here, Butch and Smokey!

Caught by surprise, Smokey protested that he hadn't brought his bass with him, but Big T leaned into the mic. "Get on up here, you big dork; your granddaughter Samantha brought it. We got you covered!" Smokey was pushed toward the stage by Wally Rupp, who had played for Smokey at the University of Richmond.

Charlie was enjoying the scene when there was a tug on his sleeve. When he turned away, he was surprised to see David Clark, the IT executive who had resigned because he didn't believe Charlie was correct with his theories. David held out his hand. "Charlie, I want to shake your hand. I'm delighted to be wrong. You were right. I congratulate you. I've changed industries and found my niche; so as it turned out, you were a blessing to me."

Charlie shook his hand. "Thank you, Mr. Clark. It's nice of you to say that. I respect you; it's all good."

"Thanks, Charlie. Enjoy the celebration. You earned it."

"Thank you, sir. I hope our paths cross again."

After thirty seconds of warm-up, "the band" was as ready as it was going to be, and Big T once again took the lead.

> **Big T:** Listen up y'all; this song goes along with the melody from 'When The Saints Go Marching In.' Y'all know that song, but we put Nashville Knights lyrics to it. I think you'll be able to see the lyrics on the screen to the side of the stage. Here we go…Kurt, you ready? Butch? Smokey? We don't have a drummer, but maybe y'all in the audience can clap and keep the beat. Let's go, y'all! A one, a two, a three….

Oh, when the Knights

Play baaaaaseball

Oh, when the Knights play baaaaaseball

I want be in the ballpark

When the Knights play baaaaseball

Charlie Collier, Big T McCraw

And the whooole team

They mastered Project Baaaaaseball

And won the World Series!

Oh, how they bunt!

And hit and run!

And how they swipe baaases too.

They run with reckless abandon

And they put the ball in plaaay.

They just said no to ana-ly-tics

Yes, they just said no.

Instead they went, they went Old School.

And now that's the new cool.

We are the champs

The Nashville champs

And we play Project Baaaaseball!

Oh, I want to be in that number

A fan of the Nashville Knights!

Big T and the band played the song twice. Kurt strummed his ukulele, and Butch Dory cut in with a BB King-ish guitar riff. Big T and the crowd delivered vocals with verve!

Charlie didn't sing. He was in deep thought, almost trance-like, even in the midst of the loud celebration. His phone vibrated in his hip pocket. It was a text from Maddy: *Congratulations, my friend. What are you going to do for an encore? xoxo, Maddy*

He texted back: *My future is like my knuckleball. I know the general direction, but it wiggles and wobbles. I'll keep you posted. You're the best, Maddy. Your future's so bright you gotta wear shades! See you around. Your Pal, Charlie*

Charlie was tired. The boy genius whom many had said had saved baseball got home that evening, made a peanut-butter sandwich, said his prayers, and fell asleep fast.

★ EPILOGUE ★

Twenty-Five Years Later

The plane lifted off from historic College Park Airport, banking right and heading for Nashville. Pilot Charlie Collier and his twelve passengers aboard *The Knuckler*, his latest aviation play toy, were heading to Nashville to his final game as a Nashville Knight, after a seventeen-year career, and winning 303 games. The aviation bug had bitten Charlie at age fourteen, when he flew from College Park to Wintergreen, and met Larry "Smooth as Silk" Fickel. The new plane, a Sintra Destiny 1500, manufactured in Portugal, had a range of 4.125 nautical miles and could carry as many as twelve passengers. Charlie put in the time to become a skilled pilot, instrument-rated (IR), and multi-engine rated (ME). Although the Colliers had strong roots in Nashville now, Charlie still loved coming back to Maryland and flying his friends to Nashville on *The Knuckler*.

Charlie had decided to hang up his cleats after this season, even though at thirty-eight, as a knuckleballer, he could probably pitch another ten or twelve years. The two ginger-headed twins, Charlie, Jr. and Charlotte, were turning six, so it was time to be a full-time dad. Besides, Maddy was on tour with Mondo Records two months out of every year, and Charlie wanted to travel more with her and the twins. Maddy's most recent single, "Heart of a Dove," was her third number-one hit, after "Slow 'n Easy on a Beautiful Day" and "You Bring the Razzle Dazzle, I'll Bring the Dazzle," and she had seventeen other hits in the top-ten.

The passenger list included Alfred Bailey, his wife Jillian, and their five-year-old son Gabe. Buddy Gibson, owner of The Germantown Black Rox, was aboard too, with his wife Sharon and daughter Indigo. Buddy had given Charlie a shot at age seventeen with his elite summer wood bat team, The Germantown Black Rox. The team was comprised solely of college players, except one. Charlie would frequently mention that Buddy helped him know he could compete at the highest level. When the plane leveled out, Buddy went up front to visit with Charlie in the cockpit.

"How ya doing, kid?" Buddy asked. He always called his former players "kid," even when they were thirty-eight.

"I'm doing great, Bud Man! Life has been so grand to me. If it all ended today, I can just count my blessings. I have friends like you, and I have Maddy and the kids. Life is good!"

"You just hold off on that 'ending today' stuff. You're flying this plane, man!"

They both laughed. "Don't worry, Bud Man; you're in good hands, and I don't mean Allstate…. The Good Lord is holding us in His hands."

"Amen to that, kid! What a joy it's been to watch your career and how well you've represented the game! Thanks, kid. You make an old man tear up. I'm gonna go back there and give everybody else a chance to come up here and make sure you're paying attention." He smiled and patted Charlie's shoulder.

"Thanks. Sounds good, Bud Man!"

A few minutes later, Alfred and Gabe came up to visit Charlie in the cockpit. Alfred slid into the co-pilot's seat while Gabe scooched down behind and between the two seats like you would in the backseat of a car. Alfred had also made it to The Show with the Knights and was Charlie's battery mate until he retired at thirty-three; the knees just couldn't take it anymore.

"It's been quite a ride, huh, Suster? Look at us, flying around in your private jet with our friends and family? And it's all built on baseball. This is unbelievable. Who would have ever thought this would happen when we were kids playing in the College Park City League?"

Before Charlie could respond, he heard an unmistakable noise from behind the pilot seats, followed by a rancid smell. Alfred looked at Charlie. Charlie looked at Alfred. Then they both looked at Gabe, who just grinned.

"Sorry, Sus; runs in the family—Boomer, Jr. What can I say? He can usually clear a room, but you have to stay here and fly this thing."

Laughing, Charlie said, "I'm trying to keep from losing consciousness, but you may have to take the boy back to coach. You don't want me to open this window!"

Fanning the air with a magazine, and pleased to make his old friend smile, Alfred changed the subject. "How are you feeling about pitching your last game tomorrow afternoon?"

"I am looking forward to every pitch, every second of the game. I have a good feeling that my knuckler is going to be doing the boogie-woogie around their bats all day long; that's what I'm feeling. Dancin' Danny is going to be in the front row behind the plate with you and Jillian, Maddy and the twins, Kate, and my mom. Danny's been so great, keeping in touch, rooting for me to surpass his strikeout record. He learned from R. A. Dickey, and I learned from him. I'm gonna teach Charlie, Jr., maybe even Charlotte; heck, stands to reason the first MLB female could be a knuckleball pitcher; you don't have to throw hard. I never thought of that before. But yeah, I'm super-excited about tomorrow, no sadness at all; I just want to relish every second, breathe the ballpark air, touch the grass, and step over the chalk line walking to the mound. I'll miss all the little things—the nuances, the games within the games. But tomorrow, I'll be a big kid having fun like we're playing under the lights at Fletcher's Field."

"Those were good times, my friend. And these are, too. These *are* the good ol' days!"

"Well, you two Boomers, we're beginning our descent into Nashville, so you better go back to your seats and prepare for landing. Don't strap that little fella in too tight; might squeeze another one out of him." Gabe smiled proudly. Ten minutes later, *The Knuckler* touched down…smooth as silk.

* * *

The following morning, as usual, Charlie was the first player to arrive at the ballpark. His legendary stretching/meditation routine wasn't timed and never rushed. Charlie had placed extra importance on his unique pre-game routine over the last few years, and his numbers had been the best of his career. Thinking of some extra edge for this game, he texted Rebecca Scully, "When you and Rammer get to the ballpark, would you text me please?"

"We'll be there in about an hour, right when the gates open," she replied.

Charlie continued through his pre-game routine on the grass in deep center field until his cell phone chirped their arrival. "Cool," he typed. "Please walk down and meet me by the dugout." Charlie walked back toward the dugout, stretching his arms as he went, not wasting a moment. He saw Timothy and Rebecca coming through the concourse and down the steps to the lower-level seats. An usher intercepted, asking to help seat them, but they pointed to Charlie walking over, and he waved them through.

"Rebecca! Timothy!" Charlie leaned over the railing and gave Rebecca a hug and Timothy a man-hug.

"Thanks for being here; I've missed seeing y'all like we used to, back in the old days! Still loving retirement?"

"It's a never-ending vacation," said Rebecca. "Six Saturdays and a Sunday every week."

"And the best part," added The Rammer, "is you don't have to worry about getting caught doing nothing."

Charlie laughed. "Well, y'all deserve it. How long you been married now? Fifteen years? It was the craziest wedding. I remember thinking, way back at Wintergreen, hmm…those two like each other." He laughed again and smiled the same smile he'd had at fourteen, minus the braces.

"Fifteen years of verbal combat and Cupid's arrows," Rebecca said. "We're both 'word' people, so we have some fun discussions, don't we, Jimothy?"

"Yep."

"Is there anything else?"

"Nope."

"Rebecca, do you have the thinking ball with you?" asked Charlie.

She smiled the sweetest smile. "In all these years, that's never changed. I carry it everywhere; it's as important as my wallet, my cell phone, and—sorry, honey—my wedding ring. The only time it has ever been out of my possession was when you needed it, Charlie."

"Wow," Charlie replied. "I didn't know I was still the only one."

She reached into her purse and pulled out the same old beat-up baseball—with one stitch missing. To her, and to Charlie, it was a ball with character, like an older person. It had scars, nicks, grass stains, and magic. Charlie, the cancer survivor and seventeen-year MLB veteran, had scars, nicks, grass stains, and *magic*. Charlie's magic was in his artistry with the knuckleball, his ticket to The Show.

"Rebecca, we have about an hour and a half until I go down to warm up in the bullpen. Would it be okay if I borrow the thinking ball until just before the game, and then I could hand it to you here before I walk out to the mound?"

"Of course, Charlie; I consider it an honor and a privilege that you would even ask." She handed it off and Charlie tossed it into his glove three times.

"Thank you! This feels good. I feel the magic. I'm pulling out all the stops today, and the thinking ball brings out my superpowers. It helped me heal and recover. You're like Wonder Woman, without the bracelets."

"I'm no Wonder Woman," she said, laughing, as Timothy nodded. "In the superhero world, I'd be Lois Lane to his Clark Kent," she added, jabbing her thumb in Timothy's direction.

Charlie said, "Thanks" and gave them a fist bump before walking back out to deep center field, with the ball in hand, to finish his stretches. Then he retreated to the far corner of the dugout for solitude and meditation in the seconds before taking the field, tossing the magic ball into the webbing rhythmically.

Soon, the stadium was filled with fans and it was time to play ball.

> **Grobins:** The Knights are taking the field to get this game started, but Charlie Collier is stopping at the railing to talk to a woman. It looks like he handed her a ball and is now walking to the mound.

After Charlie returned Rebecca's thinking ball to her, his relaxed stride out to the mound reflected the calm he felt inside. His eyes were straight ahead. He was exactly where he was supposed to be, and he felt completely at one with everything around him. Amid the noise, he had inner quiet. He was about to perform his artistry for the final time.

Charlie stood on the backside of the mound and looked at his friends and family seated all around behind home plate, mostly in the first three rows—Maddy and the twins, Alfred and Jillian, Uncle Frank,

Dustin and Leanne, Dancin' Danny, Timothy and Rebecca, and even Kate McCraw, who wanted to sit with Martha; the two had grown close over the years. The ballpark was filled to capacity; it felt like an Opening Day rather than a meaningless final regular season game against the playoff-bound Padres. Charlie looked to the sky and paused, giving thanks to God for his career. He walked up the mound and toed the rubber, focusing on catcher Brandon Ford (no relation to Florio). It was no use to use signs; every pitch would be a knuckleball. Brandon, after three years as backup, had taken over catching duties when Alfred Bailey retired. Brandon was particularly good at catching the knuckleball, and he had the biggest catcher's mitt anyone had ever seen—so big it was close to illegal. The mitt had been protested in a game early in the season, but the league had ruled it was within legal guidelines.

Charlie sneaked one final peek at his friends and family. His eyes went to Rebecca, who was subtly shaking the thinking ball like she was doing a shaka wave with it. Charlie smiled slightly, just a little upturn of the lips, and thought to himself, *Magic, here comes the magic*, as he rocked, delivered, and watched his first pitch dance erratically, catching the inside corner, at the knees. *Strike one!* The second pitch started way outside and darted over the outside corner at the last millisecond. *Strike two!* The third pitch to the Padre lead-off hitter looked like it had stopped and started, dipping and wobbling. With two strikes, the hitter had no choice but to swing. His bat was a good six inches over the ball as it darted suddenly downward, away from everything except Brandon's oversized mitt. *Strike three!* Blue rang him up and the crowd roared. Dancin' Danny was nodding approvingly in the first row. He turned to Martha, saying, "That's my boy!" Martha smiled. "No, that's *my* boy!"

"We all love Charlie!" said Kate. "He's so adorable." Charlotte and Charlie, Jr. rolled their eyes.

Charlie sailed through the first five innings, as did the Padres pitcher. Both teams had three hits, but neither had had a runner reach third base yet. Charlie's knuckler was doing what Charlie called the *Pivot Dance*—the ball was dancing, wobbling, and *pivoting* away from Padre bats. Only one ball had been solidly hit, and that was caught by rookie centerfielder Jamie Amato. The game remained scoreless until the top of the eighth when the Padres scored on a double to right-center, followed by a bloop single to go up 1-0. The double was only the second hard hit ball of the day off of Charlie. Through eight innings, Charlie had given up one run, five hits, struck out ten, and walked two. The Knights were retired quickly in the eighth so the game rolled into the ninth inning and Charlie Collier had one more inning.

Charlie was very emotional walking to the mound for the last time. It didn't show outwardly, but Maddy, Martha, and Rex, looking on from the executive suite, could see it on his face. His countenance was different. The crowd rose as one and gave him an ovation befitting one of the greats of all time. Just before the Padre leadoff man stepped in, Manager Wenzel asked for time and approached the home plate umpire.

> **Grobins:** It looks like Skipper Larry Wenzel is making a lineup change. He's talking with plate umpire Justin Fishetti and appears to be changing the lineup card. It looks like we have a switch at catcher. Brandon Ford is leaving the game, pulling off his gear and heading for the dugout. We don't know if he was injured or what the reason would be. This is unusual. Wait a minute—is that who I think it is? Oh, my! Alfred Boomer

Bailey is coming into the game to catch Charlie Collier's last inning! They've been best friends for life, played Little League together. Boomer's been retired for five years. I'm getting a note that the Knights' signed him to a one-day contract to do this. Charlie Collier is as surprised as the 67,000 fans in the ballpark. Oh, my! You can't script this; I guess you could— somebody did, but oh, my! Boomer has his mask in his right hand and he's pumping it in the air as he responds to the thunderous applause greeting him. Boomer gets to the plate and immediately asks for time to visit his pal on the mound.

Charlie was in a state of shock that Alfred was in the game. He was speechless when Alfred got to the mound.

"Here we go, Suster! You said it yesterday; today you're a kid playing under the lights at Fletcher's Field. You didn't expect your old battery mate Boomer to be here, ha! We're gonna beat Beltsville, right here, right now!" Boomer looked at the lights and said, "See? Under the lights. Look, they just came on. It's a sign."

"You always know exactly what to say, Boomer."

Boomer giggled. "Let's see how long we can talk before Blue comes and breaks us up."

Charlie laughed and put his glove over his face to conceal it. It didn't work, and Blue was on his way.

"How ya doing today, Blue? Me and Charlie were just chatting about our weekend plans, maybe a barbeque. Whatcha got going on?"

"Well, fellas, I can run my social life by you after the game. You think these fans want to pay to see us standing here talking about our weekend plans?"

Alfred answered politely, "No, sir; I think they're already wondering what the hell we could be talking about this long."

The veteran umpire laughed and continued to stand with them, letting them and the crowd extend the moment. Then he said, "Time to get back to work, fellas. Best of luck to you both, always. You've done a lot for the game."

Boomer the jokester trotted back, and as he squatted down, he whispered to the batter, "Watch out; he might throw a knuckleball."

The ninth was magical. Charlie struck out the side, all of them swinging. It was baseball bliss, but the Knights still trailed 1-0. As if the day hadn't provided enough magic, it looked like Alfred, and maybe Charlie, would get to bat in the bottom of the ninth, unless the skipper used a pinch-hitter, which would be understandable. The catcher position in the batting order would lead off, and the manager was not calling on a pinch hitter. Alfred hadn't swung a bat in a game in five years, but the skipper knew the fans wanted to see him hit.

Alfred dug in at the back of the batter's box to get all the time he could. His bat speed had been in decline five years ago, so it had to be slow-motion now. All he knew was he would be swinging; he wasn't going to watch strikes go by.

> **Grobins:** Alfred Bailey hasn't faced pitching in five years, but it's what the crowd wants to see. They're on their feet here at Knights Park. Alfred was always a crowd favorite, a gritty, tenacious player who was fun to watch and played with child-like joy, much like his pal out on the mound—two peas in a pod.

The Padres' reliever, right-hander Jason Ingram, throws one pitch, a wicked cutter. He came up as a third baseman, and his first basemen typically struggled to catch his throws to first because his throw is a natural cutter. A pitching coach along the way had the brainstorm to convert him to a reliever, and now he tops the league in strikeouts by a reliever and made the all-star team this year. Ingram looks ready and stares in at Bailey. Bailey gets tired of waiting and asks for time. Time granted. He rubs some dirt on the bat handle to get a better grip. He's old school, no batting gloves for him!

Bailey digs in. Ingram kicks and delivers. Swing and a miss. Strike one! Oh, my, Alfred was way late; the ball was by him when he swung. He'll need to make an adjustment. There ya go; just as I said that, Bailey choked up on the bat and moved back a little farther in the box. Ingram looks in, kicks, and fires. Bailey swings, and hits a line drive just over the first base bag; it hits chalk down the right field line and is rolling down into the corner. Alfred Bailey, in his first at-bat in five years, is rolling into second with a double!

The Knights have their leadoff runner on base; the crowd is going crazy, and up comes Yoshi Nakahoma, hitting left-handed against the righty Ingram. Yoshi's had an MVP kind of year, and he has the chance to be the hero in the final game. Yoshi looks down at third base coach Kevin Owens, who goes through his signs. Yoshi nods and steps back into the box. Ingram gets his sign, even though everyone in the ballpark knows what's coming. Ingram fires the cutter. 'Steeerike one!' plate umpire Justin Fishetti shouts…you probably heard that over the airways. That pitch was perfectly located just under Nakahoma's hands, a tough pitch to get a good swing on. Yoshi took it, looking for a better one. Bailey doesn't have much of a lead at second, but Ingram is keeping an eye on him anyway. He kicks and delivers. Oh, my! Yoshi connects! If it's fair, it's gone! It clangs the foul pole! Nakahoma homers! The Knights win 2 to 1 over the Padres! Charlie Collier is the winning pitcher in his final game of a sure Hall of Fame career! Listen to the crowd!

When Alfred touched home plate, the first player to greet him was Charlie. They hugged as they waited for Yoshi to step on the plate and make the win official. The players celebrated near home plate and then lined up to shake hands with the Padres. Charlie's friends and family behind home plate were joyously watching. Leanne commented to Dustin, "Isn't that nice that they shake hands with the opposing team after the game?"

"Yes," Dustin replied, "that was Alfred's idea. When he met Big T back when the boys were fourteen, Big T asked him how they would change Major League Baseball, and Alfred said that teams should shake their opponents' hands rather than their own after a game. Big T tried to get his fellow owners to go along for years, and eventually convinced them. Yep, that was Alfred Bailey's idea. Hey, it looks like Charlie's being interviewed."

Ken Rosenthal: I'm down on the field and trying to get a word with Charlie Collier. Charlie! Congratulations! What a way to end your career. What's going through your mind right now?

"What comes to mind," Charlie replied, "is what Hall of Fame pitcher

and author of *Ball Four,* maybe the best baseball book ever, Jim Bou-
ton said, 'You spend a good part of your life gripping a baseball, and
in the end, it turns out it was the other way around all the time.' I've
been blessed beyond belief to play this kids' game as a so-called job.
Ha! Best job ever."

Just then, Alfred Bailey ran up to Charlie and Rosenthal. Boomer gave
his pal a chest bump and a "Yee-haw!"

> **Ken Rosenthal:** Mr. Boomer Bailey! That was quite the sur-
> prise; how did you keep it under wraps?

"It was hard not to tell him," said Alfred. "I've known for a week, and
I've been so excited to put on the catcher's gear again for *his* big day.
He had no idea! Mr. Brainiac was clueless! You got *pranked,* Sus!"

Before Rosenthal could ask another question, Knights pitchers Kevin
Vlaming and Dan Desjardin dumped the traditional bucket of Gatorade all over Charlie, Alfred, and Rosenthal. Interview over, they headed for the dugout and the locker room celebration. Charlie was greeted beside the dugout by his family and friends from behind home
plate. Proud hugs all around! They were taking turns reaching over
the railing to hug him. Charlie tipped his cap to the crowd, still chant-
ing his name, as he descended the dugout steps.

The players lingered longer than usual in the locker room, this being
the last game of the season. It was bittersweet; they'd just missed
the playoffs, but it had been a wonderful season in so many ways.
Big T and Charlie were the last two in the locker room. Charlie, full
of emotion, had tears well up. "Big T, remember all those years ago
at the cabin when you told me about Glenn Cunningham? That day
meant the world to me, and I've carried that story in my heart since.

Remember the megaphone man? He's dead. Wanna know what the best thing about my career was? It was raising all that money for the foundation and helping the kids." Big T smiled. "I love you, Charlie." They hugged and Big T left, leaving Charlie and the locker room attendant. Charlie chatted with him, thanked and hugged him too, and then headed through the tunnel leading to the player parking lot where Maddy and the twins were waiting.

"Hey, baby, you were fabulous out there today! Dancin' Danny couldn't stop raving about it."

"Thanks. I was in the zone. What did y'all think, kiddos?"

"About what?" asked Charlie, Jr.

"You struck 'em out, Daddy! You struck 'em out!" Charlotte declared.

Charlie, Jr. and Charlotte were walking a few feet ahead. Maddy stopped Charlie, kissed him, and said, "Who could have ever imagined all that's happened to us? What's next?"

"I don't know; there's so much more, though; you just wait and see. God's always good to us."

"He sure is, Mr. Collier. I love you, Mr. Collier!"

"Love you *more*, Mrs. Collier!"

Charlie had saved baseball, and baseball had saved him.

★ NINE INNING BONUS ★

Inning #1: Develop a Positive Outlook About Life.

In our story, Charlie Collier had just awakened from surgery for brain cancer when his father asked how he felt. Charlie said, "Happy as a dog with two tails." His mom, in another chapter described herself as "happier than a bird with a French fry." Mother and son had funny ways of describing happiness, but clearly both were positive. We choose our attitudes. Choose wisely. A positive attitude throughout a lifetime will serve you well. A positive attitude gives you a leg up on your competitors. Just keep going like Glenn Cunningham and Charlie Collier.

Inning #2: Commit to Learning Your Craft.

Charlie Collier wasn't born with the ability to play baseball at a high level. He became a major league pitcher after learning and practicing the craft consistently over a long period. Remember when he'd go to Holy Redeemer School and throw the ball against the brick wall, always aiming for specific bricks? He was practicing his craft. Later, he became more specialized under the tutelage of Dancin' Danny Daneker, and he learned to throw the most difficult pitch of all, the knuckleball.

375

Success in your field is similar. Practice your craft consistently over time, seek good mentors, and good things will happen.

Inning #3: Clarify Your Vision.

Our story offered several examples of vision. Big T McCraw had big vision. His vision went against the grain, against the group-think, and he surrounded himself with a talented group of people to carry it out. Charlie had vision, too, and he held onto his dream of playing Major League Baseball, even in the darkest times. Then his vision grew after his near-death experience. If you have a big vision, nurture it, stick with it, and bring others along to help you. There are visionary leaders, and then there are those who follow the visionaries; they are necessary too…like the Knights' staff, fans, and players in our story. Everyone doesn't have to be the visionary; without followers, great ideas are never implemented. Vision is a two-edged sword; choose wisely and know when to lead and when to follow.

Inning #4: Be Bold.

We need to be bold to take advantage of opportunities. Just to play baseball at any decent level takes boldness! You have a piece of cylindrical wood in your hands, and you're trying to hit a small, hard sphere that is coming very close to you, possibly hitting you at between 70 and 100 mph. The sphere is dipping and darting to make it even more difficult to hit it with the piece of wood you're holding. Likewise, you have to be bold when taking a lead off of base. You can't steal second base with your foot on first. Be bold; venture away from base.

Good things will usually happen. If not, it's a learning experience—still a good thing.

Inning #5: Look for Answers Where Others Don't.

Big T McCraw was willing to look to fourteen-year-old Charlie for help in making his vision a reality. How many of us overlook people because they're young *or* because they're old? Wisdom and fresh ideas can be found everywhere. Big T could have said, "He's just a kid" and discounted Charlie's Project Baseball. Successful people are open to looking in what might be weird places. Look for the overlooked. What MLB franchise owner would ever cast his lot with the theories of a fourteen-year-old? Big T did, and it paid off. Yes, *The Genius Who Saved Baseball* is fiction, but it mimics real life. In the sales world, the great salespeople find ways to look for business that others overlook; they find niches. An example in our story would be Dancin' Danny and Charlie finding niches by learning to throw the knuckleball—the overlooked, difficult-to-learn pitch—well enough to have long careers.

Inning #6: Persevere Through Adversity.

Charlie persevered through the two big journeys he faced: a brain cancer diagnosis and his path to the big leagues. Then he persevered in becoming a pilot after being influenced by Larry "Smooth as Silk" Fickel, in that initial flight to Wintergreen from Historic College Park Airport.

Maddy persevered and was still in the music industry and touring twenty-five years later. She had three number-one hits and seventeen top-ten hits on the country charts.

Success rarely comes overnight. Just do what you do, do it well, and keep moving forward. You will be rewarded in due time.

Inning #7: Have Fun and Delight People.

Have you noticed how some people have a way of making you feel good just by being around them? Be that person to others. A boss of mine once said, "Doing your job well is expected. You don't score extra points for that. You score extra points by making people feel good." When you make people feel good in *unexpected* ways, that's when you hit home runs! Big T used the element of surprise twice to delight people…first when he stopped by Charlie's house and played catch, and second when he stopped by the Berwyn Café, surprising Charlie, Rex, Dustin, Uncle Frank, and Maddy. Find ways to have fun and create memories like Big T did. Good things will happen!

Inning #8: Addition by Subtraction.

Early in the story at Berwyn Café, Uncle Frank quoted Henry David Thoreau: "Our life is frittered away by detail…simplify, simplify, simplify." We gain when we subtract. We have examples in our story. David Clark resigned due to not being in step enough with his fellow executives. The team lost a member but became stronger because Clark wasn't a good fit with the organization. As we learned in the final chapter, he went on to another industry where he found his niche. A second gain by subtraction in the story involves Smokey Sam's Prodigious Pies in Nashville. You'll remember that Samantha told Rex and

Martha that her Grandpa Smokey had a broader menu but figured out they did better as "one-trick ponies with the best pizza pies in Tennessee." He simplified. The biggest example in the story is that Charlie's plan worked! It worked because he subtracted overthinking the game; he simplified. In our everyday lives, we have countless opportunities to simplify. Look for them.

Inning #9: Have Faith.

The ninth inning of a game is crunch time. You've got to be solid and have your act together at crunch time. Crunch time in our lives can come at various times, often unexpectedly. Faith gets you through, as it did for Charlie and his family as they faced the cancer monster. Nurse Emma Grace, Dr. Sievers, and the Colliers all acknowledged God as Charlie underwent brain surgery. When Charlie was in bed one night, he told his dad he was scared but "I pray and thank God for all I have." You'll remember when Rex and Martha were talking about Charlie's diagnosis that Rex also said:

"We'll keep moving and leave the rest to God."

God played a role in the lives of the characters in *The Genius Who Saved Baseball* as He does for us in real life. Believing in a Higher Power provides courage and wisdom. Faith moves mountains! Maybe the whole reason you read this book is because you needed to learn the above quote and apply it to all areas of your life. Read it over again and perhaps adapt it to your life and make it your personal philosophy. In doing so, the rest of your life will be a grand slam!

★ ABOUT THE AUTHOR ★

Robert Ingram is a former baseball coach, an award-winning speaker, and a former corporate marketing executive. He first discovered his gift for mentoring through coaching baseball. Since then, Robert has found joy in mentoring aspiring speakers and helping them grow into strong, confident presenters. As president of his local Toastmasters Club, he developed and implemented a robust mentoring program that others have followed.

The Genius Who Saved Baseball is Robert's entry into fiction. He previously co-authored *Marketing by Delight* and *Your Ultimate Sales Force*, both business books. Robert says writing this story was exhilarating. He especially loved writing dialogue for the eight main and dozens of periphery characters. Robert's humor is on full display throughout the story.

Today, Robert lives on Fox Island, Washington, with his wife Cara and dog Sonny. They are season ticket holders for the nearby Tacoma Rainiers (AAA affiliate of the Seattle Mariners) and even Sonny is allowed in on Take Your Dog to the Park Day. Robert and Cara's other passion is kayaking around the island during the summer months.

www.TheGeniusWhoSavedBaseball.com

★ BOOK ROBERT INGRAM ★
★ TO SPEAK AT YOUR NEXT EVENT ★

When it comes to choosing a professional speaker for your next event, you will find no one as unique as Robert Ingram. He combines passion, humor, and audience interaction to inspire and leave them wanting more. Robert's *Nine Inning Principles* outlined in *The Genius Who Saved Baseball* are a primer for a successful life.

Whether your audience is 10 or 10,000, award-winning speaker Robert Ingram can deliver a customized message of inspiration. If you're looking for a friendly, passionate speaker who connects with audiences, book Robert Ingram today!

Robert Ingram

Bobingram7@aol.com

(253) 651-2089